Glenapp Castle

Glenapp Castle

———————— A Scottish Intrigue

Tina Rosenberg

Illustrated by Brooke Marvin

iUniverse, Inc.

New York   Bloomington

This is a work of fiction. All of the characters, names, incidents, organizations, and dialogue in this novel are either the products of the author's imagination or are used fictitiously.

iUniverse books may be ordered through booksellers or by contacting:

iUniverse
1663 Liberty Drive
Bloomington, IN 47403
www.iuniverse.com
1-800-Authors (1-800-288-4677)

Because of the dynamic nature of the Internet, any Web addresses or links contained in this book may have changed since publication and may no longer be valid. The views expressed in this work are solely those of the author and do not necessarily reflect the views of the publisher, and the publisher hereby disclaims any responsibility for them.

ISBN: 978-1-4401-9714-7 (sc)
ISBN: 978-1-4401-9712-3 (dj)
ISBN: 978-1-4401-9713-0 (ebook)

Library of Congress Control Number: 2010900051

Printed in the United States of America

iUniverse rev. date: 12/30/09

To Jerry,
the love of my life

And to my parents,
for letting me unfurl like the White Rose of Scotland

Acknowledgements

Though this is a work of fiction, Glenapp Castle is a real place. In 1994, Graham and Fay Cowan transformed the abandoned Scottish castle into an exquisite hotel-by-the-sea. Without their generous help at every turn, this story would never have seen the light of day. On my four visits, I was welcome to roam the thirty-acre estate at will, to interview hotel and gardening staff, and to set up photographs for the illustrations when inspired to do so. From the bottom of my heart, I thank you.

No novel is successful without the unwavering support of an experienced, dedicated editor. Jennifer Sawyer Fisher is among the best in the industry and I owe her boundless appreciation for her patience, her encouragement, and her unmitigated honesty.

In my research I conducted numerous interviews, both in the United States and in Scotland. My genuine thanks to all with special gratitude to Janette McCulloch, Ballantrae's librarian extraordinaire, whose wealth of local knowledge and blood-curdling tales left me entranced, and oftentimes apoplectic; to Hammy McMillan, five-time European and one-time World Curling Champion, for both his curling expertise and inventive plotting; to Stu Cohen and Gail Verway, founders of the Columbus Curling Club for providing the opportunity to play your wonderful sport; to Susan and George Pryor who openly shared the agonizing trials and tribulations of living with a child who has suffered a severe brain injury; to Marisa Hay for tirelessly editing the Spanish passages; to Anneliesse Pearson, and the late Bill Mitchell, for their advice on matters supernatural; and to the authors listed in *Related Readings* for their contribution to my education.

My husband, Jerry, my children, Chase and Brooke, friends Marilee Nagy, and Lesley Holzer, suffered through the initial writing of *Glenapp Castle*, chapter by chapter. I requested only candor; they poured their hearts into this story. To the women in my book club of twenty-three years—Molly Ballantine, Betsy Brabb, Eleanor Geiger, Bonnie Halchin-Smith, Marisa Hay, Lesley Holzer, Sue Kent, Billie Orr, Linda Resch, Deb Tongren, Tricia Toothman and Kathleen York—who dared to review my manuscript at first offering: you are brave souls indeed. Thanks to my sister, Pam Johnson, for her sharp editorial skills, to Estelle Rodgers, who appeared like a winged avatar just when I needed her most, and to Betty Pelham, and again, Lesley Holzer, for their counsel on all things Scottish.

To Ridley Pearson, friend and author of over thirty bestsellers— thank you for loving this story, for believing in me as a writer, and for just being you.

The innovation and ingenuity of *iUniverse.com* enabled the publication of this novel. To their incredibly talented and helpful staff, I thank you sincerely.

The wonderful pen and ink illustrations for *Glenapp Castle* were drawn by my daughter, Brooke Marvin. Her steadfast commitment to this project has touched my heart beyond words. She is truly my partner in the creation of this work. To you, dear readers, we present… *Glenapp Castle*.

Author's Note

On the southwest coast of Scotland rests the tiny village of Ballantrae, defined by the vast Irish Sea to the west and rolling pastoral farms populated with black-faced sheep and Hereford cows to the east. Dominating the seascape, a dome-shaped volcanic rock named Ailsa Craig rises twelve-hundred feet above the water's surface like a newly birthed planet, ever-present, intrusively watchful. To the mystical, it is known as *The Prince of Darkness*, for it is said that the giant monolith erupted from the fiery depths of the earth's core in a single night and cooled in a single day. The seafaring call it *Paddy's Milestone*, the landmark halfway between the coastlines of Ireland and Scotland. But if you are a Believer in ancient folklore, it is revered as *Fairy Rock*.

Glenapp Castle was built just outside the village in 1870 for James Hunter, the Deputy Lord Lieutenant of Ayrshire. Typifying the Baronial style, the magnificent structure is fortified by soaring battlements and twin turret towers facing to the north and south. The true genesis of the motif is steeped in the warring Middle Ages, an era of unspeakable brutality and conflict with the English. Like many of the aristocratic homes built then, Glenapp Castle is constructed of smooth, sandy limestone block and peaked rooftops of bluish-gray slate. There are five sprawling wings in all, each with parapets strategically positioned for hurling stones and javelins of burning pitch at intruders. Of course, by the end of the nineteenth century, times of war and decimation were long forgotten. One might speculate, then, that James Hunter was a man of unusual sensitivity, for in accordance with ancient fairy tradition, he had perfectly rounded, trifoliate leaves carved in the center of each of the four circular balconies to protect his home from ill-fortune.

It is not known exactly when he designed and cultivated the two-and-a-half acre walled garden. It is, to this day, Glenapp's coda, its magnum opus, sequestered from the stalwart castle by a meandering pebbled walkway passing Chilean fire trees and a large lily pond, its banks festooned with a rainbow of blossoming azalea bushes. Once inside the walled garden, by early May, purple lupines, orange oriental poppies, and deep crimson dahlias flourish beneath the golden rain trees pre-empting the riot of color soon to appear. A canopied bridge, dripping with morning glory, spans a sparkling rivulet, separating the perennial beds from the fruit orchard and herb garden. More astonishing yet, the unsuspecting guest might be surprised by a secret, smoothly grassed nook, home to a small, stone figurine, shaded and somnolent in the shadows of tall spruce.

At this writing, Glenapp Castle is an elegant Four-Star, Relais & Chateaux hotel, heralded as one of Scotland's finest. It is, in this author's humble opinion, one of the most beautiful places on earth.

While this is a work of fiction, the physical elements of the novel's geography are accurate with one exception: the cursed north turret tower where two die in peril has but one stairwell, not two.

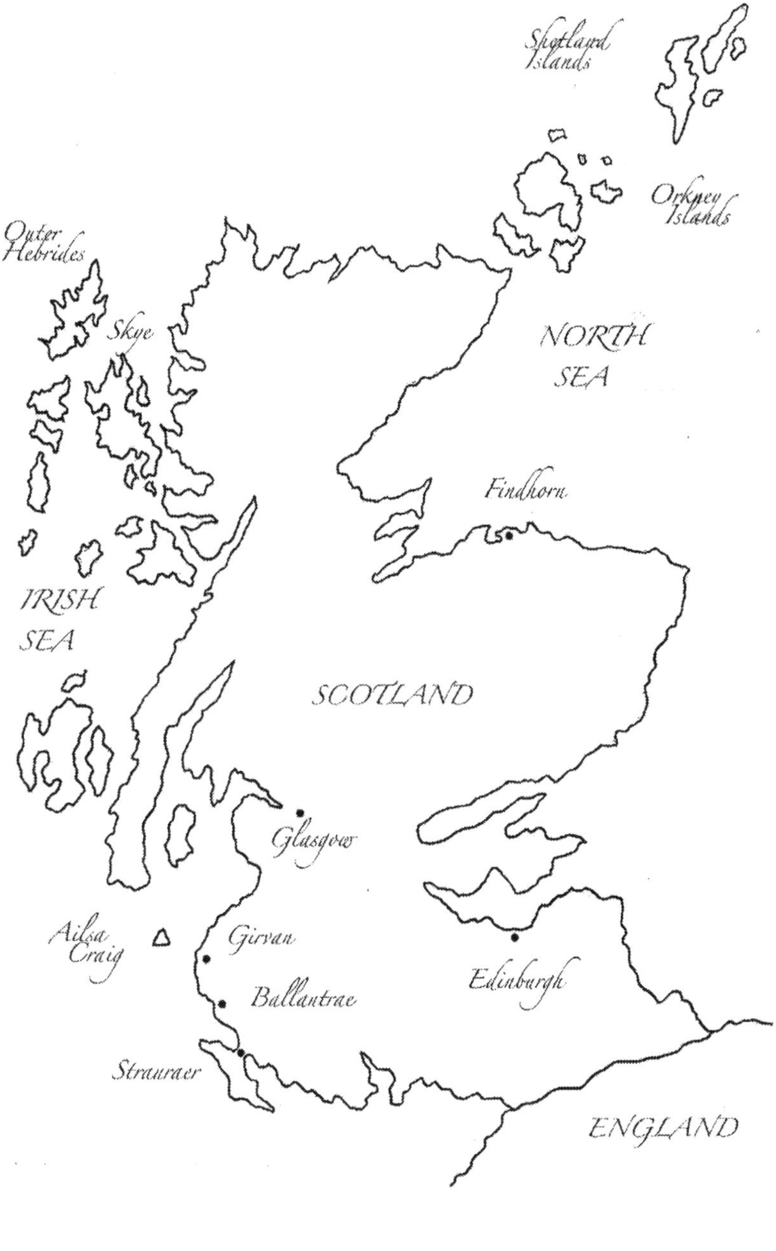
Shetland Islands
Orkney Islands
Outer Hebrides
Skye
NORTH SEA
Findhorn
IRISH SEA
SCOTLAND
Glasgow
Ailsa Craig
Girvan
Ballantrae
Edinburgh
Strauraer
ENGLAND

Ballantrae

Ballantrae: How sweet the memory
Peaceful days and placid hours
Free from care, no trace of sorrow
Lurks within thy river bowers.

Silvered willows in the sunlight
Stinchar gleaming in the main
Sparkling streams and lucid waters
Gems like these to thee pertain.

Purple seas at early dawning
Crisp waves laughing to the noon
Sheets of gold upon the waters
Paling stars neath burnished moon.

Turn, now the woods surrounded
Where Glenapp's famed forest towers
Spend thrift native here have ravished
Bridal riches as her dower.

Wealth of groves and glades extending
Arching palaces of pine
Mirrored aisles in crystal waters
Festooned with the scented vine.

Ever more shall I remember
Witching hours by Carrick's Sea
Raptured visions still will hold me
Dreaming die with thoughts of thee.

C.O.

CHAPTER ONE

TOM

I T ISN'T TRUE THAT time heals. The monotonous ticking away of minutes and hours may dull memory, but time doesn't know the first thing about mending the heart. I have thrice surrendered to time's trickery, faithfully lowering the veil of delusion, and thrice re-emerged a sorrier man. Memory is entombed in the deep recesses of the heart, not in the mind. It shackles itself to the very cells that pulsate tirelessly through the body reminding you never to forget. And it is not always for the loss of life that one grieves, for though I reference three as dead, one is among the living, still.

A ready reminder, the crimpled advertisement rests on my kitchen table, faded and yellowed from the stale, dank air that permeates my cottage.

> Needed: A Head Gardener at Glenapp Castle to
> restore two-and-a-half acre walled garden. May start
> immediately.

The haunting irony of the perfect job on the one estate I cannot bear to return to seems unjustly cruel—a twisted, perverse comedy contrived to resurrect my deepest sorrows and tempt my wildest dreams.

I am not certain why I returned to the wee village of Ballantrae, isolated as it is on the southwest coast of Scotland. Perhaps Ailsa Craig, that omnipotent sea mountain is to blame, its lurking magnetism yanking me back and forth between dread and an uncontrollable longing to live here, under its spell. Perhaps it is time to stop running away.

They say Glenapp Castle is a hotel now. I will never again step foot in the place, so it matters not to me. It is the walled garden that lures my weary spirit home—Sophie's garden.

The unrelenting April rain justifies my sense of purposelessness, and I return to my cot to contemplate how much longer I can survive without work. Lulled by the crash of my shutters in the gale, I mistake the pounding on my door for a dream remnant. But again, the dull, insistent knocks resound through the room. No doubt, it is my daily visitation from the village librarian, Nessie Brown, urging me to forgive and forget, to answer the advert and get on with my life.

What does she know of such things?

I pull on my trousers and hastily slip the advert into my pocket before opening the door. Standing before me is a woman I do not recognize. My annoyance subsides as evidently she's made some mistake.

"Are you Tom Hutcheson?" she inquires.

"Aye," I reply.

"My name is Eva Campbell. May I come in?"

She is unusually tall and has to bend forward to clear the threshold, yet does so gracefully, naturally. I gauge her to be in her mid-thirties, yet her youthful, freckled skin makes me unsure. She removes her paisley scarf and tosses her red curls to and fro, sprinkling droplets of rain to the floor. A puddle of water has formed around her feet and she smiles apologetically.

"I'm terribly sorry to bound in on you like this, but I'm really quite desperate," she says. "I'm looking for a Head Gardener and I'm told you have experience. Might you be interested? I put an advert in the paper months ago, yet I can't find anyone willing to take it on."

Unabashed by my silence she surges on. "We have two gardeners now, but they need direction. There are thirty acres in all and a vast walled garden in total disarray. My husband, Andrew, and I bought Glenapp Castle nearly eight years ago now, but repairing the damage from the fire and making the grounds presentable has consumed us, I'm afraid."

"Who are your gardeners now?" I ask, knowing the answer.

"William Hobbes, he's the one who recommended you, and Henry McGrady, from Kilmarnock."

My visitor stands quietly, her hazel green eyes watching me intently as she wipes a rogue drip of rain from her brow.

"Would you like to see the garden?" she asks.

"I'm not sure. I've been away, you see," I manage.

"Do you know the place?"

"Aye, I know the place."

"Well, then," she seems pleased. "At the first sign of sunshine, promise to come and have a look. We've totally renovated the castle, and it's a beautiful setting, as you must know. From what William tells me, you'd be perfect. Will you come?"

"I'll come, but I cannot promise…" I surrender, cursing myself.

When I open the cottage door to let her out, a red admiral butterfly fans its black, red, and white wings, then settles on her shoulder. Fairy wings, Sophie and I used to call them. Then, for the first time in weeks, the sun burns through the thick storm clouds, illuminating the flooded village streets in streaks of coppery gold and silver.

"I believe in signs, Tom Hutcheson, do you?"

Oh, I wanted to believe in signs more than anything in the world.

"I'm not sure," I say.

"Well, I do," she professes, warmly extending her hand. "I hope you'll consider my offer. The walled garden needs a savior, and I highly suspect it's you."

I watch her stroll home towards Glenapp Castle, the red admiral clinging steadfastly to her shoulder, and I pray that Eva and Andrew Campbell aren't living in the north turret wing.

CHAPTER TWO

EVA

I T WASN'T AS IF Andrew and I woke up one Sunday morning and decided to buy a Victorian castle—the notion of leaving Edinburgh was unthinkable. Not even the stifling press of humanity, the jarring screech of automobiles, the noxious fumes that seeped through our apartment windows before breakfast, not to mention the dreich weather that droned on and on for weeks at a time, could have conspired to dislodge us. It would take a series of earth-shattering, soul wrenching eruptions to awaken our dull-witted, somnolent existence, and those events began with the premature death of my beloved dad.

My father was giving a ghost tour to a group of Dutch psychics in Edinburgh's notorious underground city when his heart gave out. The medics told us he collapsed in the exact vault where the body snatchers used to stack their nocturnal cache of corpses. If my timing is right, he would have just explained that in the 1780's, the medical school had an insatiable and unquestioning appetite for cadavers—the warmer the better. Though tragic, it was an apt departure, for Dad had a lugubrious fascination with the living dead and made his real income converting haunted houses into small hotels.

For me, worse still, not six weeks later, while still missing Dad terribly, Mum insisted we sell our five family-owned hotels so she could retire to Girvan, on the southwest coast to be near her sister, leaving the divestiture for me to handle alone. Andrew was a full-time veterinary assistant to his father, the distinguished Ruaridh Campbell, Dean of the Veterinary College at the Edinburgh University. Our Sunday mornings were spent snuggled in bed, sipping coffee and reacquainting ourselves. Sadly, *that* hadn't proved as fruitful as we hoped, either.

When I worked for my dad, one of my responsibilities was to scout the Sunday papers for "Distinguished Properties", gracious-sized homes large enough to potentially convert into small hotels. Three years later, still foraging the adverts like a hungry scavenger, one in particular caught my eye—it was an auction of an old Victorian castle outside the village of Ballantrae, in Southern Ayrshire, not far from where Mum was now living. I was intrigued for the property just might overlook Ailsa Craig, that magnanimous sea mountain visible for forty miles along Scotland's southwestern coastline. The final viewing was the last Sunday in May, just a week away. I persuaded Andrew we could spend Saturday night with mother in Girvan, then drive down the coast for a look.

It was a spectacular spring day. The air was pungent with trails of sweet lilac and honeysuckle and freshly churned earth, poised for seeding. Where fields lay fallow, black-faced ewes and milking cows dotted the hillsides. Gradually, the landscape hardened into craggy-edged cliffs that dropped thousands of feet to the water's edge. As the road descended through the Carrick Hills towards the sea, I braced myself for the blast of salt air, and when it came, I hung my head out the window and let the briny scent scintillate through my every pore.

The entire village of Ballantrae must have been in church, for there was no evidence of human life to be seen when we arrived. Wee two-story houses, all connected and painted in bright seaside colors lined the main street. Just a block away, the Irish Sea spread before us like the beginning of the end of the world. And I was right—there sat Ailsa Craig like a sacred ziggurat, awash in sunshine.

Andrew and I walked the length of the beach among sanctuaries of arctic terns and gigantic man 'o war and seaweed the color of steamed red cabbage. Smooth, sun warmed, gray rocks massaged the soles of our feet as we discussed the changes we wanted to make in our lives.

After five grueling years, Andrew's frustration with still being only a salaried assistant in his father's prestigious veterinary practice had worn him to a pulp—not to mention that most fathers would have offered full partnership far sooner. Before we left the city, Andrew received the news he was now expected to "buy in" at an exorbitant price, adding salt to an already wounded relationship. I had always dreamed of opening a Bed & Breakfast by the sea—a real possibility now that I found myself a woman of generous means without a job. Lulled by the lapping waves, for a long time we silently contemplated how to work things out. It was Andrew who commented, "You know, Eva, we married because we love being together. Sundays are a start, but it's no way to run a marriage." I wholeheartedly, passionately agreed.

The only restaurant open on a Sunday was The King's Arms Hotel—an antiquated, dark-paneled establishment with cheerless photographs of men and women on ice, standing behind their curling stones—teams, one presumed, of local competitors. They certainly were a doleful lot; there wasn't a smiling face among them. We ordered homemade crab soup and forfar bridies, savoring the steak and onion pastry over a warming glass of claret. It was nearly half-past three when we finally asked for directions to Glenapp Castle.

"What's your business there?" the owner of The King's Arms wanted to know.

"We read that it's going up for auction tomorrow," Andrew replied.

"You won't find anyone from these parts bidding against you, that's for certain," he snarled. "No one in their right mind would buy that place."

"We're not going to buy it," Andrew clarified, politely. "We just want to have a look." The proprietor mumbled something about young people these days being bloody fools and after settling the bill, left us standing alone in the bar, without directions.

We hadn't seen the castle driving into the village, so we headed south across the Stinchar River, then took the first lane to the right towards the sea. The road ended abruptly at a spiked wrought-iron gate, secured with a steel padlock large enough to safeguard a county prison. On the stone pillar, *Glenapp Castle* was engraved in deeply grooved block letters, barely visible beneath the gridlock of overgrown ivy.

"If this is the last day for viewing before the auction," Andrew commented, "you'd think they'd leave the gate open for prospective bidders. Is there a gatekeeper to ring up?"

Before I could reach into my handbag to retrieve the advert, three gigantic ravens stealthy swooped down and landed all aflutter on the stone pillar. Spellbound, we watched the riotous trio tussle and shove one another, then rivet their beady green eyes on ours. The largest had lost a hefty portion of its tongue in a fight; its black tip was shredded and caked with dried blood.

"Not welcome," I meekly observed, recoiling behind Andrew's back.

"Nonsense," he replied, grasping my hand. "We'll simply walk across the ditch and bypass the gate altogether." But within seconds, the ravens edged closer, nipping at our heels. When one finally sunk his beak into Andrew's ankle, he shooed the pests to the nearby conifers.

"I don't understand it," he puzzled. "Ravens typically shy away from humans. And those queer eyes—ravens are born with bright blue eyes that turn gray, then brown, never green."

Nearly a quarter of a mile later, we came upon an enormous monkey puzzle tree around which the driveway split. Our intuition led us to the right towards the brighter opening of pointed firs. Then, after another hundred yards, we saw it.

"My God!" Andrew exclaimed. "Just look at this!"

The afternoon shadows part and parceled the five sprawling wings into slanting, geometric shapes, teasing me off balance at first glance. Constructed of sand-colored limestone, the castle floated on air like a mirage with no beginning and no end, melding with the cloudless lapis sky in a blurred, edgeless watercolor. With twin turret towers poised like regal bookends, Glenapp Castle seemed the most beautifully proportioned house I had ever seen.

It was the crescendo of birdsong that finally reeled in our senses. Like the climax of a great choral symphony, hundreds upon hundreds of birds—thrushes, warblers, woodcocks, swallows, and others I could not identify, joined in the dizzying swell of music above our heads. From the soaring parapets to the peaks of the twin turret roofs, from the precipice of the battlements to the blossoming, blood-red rhododendrons they soared, all in song, all at home.

"There must be a thousand birds here," I marveled.

"I've never seen, or heard, anything like it. What on earth do you suppose they're doing here?"

"I'm not sure," I said. "But I bet I know where they all sleep."

Astonishingly, the massive front door to the castle was unlocked, yet curiously fortified on the inside by several heavy curling stones. I was not entirely surprised; it is well-known that most of the world's curling rocks were forged from granite quarried on Ailsa Craig. Once inside, we brushed a sticky morgue of decomposing insects from our hair as several mice scurried across the floor.

"Think beyond the mess, Eva," Andrew encouraged. "Will you look at this oak paneling?"

"What oak paneling? Everything's covered in bird droppings." It was true—there were as many birds inside as out, cooing and cackling, roosting in corners, waddling across the dusty floor oblivious to the mice, and of us. Andrew shook his head in wonderment. "My God, Eva, look at the size of these windows! Can you imagine what this place could look like renovated?" Indeed, I could.

We wandered through the gracious entry hall to a drawing room flooded with dappled sunlight. Andrew pointed out the intricately carved, pine mantelpiece depicting four scenes of a stag hunt. Someone had attempted to pry it free leaving deep chisel marks along the wall. The rest of the room had been stripped bare of anything not attached to the walls, including the door to a lovely Queen Anne corner cabinet, the shelves now platform to several colonies of nesting birds.

Andrew was exploring the adjacent dining room when I caught my first glimpse of her, dressed in a tidy maid's uniform, leaning over a round pedestal table, arranging invisible flowers in an invisible vase. As my heart thrashed against my ribcage, the green, waif-like apparition turned and smiled, then drew her finger to her lips as if a great secret were being shared. Before I caught my breath, she'd vaporized in the lofty labyrinth of cobwebs. Despite my father's penchant for the incorporeal, in that department I was strictly prohibited from any involvement. Now I had seen the visible dead for myself. And she saw me, too.

"Wait," I implored, too loudly.

"Sorry?" It was Andrew, peeking around the corner like a court jester.

"Amazing how the light plays tricks, sometimes," I remarked, offhandedly.

"Ooooooooooo," he teased. "Seeing ghosts already, are we? A wee gallus to show themselves in broad daylight, wouldn't you think?"

Ignoring the jibe, I retorted with an equal dash of sarcasm, "So how do curling stones wedge themselves on the inside of the front door?"

Andrew, his ringlets the color of orange-blossom honey forever falling over his brow, peered at me through his rimless specs and conjectured, "Kids—if we could get in, so could they. We'd best move along if we want to see the rest before sunset."

I promised myself that on the way home to Edinburgh, I would tell him what I had seen. He deserved to know the truth. All in time.

We trudged on through the unfathomable filth, retracing our footsteps along the hallway to the main staircase, but soon discovered it was cordoned off with yellow police tape printed with DO NOT ENTER in bold, black lettering. The cobalt blue wall covering was peeling off in sheets, and several wooden steps, easily six feet wide, had rotted straight through leaving gaping holes in the treads.

"There's been a fire here, Eva. Look how the wood's warped from residual water damage. No wonder no one wants to buy this place. Fires spook people. The stairs look intact enough. Let's go up."

"Sweetheart, no!" I objected. "We could fall through the floor, and no one knows we're here."

"Our friend at The King's Arms does," he playfully reminded me. "Come on, we'll be careful, I promise."

Hugging the edge of each step, we tenaciously progressed to the landing, only to discover the same police tape blocking the hallway to the left. "Ah…that's why we didn't see it from the front," Andrew observed. "Most of the visible fire damage is at the back of the castle. I wish we could get in there."

"Not I."

We explored the rest of the castle, peeking into closets the size of bedrooms, bedrooms the size of small flats, counting seventy-three rooms in all. The castle had been deserted in a flurry; several beds were sheeted and there were curious odds and ends still strewn about: a vintage ship's lamp, a bedside table inlaid with a map of South America, assorted books and artifacts. I even discovered linens with the initial "M" in a hallway closet, fastidiously folded as if someone tidied them up each morning.

The rear of the castle spilled onto a terraced garden that in its day must have been splendid, but now revealed abandoned campfires and empty beer bottles scattered across the lawn. It was easy to see why young revelers would frequent this spot. Glenapp Castle sat high on a knoll with a perfect view of Ailsa Craig.

"Look here!" Andrew pointed to the north turret wing. The second floor windows were charred black and shattered as if blown out by an explosion. There sat our three ravens, posted like sentinels on the ledge.

"I can't figure it out," Andrew softly intoned, as if the sinister birds might overhear. "Why do you suppose the ravens are perched only on the wing damaged by the fire? I didn't see them among the other birds in the front of the castle, did you?"

"Do they bother you?" I asked.

Andrew turned to face me, surprised. "Not particularly," he said. "Eva, what are you thinking?"

"Can you imagine what a magnificent hotel this would make?" I asked. "The castle needs a lot of work, but it's not insurmountable. We'll have to secure a loan. You could manage the construction crews, the business aspects, and the correspondence; you're much better at that than I am. I could handle the day-to-day details, the staff, and the kitchen."

"And relinquish my veterinary practice all together?" he replied, astounded.

"Maybe. We'd make a grand team, don't you think?"

"I do, sweetheart," he agreed. "But we're talking about making a decision overnight. The auction is tomorrow."

"What else do we need to consider?" I begged to know. "We have enough money to get started, and I have the hotel managerial experience. Neither of us is afraid of hard work. Someone's got to make something of this place."

"You amaze me," Andrew laughed. I amazed myself. But he was thinking about it, I could tell.

We strolled down the hill passed the terraced garden until we came upon a lily pond edged by blooming yellow, orange, and pink azalea bushes. A half-rotted wooden rowboat, listing with rainwater, drifted among the lily pads.

And there was more to come. Down the knoll to our left, Andrew noticed an arched doorway set in a twenty-foot stone wall. When we pried it open, we discovered a two-and-a-half acre garden—unattended, unloved, and screaming for revitalization.

Until the day I die, I will remember the first time I saw Glenapp's garden. I believe an angel took my hand and swept me along the rows and rows of flower beds, all bursting with blossoming perennials poking through the undergrowth in a plea for revival.

Within the walled enclosure, there was a fruit orchard, an herb garden, a glass conservatory, even a Head Gardener's cottage wrapped in clematis and ivy.

I found Andrew standing over a miniature, stone statuette of a little boy sitting on a pedestal, reading, encircled by a patch of pink candelabra primrose.

"This is a sacred place," he whispered. "We'd best find a room at The King's Arms."

The King's Arms—the perfect place to tell him what I had seen.

CHAPTER THREE

ANDREW

I WAS FOURTEEN WHEN my mother slipped a copy of Robert Louis Stevenson's *The Master of Ballantrae* beneath my pillow. My father had just forbidden me to play rugby and I was at war with the world. "An adventure of a different kind," my mother had scribed on the inside cover. Though it was primarily a seafaring tale, I became enamored of the small village-by-the-sea in Southern Ayrshire. This was the land that spawned the likes of Robert the Bruce and William Wallace, of National poet, Robert Burns, and of no small consequence, Johnny Walker.

But most alluring to my young, impressionable mind was the sixteenth-century tale of Sawney Bean. Over a twenty-five year period, during the reign of King James VI, Sawney and his brood slaughtered and dined on hundreds of unsuspecting travelers. The son of a ditcher, Scotland's most famous cannibal settled in the coastal caves below Bennane Head where his incestuous flock begat a colony of forty-six bloodthirsty offspring. At first, reports of appendages washed up on the beaches were attributed to shipwrecks off Ailsa Craig, but when the lighthouse keeper vehemently denied it, several local innkeepers were hung, tragically, to no avail.

Finally, a lone traveler, weary from a long day's trek, decided to bed in the forest alongside the road not far from Bennane Head. But sleep eluded him and he leaned against a chestnut tree, waiting out the pre-dawn hours. For moments at a time he dozed, but when he heard screams from the direction of the road, he scampered to see what trouble brewed. What he witnessed both repulsed and fascinated him. A young couple, traveling in the night, was accosted and ruthlessly murdered right before his disbelieving eyes. He watched the clan of twenty drag the still-warm bodies down a steep cliff path towards the sea, then disappear into the mouth of a cave. Several hundred yards behind he followed, and what he saw, he would never forget. The Bean women cut their victim's throats and drank their tepid blood while the men feasted on the dismembered arms and legs. The fleshy remnants of fingers and toes were tossed to the children.

The eyewitness ran the five long miles to Ballantrae and reported what he had seen to the authorities. At last, King James sent his royal hounds to root out Sawney Bean and his family, once and for all. Upon discovery, they were transported to Edinburgh where the men's limbs were severed and their bodies left to bleed in the public square. The women, forced to watch, were then burned at the stake. When the King's men returned to Sawney's cave, they discovered human appendages, soaking in pickled barrels, and strips of human flesh, smoked and cured like bacon. Tucked into the deeper recesses, rat-infested pyramids of bones, suckled to the marrow, reached to the ceiling.

At fourteen, it seemed a compelling tale. Little did I imagine Eva and I would buy a castle just five miles down the coastline. Glenapp Castle seemed a strange dichotomy of joyous birdsong and mysterious tragedy, rekindling my dormant childhood imagination. I fell in love with the place the moment I saw it.

So, on 17 May, 1998, Eva and I bought Glenapp Castle, its four staff cottages, and the surrounding thirty acres for a song. The auctioneer thought we were bloody fools and pointedly told us so.

"What in God's name do you want with this monstrosity?" he queried. "Bad history, you know. Some say they've seen ghosts."

"How could anyone have seen ghosts when no one lives here?" I asked, amazed that a grown man would echo such nonsense.

"Well, it's certainly not a proper place to be raising a family," he grumbled.

"You needn't worry about that; it's just us," Eva remarked with a tinge of sadness.

"What actually happened here?" I asked.

"Fire."

"So we see. Were there fatalities?"

"Aye, two…one we all miss, and one who's surely burning in hell." He spat for emphasis, splattering droplets of spittle on my shoe.

The owner of The King's Arms had been right—Eva and I were the sole bidders. But as we strolled about, quite pleased with ourselves, we noticed a lone woman standing by the gazebo behind the walled garden, her eyes cast to the ground. Beneath her floral scarf, a long, silver braid cascaded down the middle of her back. I would have liked to have spoken with the lady, asked her a few questions about Glenapp's history, yet the mere sight of us sent her scurrying away through the wooded glen.

*   *   *

Much to my father's consternation, I resigned immediately from my vet practice. Eva packed our things, and we moved to the south turret apartment until the two, fire-damaged north turret suites were readied for permanent residence.

Eva and I were determined to transform Glenapp Castle into the most magnificent hotel in Scotland. The infrastructure was there—large, gracious rooms, well-lit with magnificent views in every direction, and grounds that rivaled the loveliest in Great Britain. We pulled up the rotted wooden flooring, replaced the plumbing and electricity, designed and built a new kitchen, and decorated all seventy-three rooms with antique furnishings found exclusively in Scotland. Thus done, it was time to introduce ourselves to the travel bureaus throughout Europe.

Our last night in Paris, over dinner, Eva and I were lamenting that despite our best efforts, and with only three weeks until our grand opening, we still hadn't procured a superior chef. Glenapp Castle was "too isolated, too large, too new, too risky an endeavor."

It was ten o'clock when we approached the dark alleyway behind the restaurant en route to our hotel. Eva saw his shadow first, slumped against the dimly lit wall, chef's cap in hand. So still was the body, it wasn't immediately apparent if he was among the living or dead. Then the silhouette lit a cigarette, and in the flash of match light, betraying his youth, we glimpsed a sandy-haired figure with a newly fashioned goatee about his chin. He couldn't have been more than twenty-five. As we had to step over him to pass, it seemed uncivilized not to ask of his plight. Eva's French was better than mine, and she soon discovered he was a Scot!

"Where are you from, then?" she asked.

"From Wigtown—you've never heard of it."

"Nonsense, it's not far from us at all," she informed him. "What happened to you?"

"I've been sacked, if you must know. Now leave me alone—I'm depressed."

In spite of myself, I couldn't help but wonder, "Are you the one who prepared our supper this evening? It was splendid."

"*Oui, bien sûr,*" he replied, his eyes lighting up. "I trained at the Cordon Bleu, not that anyone in Paris appreciates the fact."

"That's impressive. Why were you sacked, then?" Eva wanted to know.

I hadn't expected the truth. "For flirting with the waiters. So now you know. Leave me alone, *non?*"

From my perspective, and I knew from Eva's as well, this was hardly an insurmountable problem. "Well…" I consoled, "Perhaps you need another chance. We're starting a new castle hotel in Ballantrae. We open in just over three weeks. You're clearly talented; why don't you consider coming home with us?"

"Return to Scotland? *Merde,* why would I do such an idiotic thing?" he rebuked.

Eva perked up. "Because if no one appreciates your gifts in Paris, you may as well come home. We'll pay you well, as long as you refrain from propositioning our staff, and you quit smoking."

"I am bored with sex," he sulked. "Smoking…they go hand in hand, *n'est-ce pas?*"

I handed him my business card. "We're staying at the Hotel de Louvre. If you want to come, be in the hotel lobby by nine. We're flying home to Glasgow tomorrow."

Desperate as we were, we had little hope he would actually show up. In fact, we weren't sure we wanted him to, but the next morning, when I went to check out, there he was, sitting alone in the lobby with a mahogany box of culinary knives resting at his feet.

"I promise to behave," he said, "but you'll have to pay for my flight."

"And what name should I book it under, pray tell?"

"Kevin. Kevin MacCraig Murray."

*   *   *

The walled garden Eva and I saved for last. It was William who suggested there was a chap in the village who would be perfect for the job of Head Gardener. Returning from her interview with him just this morning, Eva agrees.

"He's a wee bit odd but I like him. His name is Tom Hutcheson. Do you want to meet him? He's the only prospect we have, I'm afraid."

"I don't suppose William and Henry can manage it with all they have to do, can they? What's so peculiar about him?"

"I can't describe it, exactly," she says. "He's average in appearance, in his mid-to-late twenties, I suppose, yet his demeanor is so reserved one wonders what he's thinking."

"Maybe he's not," I jest.

"No, his mind is racing; you can see it in his extraordinary blue eyes. And something happened to his right hand. It's hardened with scar tissue. Anyway, you're going to think me silly but what really sold me were the bagpipes sitting on his table. It would be fun to have a piper here at the castle, don't you think? And don't be surprised if you see him wandering about the garden; I've invited him."

After lunch, I happen to glance out our bedroom window in the north turret wing, the only one that commands a view of the walled garden from above, and there he is, sitting on the bench, staring at the Head Gardener's cottage, his body seemingly locked in a still life of memory. Then, to my astonishment, he stands up and bows to each species of flower, deeply inhaling their fragrance, then nods in reverence as if greeting an old friend. Like a man released from prison, he weaves his way along the garden paths reclaiming something lost, something dear. As he does so, he caresses each newly sprouted leaf with a tenderness rarely seen publicly in a man's touch. One thing is certain: Tom Hutcheson is familiar with this walled enclosure and with its cottage. Of this I am sure. Thinking that perhaps he might decide to leave, I hurry outside and down the hill.

"I'm Andrew Campbell," I introduce myself. "Eva told me you might be coming."

I have startled him. Pebbles spewing beneath his feet, he turns abruptly to face me, yet does not reply in kind. He's of medium height with a head of straight, light brown hair parted in the middle like a schoolboy. His complexion is pasty white as if he hasn't seen the sun for months. Odd for a gardener.

"She and I have decided that since I'm the one most attached to the garden, you'll be working with me, if that's all right."

Like a bolt of lightning, Tom Hutcheson meets my gaze. His eyes are droopy and keen like a foxhound's, yet their color is a catapulting, crystalline blue. I do not envy him this, for while transfixing, they bear an expression of unspeakable melancholy.

Suddenly I'm frightened he might leave. "The Head Gardener's cottage has been terribly neglected, but I've often thought it a nice spot, edging the garden as it does. William and Henry can have it fixed up in no time."

Disarmed by his lack of response, I surrender to the cold, hard facts. "We genuinely need you here, Mr. Hutcheson."

Nothing.

Thinking that perhaps Eva had failed to mention that the lad is mute, I conclude, "Well...I suppose we're lucky to have found you, then."

"No..." he falters. "I'm the fortunate one. It feels good to be back."

"I'm glad of it," I reply.

"You needn't bother William and Henry; I'll manage the cottage."

"Are you sure?"

"Aye, I'm sure."

The young man picks up his leather satchel and bagpipes and walks directly towards the cottage. I watch him push open the door with his shoulder and let drop his belongings to the floor.

"Come on, Rosie," he beckons, and to my stark surprise, a dog, white as a seagull's underbelly, scrambles from beneath the garden bench and runs into his waiting arms. "Is it all right?" he asks.

"Of course," I say. "How old is she?"

"I'm not sure. She was a gift from a friend where I apprenticed. She's my mate, Mr. Campbell; I couldn't leave her behind."

"She's welcome to stay."

As I climb the hill towards Glenapp, it occurs to me that in Celtic lore white dogs are imbued with magical healing powers.

And ravens are harbingers of death.

CHAPTER FOUR

TOM

EVA AND ANDREW CAMPBELL are unaware that Hutchesons have worked at Glenapp Castle since 1882, starting with my great-grandfather. When it became apparent he possessed an extraordinary way with plant life, he was promoted to Head Gardener—the very same position I have just accepted, over a century later.

When out of sorts as a youngster, my father often consoled me with legendary yarns about my great-grandfather's life. One tale changed my life forever.

"It was early spring," Dad would begin, "and the March rains had saturated the earth. When your great-grandfather Thomas became Head Gardener at Glenapp Castle, he would pace back and forth, pining to be outside in his garden. He was a restless soul and oftentimes your great-grandmother, Effie, woke in the heart of night to find her husband gone from their bed. A shawl wrapped around her narrow shoulders, she peered out the window in search of him. What she saw both troubled and amazed her, for her husband was conversing with the plants, chatting casually as if they'd come to tea. In the morning, he slept late, making excuses that the right time to plant this, and to transplant that, was not in the heat of the day, but at dusk, or in the rain at two in the morning. He would get up at all hours of the day and night, skipping meals, even his afternoon tea. His most frequent absences marked the lunar cycles when he would plant all through the moonlit nights, never pausing to rest. At first she was beside herself with his peculiar behavior, but she loved him, and the walled garden at Glenapp Castle became the envy of Ayrshire."

"How did he do it, Dad?" I begged to know.

"Your great-grandfather understood that all living things share a common language if only you know how to listen properly."

On the edge of my seat, I'd plead, "Tell me the best part."

At this juncture, leaning forward, Dad lowered his voice to a hushed whisper. "When the moon waned, shining no light on the garden at night, and if the plant spirits told your great-grandfather Thomas that there was work to be done, hundreds upon hundreds of sparkling fairies with red admiral butterfly wings would illuminate the entire walled garden for him. And on those nights, Ailsa Craig, the island the Celts named Fairy Rock, remained lit until he had finished and gone to bed. Then all went dark. Poof!"

"And?"

"Well, they say there's a garden near Findhorn Bay, on the northeastern coast of Scotland, where the gardeners communicate with the plant spirits and grow the grandest vegetables the world has ever seen."

I simply could not imagine anything more fantastic than that! Someday I would see the plant fairies for myself, then return to Glenapp Castle and create the most beautiful garden in all of Scotland. It was my birthright.

In two years, my father would die of cancer of the colon. I was ten. The very day he received his terminal diagnosis, he beckoned me to his side.

"Listen carefully, Thomas," he commanded. "Don't ever forget what I am about to tell you. Never build a house on the traditional route of the fairy procession, for to do so is very bad luck."

For a moment, I thought he was hallucinating, yet the clarity of what followed proved otherwise. "Glenapp Castle," he explained, "was originally protected because the first owner, James Hunter, consulted the village elders regarding where the fairy path crossed his property. He understood that fairies are local avatars of good fortune and that three times a year they travel, always in a triangle—from the village, to Glenapp Castle, and back to Ailsa Craig, bestowing their magic on all who dwell within their locality. This was the reason James Hunter had trifoliate leaves carved in the center of each balcony, Thomas, as homage to the fairies."

"Why are you telling me fairy stories, Dad?" I asked. "You should rest."

"No, no," he cautioned. "Listen carefully, my son…when the current owner, Sir John McPhee, purchased the castle in 1967, he built the north turret wing directly over the sacred trail placing those who live there in grave danger. You must promise me, Thomas: never cross the threshold of the north turret wing."

"What about Mum?" I'd protested. "She's there tidying up after Sir John every day."

"She's a Non-Believer," Dad decried.

"How could she be?" I gasped.

"She's not from these parts," was all he would say.

"And are there no houses in the village built on the fairy path, then?"

"There was one," Dad revealed. "Ardstinchar Castle, just outside the village, had been the stronghold of the Kennedys of Bargany for two-hundred-and-fifty years. In the late fifteenth century, at the height of their clan wars with the House of Cassillis, they constructed a watch tower directly on the fairy path to prove that bricks and mortar, not fairy legend, would ensure their sovereignty over Ayrshire. But they paid a fatal price, my boy—Ardstinchar Castle burned down, and all the Kennedys of Bargany with it."

*   *   *

It was an easy promise to make; the staff children weren't allowed to play freely on the castle grounds, anyway. Instead, we retreated to the wooded glen, a gentle ravine forested by birch trees and blossoming rhododendrons and gigantic redwoods that grew so tall they blotted out the sky. Through the valley flowed the Garleffin Burn, a tributary of the River Stinchar that formed deep pools perfect for swimming in the sultry heat of summer. It was a child's paradise, my second home, and the one place where I was free to run and play unsupervised.

We were allowed to remain in our staff cottage because my mother,

Judith, continued to work at Glenapp Castle, first as a housemaid, then as Head of Staff in recognition of her competence and, I realized later, her unwavering discretion.

My dad's last dying wish was that I be made an apprentice to Mr. Colin Dunbar, his best friend and resident Head Gardener. He had only one child, a daughter, Sophie, six months younger than me. She had been my best friend since the age of four, and when I think of my father's death I cannot avoid the reality that, without her, I might never have survived the ensuing feeling that he abandoned me just when I needed him most.

"You mustn't be sad," Sophie would console me, taking my hand and dragging me into the glen to play. "He isn't really *gone*; he's just not *here*."

"Where is he, then?" I'd beg to know.

"He's with the fairies. Where else would he be?"

Day after day, Sophie enfolded me in her world of fantasy, filling the empty crater of my heart with hope that I might one day be whole again. And she was right; the dead are never really gone—you can hear and see them, and even catch a fleeting whiff of their essence when you least expect it. So many times, coming home from the glen, I'd smell the sweet, black-raspberry aroma of Dad's pipe tobacco enticing me home, and before I knew it, I'd retreat to my bedroom and pick up his old bagpipes, only to hear the metronomic tapping of his foot as I fumbled my way through *Scotland the Brave*. "Slow down, Thomas," he'd entreat. "Piping is rhythmic; the cadence demands patience, my boy." By the time I'd warmed up to *The Gay Gordans*, or *Strip the Willow*, gigs he'd taught me himself, he was gaily clapping the beat and laughing from the sheer joy of it.

It was piping that bonded us in life, and in his honor I pledged never to play in public, only with him.

Hutchesons were once celebrated clan pipers on the Isle of Skye. In 1803, the clan chieftains heartlessly evicted over forty-thousand families, replacing generations of crofters with sheep and cattle. The Diaspora came to be known as "The Clearances" and Highlanders throughout northern Scotland were forced to emigrate all over the world, looking for work. My father's great-grandfather refused to abandon his native Scotland and moved with his family to the lowlands to become the Burgh Piper of Dumfries. For playing twice daily in the town square, he was provided a house and respectable wages. Then the Burgh Reform Act of 1833 relegated all funds for general utility and the last of the Burgh Pipers disappeared. Now an old man, my great, great-grandfather lay down his pipes and turned to the earth to make his living as a gardener. It was his son who later became Glenapp Castle's first Head Gardener. It was his great, great-grandson, my father, who, one day, came home with a set of bagpipes and demanded he be taught to play. He placed them in my hands when I was four.

On my thirteenth birthday, my mother planned a small celebration in our staff cottage. Sophie and her parents, Victoria and Colin Dunbar, were there, along with a few friends from school. When we'd finished our cake and tea, Mum offhandedly suggested I play a tune on Dad's pipes. The only other person who knew of my pledge not to play without Dad was Sophie. She was standing in the back of the room shaking her head as if to say, "No, no…this can't be happening."

"He can't," she blurted, surprising everyone, including myself.

"Nonsense," my mother objected. "He's every bit as good as his father was."

"Aye, but you have a bad sore throat, don't you, Tom?" Sophie announced with conviction. "You told me so this morning."

"She's right, Mum—I couldn't possibly play," I murmured, clutching my throat with both hands.

"See?" Sophie echoed, triumphantly. "It's impossible."

That was the moment I realized that Sophie Dunbar, my one and only true friend, was extraordinarily beautiful. Why had I not noticed this before? We were together every waking minute and yet, like a blind idiot, I had not. Her wavy mane of cherry-blond hair, had she ever cut it? There she stood, smiling at me with such unconditional love and devotion I wanted to cry. Despite the onlookers, all I could think about were the streaks of violet that flashed across her eyes in the late afternoon sunlight, how her laugh deepened ever so slightly just before she really let loose, and the way she tilted her head to the right when cast in a daydream. In that second, our hearts melded into one, and when our eyes locked, we were doomed.

*   *   *

In matters of romance, Sophie and I were young and inexperienced,

so for days we simply ignored one another. At the end of school, she
would leave promptly to avoid walking home with me; I'd pretend I
had too much homework to play. Suddenly, her dad had her working
in the walled garden, my garden. She preferred the wildness of the
woods and must have known it was the only place I could go. Our
chance conversations became stilted and awkward. Two torturous
weeks later, purely by chance, we happened on one another in the glen
by our favorite redwood. Between the bulging roots I sat, watching
the flowing stream, feeling mighty sorry for myself. Unknowingly, she
walked right up to me.

I sprung to my feet. "Soph! What are you doing here?"

"What are *you* doing here?" she demanded to know, arms
akimbo.

"I don't know where else to go," I stammered, inconsolable and
sulking like the miserable adolescent that I was.

Debating what to do, Sophie fixed her gaze on the roaring
burn. If only we'd had the confidence to talk everything might have
been different, but I was gripped with cowardice, and she, I would
discover years later, with fear of reprisals, both physical and emotional.
Suddenly she took off running so fast her feet got tangled in the tree
roots. Without even pausing to recover, she bolted again, and oh…my
Sophie could run! We'd raced through those woods a thousand times,
knew every root, every turn and dip in the soft forest floor. In our daily
competition as to who could reach the monkey puzzle tree first, she
was one up.

"Sophie! Wait!" I wretchedly pleaded, but she wasn't stopping. As I
drew closer and closer, I watched her hair, loosely gathered with garden
twine, dance across her back. Then, with a crushing sadness, I realized
that I couldn't tackle her around the waist as I always had, for the
days of playfulness and folly were gone forever. I halted, slammed the
ground with my clenched fists and wept out of pure, unadulterated
self-pity. Somehow, I had managed to lose the two people I loved the
most.

*   *   *

Sophie and I lived on the same estate awkwardly estranged from
one another until we were nearly eighteen. She became more involved

in school activities, and I apprenticed with her father, Mr. Dunbar, at the very least justifying my presence in the walled garden. Did I forget her? Nay, she was the entity around which everything else revolved. She was the rising sun's sparkle on the ocean surface at dawn, and the illumination of the moon through my bedroom window at night. I saw her wondrous eyes in every girl I met and lost heart again and again when I acknowledged how desperately I missed her, needed her. I navigated my way through the dense fog of daylight while at night surrendered to dreams too intimate to share. The truth is, everyone loved Sophie. She excelled at everything she touched, securing her popularity at school, and was, with one exception, kind to everyone. To me she was cold and brusque, ensuring my unpopularity. I didn't care as some might think. I was a loner and preferred the solitude of the garden enclosure. What tormented me was watching her come and go as she pleased with my heart shackled to her every move.

*   *   *

After my father died in 1989, my mother's responsibilities at Glenapp Castle became more extensive. By the time I was in high school, she was in charge of hiring and training the in-house staff, in addition to her own duties as private servant to Lady Sylvia McPhee.

Each evening my mother came home to cook my supper, then dutifully returned to the castle until long after I'd gone to bed. I was to be home by sundown, hands washed, ready to eat. We'd dispassionately discuss the events of the day, then off again she'd go. I never questioned her obligations there, neither did she pry into my affairs, for which I was eternally grateful. My mother was an introvert, trudging through life as best she could as a gratefully employed, single parent. Neither of us pretended to be happy, nor did we analyze why we were chronically despondent. Tragically, this left me with little understanding of what happened between her and Sir John McPhee, her master and employer. On the rare occasion when I asked where she disappeared to twice a year for several days at a time, she'd only reply, "It's a delicate matter, Thomas, but I'm doing good works. Worry not."

I never liked Sir John. He was arrogant and possessed no love of children. Never having had his own, he begrudgingly tolerated our presence, and we strategically avoided his. Sophie and I used to play scout: a sighting of Sir John McPhee's white beard and ample paunch sent us scurrying to the glen like wild Indians. Though my mother never expressed her own feelings, she was liberal in lecturing me on the proper behavior regarding Sir John. To this day, I'm not certain whether she was protecting her employer…or her son. I knew one thing: I didn't like the way he looked at her. His eyes stalked her when she brought him his tea on the lawn, then he needlessly engaged her in conversation once there. Several times, Sophie and I hid behind the rhododendrons to listen—the chatter was trivial enough—some nonsense about saving children from the jaws of Satan. Whatever the topic, I resented his flirtations, for about the time I realized how pretty Sophie was, so too did I recognize my mother as a woman of attractive qualities. Unlike me, she had olive-toned skin and thick, wavy, dark hair. In fact, she looked more Mediterranean than Scottish. I always wished I had inherited her exotic features—no luck there; I looked just like my dad, scrawny and fair with those droopy Hutcheson eyes that inspired my classmates to howl when I passed in the hall. Anyway, to her credit, Mum was the perfect servant, loyally performing her duties which appeared to include tolerating Sir John's salacious overtures. As I drowned in the abyss of my own sexual fantasies, I knew exactly what he was thinking, and I despised him for it.

CHAPTER FIVE

EVA

I SIMPLY COULDN'T TELL him. Andrew was so enthused over the prospects of buying Glenapp, it hardly seemed fair to discourage him over such a minor detail. In any case, he doesn't believe in ghosts, and thus far, my fair lady only reveals herself to me on the rare occasion I glimpse her neatening up the linen closet or remaking our bed. I can certainly use the help—one can hardly imagine all that goes on here. Guests up at dawn wanting coffee, travelers from all over the world checking in and checking out, directions needed to go here and there, staff to be looked after, seventeen guest rooms to be tidied, fresh flowers to be put out each morning, shooting, falconry, golf, and ferry rides to Ailsa Craig to be arranged. At present, I wish my illusive specter would answer the telephone. Worried the earsplitting ring might awaken our guests, I hastily pick up the nearest phone at the bottom of the hotel staircase.

"Hello…Glenapp Castle Hotel."

"Is Andrew Campbell there, please?"

"He's not available at the moment. This is Eva. May I help you?"

"Eva, this is Helen Campbell." I can't recall exactly who the woman is. Helen Campbell—Andrew's cousin twice removed by marriage? I'm not sure.

"Listen," she continues, "can you and Andrew come to Glasgow in the next couple of days?"

"If you're just visiting, come lodge with us," I offer. "We're only an hour and a half south. It's frightfully difficult for us to get away this time of year; we run a hotel, you see, and…"

"I know this is a monstrous imposition," she apologizes. "I'm not quite sure how to say this. The fact is…it's a legal matter."

"What sort of legal matter?" I inquire, alarmed a guest may have lodged a complaint with the authorities.

Her exhalation sends a gale through the receiver. "Do you remember Kitty, Andrew's first cousin?"

"Certainly," I reply. "She came to our wedding." I remember her well. She was inebriated and had to be escorted out the back door at our reception. Last I'd heard she'd moved to London with some wayward character who amply supplied her with drugs. Is there a child out of wedlock? I can't remember.

"Kitty was killed in a car accident near my home here in southern England, in the New Forest area," Helen informs me. "Her car was sideswiped by a lorry and knocked off the road. It's all too horrid."

"I'm awfully sorry," I sympathize. "Are you coming to Glasgow for the funeral?"

"No, it's all rather complicated—her body was flown to London, you see. What I'm trying to say is that you need to go to Glasgow because according to Kitty's will, Andrew is the legal guardian of her five-year-old daughter, Isobel."

A forced, unrecognizable laugh erupts from my throat. "There must be some mistake, Helen. We don't even know her, and Andrew would never agree to something like that without discussing it with me first. This is a misunderstanding, I'm sure."

"I'm afraid there's no question as to the legality of the will," she assures me. "I've just spoken with Kitty's solicitor in Glasgow. He'll be ringing you up this afternoon."

My entire body goes numb, for all the blood has drained to my feet. The phone receiver slips from my grasp; it crashes and bangs against the table leg like the executioner's drumbeat, swinging in wide loopy arcs— like an empty noose, I think to myself. The possibility that Andrew could have made such an arrangement behind my back, knowing that we haven't been able to conceive a child…it is incomprehensible, and yet Helen says it's true. The solicitor is contacting us today.

Behind me, Andrew is descending the stairs. "I've taken Mrs. McBride her breakfast," he merrily informs me.

Warm as an iceberg, I choke out, "Tell me it's not true."

"What?"

"That you're the legal guardian of your cousin Kitty's daughter?"

Wide-eyed, Andrew clumsily replaces the phone receiver, grabs me by the elbow, and pulls me into the library, locking the door behind us. I stand stoically rigid with my back to him, staring at Ailsa Craig, marveling how the mammoth stone pyramid can remain unaffected while my life spirals out of control.

"Eva, turn around, please."

With fire in my eyes, we are face to face, husband and wife. I pray this is some godforsaken muddle, but I can see from his aggrieved, contorted expression that it is not.

"What happened?" he asks.

"Helen Campbell rang to say that Kitty was killed in a car crash, and that you are, incredulously, her little girl's legal guardian. Tell me it's a lie!"

Smitten, Andrew collapses in the chair. "Oh my God," he groans. When he finally explains, his voice is muffled and windless.

"After her parents died, Dad was appointed Kitty's legal guardian until she came of age herself. When she gave birth to a daughter, and because she wasn't married, Dad wanted to be sure his great-niece would be cared for but felt he was getting too old to take on the responsibility. He called me one day, several years ago, and asked if I would assume Issie's guardianship, and I reluctantly agreed. I swear, Eva, I could not for the life of me have imagined this would happen."

"This was just five years ago!" I rage. "Why didn't you consult me?"

"Please don't shout. You'll wake the guests," he begs for restraint.

"I don't care! There's no way we can manage a hotel, *and a child*, especially one that's not even our own."

"We're not able to have our own," he declares. The reminder that due to a weak uterine wall I am unable to carry a baby full-term only adds to the miserable state of affairs. Seeing my stung expression, he apologizes, "I'm sorry, Eva, I just think we should take some time to consider that this might be good for us."

"What do you mean...*good* for us?"

"Well...it's possible a child might add some richness to our lives," he has the audacity to suggest.

There is only one explanation. "Tell me the truth, Andrew. Don't lie to me. Are you her father?"

Infuriated by my accusation, he spews, "Christ, Eva! What do you take me for?"

"Then why didn't you tell me?" I beg to know.

"It was horrible of me not to. I'm sorry, sweetheart, truly I am," he apologizes in earnest. "Dad caught me at a busy time, and if you must know the truth, its actuality seemed so obscure, I somehow forgot all about it."

Really, I am speechless. It is so typically Andrew—kind-hearted, generous, and incurably absent-minded—it is why I love him and why he leaves me apoplectic.

"Look, sweetheart," he says, "I love you. I wouldn't jeopardize our marriage for anything. Ultimately, it's up to you. You'll be her mum. If you're totally opposed, we'll explore the alternatives."

"Alternatives? Such as what?"

"Well...I suppose the only option is to put her up for adoption?"

"Oh Andrew, I couldn't imagine..."

"I agree," he says, "then we should talk."

"I'm too angry and hurt to discuss this right now," I fume. "Besides which, half our guests are checking out this morning. There's a group of Japanese golfers scheduled to arrive any moment for a noon tee time at Turnberry, and in case you've forgotten, we have a wedding here next weekend and Kevin refuses to prepare haggis for the two hundred guests. Which one would you like to handle first? And by the way... expect a call from Kitty's solicitor this afternoon. He'll be ringing you up with the good news."

I am crazed, irate, and hopelessly confused. I sound like the bitch of Eastwick. Andrew looks as if he's been zapped by a taser.

CHAPTER SIX

ANDREW

S HE MAY HAVE PURGED herself, but I can tell by the way her freckles multiply across the bridge of her nose that she is still enraged. No doubt she is contemplating strangulation, or perhaps dangling me over the side of a cliff, or worse yet, denial of her. For now, slamming the library door seems sufficient retribution.

The call came late in the afternoon. The child is apparently already in Glasgow; we have but three days to make up our minds. It is nearly midnight before we crawl into bed to talk it over. Eva reassures me she has always wanted children; it was the betrayal that I never consulted her that hurts her the most. "It felt like a manipulative, premeditated lie," she contends.

"I never lied to you," I weakly object.

"Guilty by omission," she counters, docking her head on my shoulder. "Now, leave me alone. I'm exhausted."

"You sound more like Kevin every day," I remark. She is smiling, and I know she's made her decision. I am elated. A child of our own to raise, to love, to guide through the vicissitudes of life—such a gift bestowed on the infertile is a miracle, is it not?

*   *   *

We are to meet a certain Judge Sinclair in his chambers in Glasgow, first alone, then to meet Issie. I am grateful for the private interview as Eva and I have a number of pressing inquiries. For reasons unknown, Kitty abruptly moved to London eight years ago. Eva and I haven't an inkling what her life was like there, or what Issie may have been exposed to in her first five years. I called Helen yesterday in hopes she might enlighten us.

"She rang me up out of the blue and said there was a Robert Burns festival here in Lymington, of all places, and could she come stay for the weekend?" my cousin relayed. "You can imagine my surprise when she arrived with a child in tow. Quite precocious, Issie is. Bright as a button. When Kitty asked me if I would watch her for the evening, I was happy to oblige. That was the last time I saw Kitty alive."

"Was she drinking when the accident occurred?" I asked.

"No, she said she hadn't had any alcohol or drugs since she moved to London, and I believe her. She really looked quite splendid, I will say. And she adored Issie; you could tell by the intimate way they communicated—always holding hands and giggling, finishing each other's sentences. Kitty told me she refused to leave Issie's side in London. Coming down here was a wee holiday and an excuse to reconnect with her literary friends, I imagine. Tragic, isn't it, dying so young?"

Sounding artificially offhanded, I pressed, "Any clue who, or where, the father might be?"

"I had only one afternoon with Kitty," Helen reminded me. "There was no mention of a father."

*   *   *

Judge Sinclair is a walrus of a man with a thick crop of wiry silver hair and a sweeping handlebar moustache. Still in his court robes, his skewed wig at his elbow, he makes little effort to heave himself from the depths of his chair. "Ahhh…good afternoon. Mr. and Mrs. Campbell, I presume?"

"Good afternoon, M' Lord," we reply in kind.

He gestures for us to sit across from his desk. "There's no point in wasting time," he proceeds with alacrity. "You have, Mr. Campbell, assumed legal responsibility for the welfare of Kitty Campbell's daughter, Isobel, age five-and-a-half, orphaned as a result of her mother's untimely death."

"Yes, M' Lord."

"I do not generally take cases regarding guardianship," he tells us, "but I have a special interest in this matter. I was very close friends with Kitty's parents. It's a tragic occurrence when a young, single mother is killed. Did you know Kitty well?"

"No," I reply, understanding now why the child is in his custody. "When both her parents died, at my father's request, I agreed to take on Isobel's guardianship. Little did I imagine…"

"Surely not," the Judge sympathizes. "I have not seen Kitty myself in quite some time, though I will share with you she was not a stranger to this court. On two occasions she was arrested for possession of cocaine. I'd like to believe she was a victim of her own vulnerability; some women simply choose bad company. Relative to the accident, we'll know more after the autopsy."

"Why is one necessary?" Eva asks.

"Kitty requested her organs be donated upon death, which automatically requires an autopsy. I have not yet seen the reports. Her body was flown to London immediately to harvest any organs viable for transplant. We can feel thankful she was able to contribute to the life of others despite her own tragic end.

"But now…" he demurs, "I'm sure you have questions of your own."

"What do you know about the father?" I ask.

The Judge hands us Issie's birth certificate. "His name is Vicente Flor. Beyond that, I know nothing. It appears he's out of the picture, at any rate. Issie's full name is Isobel Flor Campbell which may imply Kitty was fond of him."

"Flor?" I ask. "It's rather unusual."

"It means 'flower' in Spanish," Eva contributes.

There are more questions, more vague answers, and endless papers to sign. Nearly an hour later, sensing our eagerness to meet Issie, the Judge says, "One last question, if you don't mind my asking—is it your intention to formally adopt Issie?"

Eva and I are unprepared for the question. "Does one need to?" I ask.

"No. Issie's legal guardianship is granted to you by virtue of the will and approval by the court. However, Issie is not legally entitled to your estate upon your death unless she is formally adopted."

"I see. Well, surely…" I glance at Eva before saying more. "We'll let you know as soon as we've had time to discuss it."

"There is only one last detail. There's a family pet, a basset hound named Grimshaw. He and Issie seem quite attached. For continuity's sake, I was hopeful the dog might accompany her to her new home."

"Of course," we answer in unison.

"Then I shall return momentarily." He hoists his immense frame out of his leather chair, stands idly for several seconds to catch his breath, and strides towards the door.

My mother often warned me not to make assumptions in life. I most certainly expected Issie to look like her mother; it never occurred to me that her genetic composition would reflect her father's almost entirely.

"This is Issie Campbell," Judge Sinclair announces with unexpected tenderness in his voice, "and these are your new parents, Eva and Andrew Campbell."

She is the color of melted caramel. Her shiny, jet-black hair, cut bluntly just below her pierced ears, is so luminescent it harnesses all the light in the room. Two dazzling orbs of whisky quartz, transfixing in their feline stillness, gaze upon us with such hopeful optimism Eva and I are brought to our knees. Two thoughts pass through my mind—it's strange what one thinks about in such situations. First, how could a father abandon such a beautiful little girl? And second, that Kitty's parents would levitate from their graves if they knew their grandchild evidenced almost no physical resemblance to their daughter. In fact, no resemblance at all.

In a surprisingly English accent, she asks, "Can Grimmey come?"

Next to her stands a brown, black, and white basset hound, his elongated, tubular body six inches off the ground, the loose folds of his pendulous ears skirting the floor like a dry mop. When Issie wraps her arms around his neck, his somnambulant eyes sparkle with love and adulation.

"Of course," Eva replies. "Our new gardener has a beautiful white dog named Rosie and I'm sure she'll love the company."

Suddenly I want another word with the Judge. "May we have a moment?"

"Certainly," he says, joining me in the corridor.

There is something I need to know. "Forgive my asking, but what nationality was the father?"

"I see you didn't know Issie is of mixed heritage."

"No, no one told us. I might have guessed from his surname, I suppose. I see now it was terribly presumptuous of me to think she'd look like Kitty."

"Not at all. As I said, I do not know the father, though I presume he was of South American descent. Unless you do DNA testing, you will never be sure. She certainly is an attractive child. You can feel relieved in that regard."

*   *   *

We are quiet on the drive home. I try to recall the times my cousin Kitty and I played together as children. I hadn't liked her much. She was bossy and quarrelsome, if not a bit perverse. We survived our infrequent visits solely by our love of animals. Invariably, Kitty would confine our cats to my bedroom and try to make them drink copious amounts of water so she could watch them urinate. Of course, it rarely worked in time to her satisfaction, and as soon as she went home, they'd relieve themselves all over my bed. While waiting, she'd suggest we play *doctor*. When I'd balk, she would profess me a sissy, proceed to disrobe, then instruct me on the ins and outs of the female anatomy. When Kitty physically matured, and I did not, for obvious reasons, I avoided her company altogether. She did, however, have two redeeming attributes: a love of Robert Burns' poetry (I believe she possessed his entire collection and could mesmerize an entire room with her readings), and an extraordinary gift of musical talent.

Eva is pointing out notable landmarks to Issie along the way, but Ailsa Craig alone arouses her. Even Grimshaw, seemingly catatonic in the back seat, is resurrected.

"Grimmey, that's where the fairies live," Issie exclaims. "Right?"

"I've heard something to that effect," I play along.

"My mum told me that the fairies live there because an evil man built his house on the fairy path and they got angry and won't come back until he's gone."

"Well, no one lives forever," I cheerfully point out. "Perhaps they'll return when he dies, or better yet, maybe someone should tear down the house."

"Noooo," says Issie, emphatically shaking her head. "Mummy said it isn't that the fairies can't walk around the house; it's that there's a Non-Believer still living there."

I am not familiar with the intricacies of fairy magic, but it doesn't seem logical. "It's an old tale, is it not? Surely the Non-Believer, as you call him, is dead by now."

"Are you a Believer?" she asks me.

"I suppose I had better be," I reply, puzzled over exactly what it is I'm supposed to believe in.

Issie swivels in her seat to face Eva.

"Absolutely," Eva confirms. "So was my father."

We are almost home and I am in a jovial mood. "Your father? Well…nothing would surprise me with him."

"I'm a Believer," Issie announces. "Absolutely."

It is nearly evening by the time we reach Glenapp Castle. I am about to point out the monkey puzzle tree at the fork when without provocation, Issie asks, "Who's Tom?"

How on earth would she know Tom Hutcheson? "He's our new Head Gardener, sweetheart," I answer. "Why do you ask?"

"Because he's very sad."

"What do you mean, Issie?" Eva asks, nonplussed.

"I mean he's lost someone he loves, just like me."

CHAPTER SEVEN

TOM

S OPHIE AND I CONTINUED to dance around the awkwardness of our paths crisscrossing every day. It was simply unavoidable. In our last year of high school we were in all the same classes, and we both competed for our local Curling Club two evenings a week. Our mutual commitment to the sport, and the heartfelt pride of coming from two prominent curling families, threw us together again and again. My late father, Duncan Hutcheson, (Doon to his friends), and her father, Colin Dunbar, were once co-captains of the Ballantrae Curling Club before Dad's cancer ended his career. Even Sophie's mum curled. The truth of it is everyone in Ballantrae, young and old, male and female, has, at one time, enjoyed the thrill of attending a local bonspiel. For most, it was the pinnacle of their social life.

Speculation as to the origin of curling is an ongoing debate to all but my father. "Curling originated in Scotland, my boy," he'd lecture, "and don't let anyone tell you otherwise. The first curling rock was found in a tern in Dunblane, just north of Glasgow in 1511. End of discussion!"

I'd heard this argument since I could walk. The history of curling was branded in my memory, even penetrating my dream life at times. Dad had a print of Pieter Bruegel's *Hunters in the Snow* just to illustrate the obvious difference between true curling and the related "ice-shooting" as the Dutch call it. Though I no longer remember my father's features, I vividly recall his impassioned voice when talking about the sport he adored.

The great appeal of curling is that it's easy to play. The rectangular, iced playing field is called a *sheet*. Two opposing teams of four each attempt, one player at a time, to throw their stone closest to the center of the circular target, called the *house*, at the opposite end of the sheet. The team with the most stones closest to the *button*, the center of the circle, wins. The *sweepers* broom the path of the stone so it bends less and travels further.

It is no exaggeration to say that on Tuesday and Friday evenings from October to the end of March, most of Ballantrae could be found at the rink. The ladies played first, then the gent's league took over. Though the league nights ended in casual socializing, the passion and competitiveness ran deep. Too deep, sometimes.

Remarkably enough, Ballantrae fielded two men's curling teams, one sponsored by Bristols of Scotland, the curling rock excavating company, and the other by Sir John McPhee, the owner of Glenapp Castle. My mother's employer claimed he curled for the Edinburgh Curling Club while at university. The standard joke was that no one was still alive to verify his story. Nonetheless, he was an avid curling enthusiast, and his generosity was appreciated by many. It did nothing to endear me to him, or him to me, but that's another matter.

Ballantrae's youth teams practiced on Monday and Thursday evenings with our games usually scheduled for Saturdays. Sophie's prowess in curling was matched only by my own. By our last season in high school she and I were the best curlers in the district, and we took our positions as separate team captains very seriously.

Sophie didn't have a car so for four torturous years we were forced to ride to and from practices together in my dad's old pickup. We'd discuss local gossip or the strange hours Sir John McPhee seemed to keep, wandering back and forth between his twin turret apartments, then we'd fade into a silence so loud sometimes I could barely breathe. They were the worst hours of my life, and as we wrapped up our final season, I felt as if I'd been unshackled from the town pillory. In my crazed, jealous mind my sole consolation was that Sophie didn't seem to date anyone more than once or twice. I didn't even bother. Why should I? By the end of July, I would be off to Findhorn Gardens to study landscape design. Then, at least, I wouldn't have to look at her beautiful face every single day wishing to God, just once, she'd beg me to kiss her.

Do you know what it's like to love someone and not be able to tell her? Throughout high school I felt suspended in another galaxy with no solid ground under my feet. A chronic insomniac, I'd get up, go to school and think about Sophie all day long. The hopelessness of my situation didn't prod me forward; I stagnated, obsessing over what could have possibly caused her to hate me so much. I told myself it was better than indifference—indifference relegates one to non-existence. To loathe someone means they're still in your thoughts.

Our last tournament of the season was in Stranraer, a larger town nineteen miles to the south. Both the girls' and boys' teams were in an excellent position to win the Youth Districts Championships.

The girls competed first. Their opponent was the team from Barrhill. Sophie's team won the toss, and elected to throw the *hammer*, the last stone of the first round—always a strategic advantage. There would be ten rounds or *ends* in all, and whichever team had the most points took home the championship. One by one, the players alternately threw their curling stones down the icy, pebbled sheet. The skips, usually the team's captain, gave directions to their teammates where to aim their stones, as well as calling to the *sweepers* whether or not to brush the stone's path. Barrhill won the first three ends and I was beginning to lose hope our girls could pull it out. I could see the frustration on Sophie's face as their rocks missed the mark again and again. They were down by six after five ends. At the fifth end break, she gathered her three teammates. I was sitting with my team, next to play, just behind her as she tried to spirit their efforts. "Look now," she counseled. "We mustn't lose faith. We're not playing our best, myself included. Let's try to relax a wee bit. The ice will be faster now with the pebbles gone, so go easy. This championship belongs to us. Let's make our village proud." I wanted to kiss her. So what else was new?

By the finish of the ninth end the teams were tied. Ballantrae had lost the last end so got to throw the final stone. As *skip*, it was Sophie's last shot to win, or lose. There were only four stones remaining in the round house, and she needed to either take one out or land hers closest to the button in the center. Not a whisper could be heard. Slowly, taking a deep breath, she slid across the ice releasing her stone at the perfect time. Every eye in the rink watched her stone careen into her opponent's, sending it flying outside the house for a Ballantrae victory.

It was the first time Ballantrae Girls had ever won the Youth Districts Championship. The home crowd erupted.

Now it was our turn. We played Colmonell, our neighboring village, a team we knew well. I won't recount the details of our match at length because we won easily, but the melee that followed is worthy of note.

Never in the history of our village had both the boys' and girls' teams captured the much-coveted title. We all screamed and whooped like crazed idiots, hugging and crying in disbelief. Our teammates hoisted Sophie and me onto their shoulders and paraded us around the rink as if we'd just won the World Cup. Sophie grabbed my hand to steady herself as we raised our arms in triumph.

It was the first time we'd touched in five years.

When the fever cooled, we all hurried through the rain and tumbled onto the bus. As my coach delayed me with congratulations, I was the last one on and wove my way down the aisle in the dark, looking for a vacant seat. There was only one. It was in the back corner next to Sophie. Now how was it that the most popular girl in school was sitting alone?

"There's nowhere else for me to sit," I stated the obvious.

"Sit here, then," she said. Careful that our thighs didn't touch, we listened to our teammate's revelry. Finally, their adrenalin sapped, a welcomed quiet settled over the bus.

Then, God in Heaven, what did I do to deserve what happened next? Sophie leaned over and whispered so close to my ear I could feel the brush of her warm breath on my neck. "Tom, I've been so awful to you at times. I'm sorry."

"At times?" I objected.

"Most of the time," she admitted.

I didn't know what to say. Part of me wanted to rant how her aloofness had ruined my entire time in high school, yet another, wiser part of me knew forgiveness was the only avenue to any future we might have. Above all, I prayed the conversation would continue unabated forever.

"You're forgiven, Soph. I'm partially responsible, I suppose," not exactly seeing how.

Rain pattered against our window as the lights passed in a smoky blur. Then, as if a simply apology had miraculously dissolved five years of unmitigated torture, Sophie laid her head on my shoulder. It wasn't me who raised his arm so she could nestle closer—it was someone else, some debonair Casanova from the cinema pictures. Only when I felt my chest implode did I realize it wasn't a dream. So close was her hair, I could smell the sweet essence of lavender from her shampoo. Under no control of my own, my hand brushed the loose strands from her face, and when I gazed down at her long lashes, I saw that her eyes were closed. Without her knowing, I gently kissed the crown of her head. Forgive her? There was no question of forgiveness—I would have cut off my throwing arm for her love.

During the last few miles driving home to Glenapp in my pickup, there seemed to be no end to my recklessness. "I need to talk to you," I said.

"What about?" she asked.

"I don't want to start now. It's late, and Mum will be waiting to hear the news."

"All right," she agreed.

"Will you meet me in the glen tomorrow, by the redwood?"

"It's supposed to rain," she hedged.

"You could wear a raincoat."

Sophie smiled that smile I hoped to wake up to one day. "I guess I could do that. What time?"

"I have to work until three o'clock. Could you meet me at half-past?"

She climbed out of the pickup, shut the door and, leaning through the window, said, "I wish your dad could have been there tonight."

"Me, too."

"Maybe he was."

"It's hard to imagine he'd miss the District Championships," I joked.

"I think he was there, Tom. He loved you so much." And imitating my dad's throaty voice, she added, "You've made me proud, son."

"Thanks, Soph."

"Good night, Tom."

"Good night."

I watched the gatekeeper of my heart run through the rain to her cottage. Sophie opened her door, stepped inside the pool of soft, buttery light, and looked back just long enough for me to see her touch the crown of her head where I had kissed her.

CHAPTER EIGHT

EVA

I T WAS THE VERSE from Kahlil Gibran's *The Prophet* that forged a new frontier in my thinking. Andrew recited it to me (how *does* he remember these things?) the night before we drove to Glasgow to meet Issie for the first time. "Remember, Eva," he'd said,

> Your children are not your children.
> They are the sons and daughters of Life's longing for itself.
> They come through you but not from you,
> And though they are with you yet they belong not to you.

"But Issie *didn't* come through me," I'd pointed out.

"Don't you see? That's exactly it!" he'd explained. "If children are life's longing for itself, it doesn't matter if they come through you. What's important is that we embrace the opportunity to be loving guardians throughout our child's life journey."

Put that way, I wasn't sure how equipped I was to be a mother of a five-year-old, especially one I didn't conceive or birth. What if Issie flat out didn't like me? Or worse, what if I didn't like *her*? The prospect was terrifying. By morning, I had conjured up a castle-full of reasons why we were making a colossal mistake. By the time we left Judge Sinclair's chambers, I couldn't recall what they were. The child is beguiling. Personally, I'm grateful she doesn't look like her birth mother. Though Kitty was lovely, I don't want to look at Issie every day wondering if I'm equal to the job of mothering her daughter. I like to think Issie's foreign looks untether her from her past, for I will never have to meet her father, and Kitty is, sadly, gone forever.

When we arrive at Glenapp in the gloaming cast, a herd of deer are nibbling on the boxwood hedge. Andrew playfully drives around the courtyard fountain twice before parking.

"Is this where you *live*?" Issie gasps.

"We live in the north turret wing," Andrew explains. "The rest is a hotel."

"Other people live here, too?"

"Well…" I laugh. "Only for a night or two—it's too expensive to stay much longer."

*   *   *

With only a few days notice, Andrew and I did our very best to convert our spare bedroom into a cozy nest for Issie. It is actually the brightest room in our section of the castle with two, full-length windows overlooking the terraced garden, and the expanse of sea beyond. Issie, anxious to see where she and Grimshaw will sleep, walks right in. There is an antique trunk at the foot of her canopy bed, and more surprising still, a scribbled note resting on top. She hands it to me to read as she excitedly lifts the rounded lid.

> *Dear Miss Campbell,*
> *These clothes belonged to my daughter, Lucy, when she was six. I thought you might like to have them.*
>
> *Respectfully yours,*
> *William Hobbes*

"Who's he?" Issie asks.

"He's one of our gardeners," I reply, not a little nonplussed. Of all our employees here at Glenapp, William is the most remote. A singular nod is the common response to my inquiries about the state of the kitchen garden or how things are going with Tom Hutcheson.

"Something bad happened to his little girl here at the castle, didn't it?" Issie remarks.

"Did it? I'm not so sure here at the castle…" I start to say, but Issie is already spreading the first layer of clothing on the floor.

William's daughter must have had extraordinary taste as each article is brightly patterned in wildly bold designs. Delighted, Issie wiggles into a pair of Lucy's black and white polka-dotted shorts and a yellow blouse, then rummages further until she reaches a layer of buff-colored tissue paper. Beneath is a cache of old-fashioned accouterments, among them a fox-fur scarf, a black-feathered boa, and a felt hat festooned with quail feathers and glistening fake jewels sewn into the fabric. There are costume-beaded necklaces, gemmed brooches, and Indian silk sashes. Issie puts on a pair of elbow-length kid gloves, then runs her small fingers along the sides of the trunk to ensure she hasn't missed anything. Carefully, she slips her hand beneath the loosened fleur-de-lis paper lining and lifts out a photograph.

It's a photograph of a dead infant. "Oh my!" I gasp, snatching it away.

But I am too late. "That baby doesn't look right," Issie grimaces.

"No, it certainly doesn't. I'm sorry, sweetheart. I don't know where this came from."

Whatever was William thinking? This is not your typical turn-of-the-century, sepia-toned image of a deceased infant; it is a color Polaroid taken with a flash at night of a baby wrapped in a burlap bag. The date on the lower right hand corner is 17 October, 1971—nearly twenty-five years ago. I hastily hand it off to Andrew.

Meanwhile, Issie is spinning around the room bejeweled in necklaces and rings and the fox fur collar about her neck. It's remarkable how a phone call can alter one's life. Four days ago, I was childless. Today, I am the mother of a swirling dervish.

*   *   *

Aside from Grimshaw howling like a foxhound on scent, we all slept reasonably well. Andrew rose early and introduced Issie to Kevin while I dressed. I can hardly wait to be with her. Glenapp's vast acreage might be a wee intimidating at first. Hand in hand we'll meet the staff and explore the property top to bottom—maybe even take a row in the lily pond, Grimshaw in tow. Since she already seems to know Tom, we'll start in the walled garden.

But she is not in the kitchen. Kevin informs me that William Hobbes, of all people, came to the pantry door and offered to show Issie around the property.

"William? Surely not!"

Kevin laughs. "He's not going to *eat* her, Eva."

"Don't you think it strange?" I contest. "The man has spoken but one sentence to me in three years, and now, within twenty-four hours, he offers to give Issie a tour?" I cannot account for it.

"I don't think it the slightest bit unusual—William gives tours all the time," Kevin replies in jest. "She's adorable, Eva."

"Isn't she? I never thought I'd feel this way about a child," I confess uneasily.

"I'm happy for you," Kevin says, "though I could do without the dog."

"Grimshaw? He won't eat you," I reply.

"He drools, and he continuously plops his elongated protuberance of a body directly in front of my cellar door. And he whines. You know how I hate whiners."

"Where did William take Issie, do you know?" I ask.

"William said he wanted to show her the walled garden."

"I'll be back," I promise. "Let's review the menus for next week when I return."

"Eva, let me handle it," he offers. "You're a mother now. Take the morning off, for heaven's sake."

*   *   *

It is early yet. I can see their footsteps imprinted in the dew-laden grass; they are side-by-side, close, as if something of great importance were being discussed. Perhaps William will know my daughter better than I by morning's end.

A stiff, bracing wind sweeps in from the sea. To my left, the wooden door to the walled garden repeatedly bangs against the stone edifice. I debate whether or not to interfere. I will decide once I see for myself that Issie is all right. Surely so—William is, after all, a father himself. Perhaps he just misses his daughter and seeks comfort in knowing another child has arrived on the scene. I edge closer. I see them now—they are just inside the nearest glass conservatory. William is on his knees ardently holding Issie's hands in his.

"But I already *am* a Believer," I hear her say.

"And your new mum and dad?" William eagerly asks. *The nerve to ask a little girl such a thing!*

"My new mum, yes," Issie replies. "My new dad...not so sure."

William considers her answer. "That's not good," he mumbles. "No matter, you're the one we've been waiting for. My cousin, Nessie, says children haven't forgotten where they came from and possess the power..."

I've heard enough. Just as I decide to reveal myself, William says, "Run along now and find your mum. She'll be wanting to see you first thing this morning, I expect."

"I'm right here," I say.

Abruptly he stands up. "Morning, Mrs. Campbell."

"Good morning, William. Thank you for showing Issie the garden." My tone is disingenuous, born of guilt and jealousy and possessiveness of a child I have yet to know.

"Pleasure. I hope she comes here often," he says.

Issie looks at me expectantly. "May I? Oh, please..."

"Of course, sweetheart," I say. "This is your home now."

Pointing to William, she says, "He's the one who left me the trunk of clothes."

And the picture of the dead baby. "Yes, I know. Thank you so much, William. It was extremely kind of you," I say, but he is already walking away.

"Good morning, sunshine," I rejoice, giving my new daughter a hug. "And what does William have to say this morning?" *I cannot help myself.*

"He told me that I should come to the walled garden as much as I can because the fairies need me here, and I told him I would."

"*Need* you here?"

"He said the walled garden was the fairy portal, whatever that means, and that his cousin Nessie says children have a double dose of magic, and I don't know—it was confusing. What's a portal?"

"A portal? It's an opening, like a doorway. William must mean…"

that the walled garden is the portal the fairies enter through, but they can't return because there's a Non-Believer residing in the house, and that must mean the house is Glenapp Castle, and the building in question is the north turret wing, and the Non-Believer is…

"Andrew!"

"No, no… not *him*—someone named McPhee," she corrects me.

How does Issie know what I am thinking? Are my thoughts scribed across the cloudless sky, visible for all to see, or does she possess a gift?

"William says McPhee means, *Son of the Black Fairy*," she adds hastily.

She is right.

CHAPTER NINE

TOM

SOPHIE HAD AGREED TO meet me by the redwood the following afternoon. Exactly what I was going to say to her, I didn't yet know, but I had time. My immediate goal was to avoid a long interview over the curling matches. But that night was to be full of surprises! Gathered around the kitchen table was my mum, my Uncle Roddie, and, of all people, Sophie's dad—a sight for the Guinness Book, it was, and one that almost sent me back to my truck.

Uncle Roddie is my Dad's older brother. He runs the sightseeing ferry from Girvan to Ailsa Craig in the old fishing rig Dad gave him before he died. Dad always called her *Judy*, for my mother, of course, but Roddie renamed her *Red Runner*. Curling stones have different colored handles, usually red or yellow. Roddie's lucky color was red.

Like a typical Hutcheson, my uncle is slight in build, fair-haired, and earned the sobriquet Captain Hound for his shadowy, bloodhound eyes. After my father died, Roddie would appear unannounced at our cottage, something he never would have done when Dad was alive. The history there wasn't complicated—Roddie had been the first to discover my mother, the pretty newcomer who started working at Ferguson's Bakery in town. It took him three weeks and dozens of currant scones to conjure up the nerve to ask her out. They dated only twice before he made the fateful error of introducing her to his dapper younger brother, my dad, Doon Hutcheson. Eight years after Dad died, and with no forewarning, Uncle Roddie would appear at our house, silently leaning against the door jamb until somebody noticed him. It drove Mum crazy. Over coffee they'd sit at the kitchen table sharing gossip. Roddie would tell jokes I knew he hadn't laughed at himself. By the time I was in high school, he no longer pretended the visits were to see me. Soon, as my hapless situation with Sophie paralleled his with my mum, I understood how desolate he felt. I also grew to emulate his handling of unrequited love—feign a steel-clad heart while dying of loneliness inside.

My mother, always cordial, welcomed my uncle, sober or inebriated. I never could figure out if she actually liked his company or tolerated him because he reminded her of Dad. Either way, on this particular night, it was not his presence that astonished me. Nor was it Mr. Dunbar's. It was the two of them together.

There were two factors worth noting here. First, my father and Uncle Roddie grew up in the cottage that Colin Dunbar presently inhabited. My grandfather had been the Head Gardener as was his father before him. This incensed my uncle. Each time he visited, he would count the days before I could take Colin Dunbar's job as Head Gardener and reclaim Hutcheson House, as he called it. His boyhood abode held strong remembrances of better times, and it irked him that the likes of Colin Dunbar resided there.

Second, my dad and Colin Dunbar had been best of friends and were considered the two best curlers in southwestern Scotland. When Dad was alive, they co-captained one of Ballantrae's curling teams while Uncle Roddie captained the other. After Dad passed on, Mr. Dunbar captained the team alone and the rivalry between these two men sipping coffee in my kitchen was legendary. The 1997 curling season was concluding and both men's teams from Ballantrae were undefeated. The final match was the following Saturday and the winning team would qualify for the National Title, and if successful there, would go on to compete in the World Cup. Ultimately, Uncle Roddie and Mr. Dunbar both knew the winning captain would likely earn a spot on the Olympic team in Nagano, Japan the next year. The stakes were high. Very high.

Sir John McPhee sponsored Mr. Dunbar's team. Bristols of

Scotland sponsored Uncle Roddie's. Whoever won, there was to be a huge celebration at Glenapp Castle after the tournament. To further complicate matters, Colin Dunbar had been visiting my kitchen too often lately, and he wasn't there to see me. We saw plenty of one another in the walled garden.

"Well, how did you do?" my uncle asked when I entered the kitchen.

"We won," I answered without any of the emotion I'd felt earlier.

"And the girls?" Mr. Dunbar inquired, anxiously.

I wondered why he wasn't home congratulating Sophie himself. "They won, too."

"Congratulations, Tom," Mum said as she prepared a dinner plate for me.

Mr. Dunbar rose to leave. "What time would you like me to be there tomorrow?" I asked.

"Sleep in, Tom. You've had a long day. How about starting at ten?"

"I need to be done by three o'clock, but I'll make up the time another day, if that's all right."

"I'll see you in the morning, son," emphasizing *son* as he riveted his cold eyes on my uncle. "Your dad and I are mighty proud of you."

I thought Roddie was going to throttle him right then and there. God in Heaven, what was Mr. Dunbar trying to do, annihilate himself?

"Thank you," I replied as he headed out the door.

"Tommy, how on earth do you work for that tyrant?" Uncle Roddie rebuked.

"He's all right. I just show up for work and do whatever he asks. I have to admit, he's taught me a lot about gardening." I turned to my mother. "Mum, what was Mr. Dunbar doing here, anyway?"

"Sir John asked if Colin and I would coordinate the castle staff, indoors and out, for the Gala Affair, as he calls it."

"Bloody hell, Judy," Roddie snapped. "What do you need Colin for? You run things at Glenapp."

"Roddie, you're very flattering, but I only manage the staff inside the castle, not all the groundskeepers. That's Colin's department."

"That slippery fool! I wouldn't trust him with my rusty shovel." Mum and I smiled at one another. "And what the devil is he doing here on a Friday night? He should be home with his family." Rather an odd statement coming from the likes of my aloof uncle, but I agreed wholeheartedly.

Then suddenly, Roddie's expression changed. "What about Sir John, Judy? Does he still bother you? I swear, if he puts his hands on you, I'll kill him."

"Now, Roddie, calm yourself. I can handle him. He's harmless, really."

"He's NOT harmless!" Roddie bellowed, slamming his fist on the table. "I don't like the way he looks at you, and you haven't answered my question."

"It's not any different from the way *you* look at me," she jibed, irritated now by his inquisition. Uncle Roddie looked embarrassed yet unconvinced. That was exactly the point. He knew precisely what Sir John was thinking.

"Why do you keep it a secret where you disappear to twice a year? Are you working for him?"

"No, Roddie, I'm working *with* him. It's a special project to save…" She turned away. "I can't talk about it."

"Why not, if it's such a worthy cause? Out with it, Judy," Roddie harassed.

Having heard this exchange countless times, I yawned and headed to bed.

"Good night, Tommy," Uncle Roddie said, giving me a hug. "I'm proud you're my nephew."

"Thanks, Uncle Roddie."

*   *   *

As I readied for bed, I wondered if the long, sordid history between these two men wasn't coming to a head. There was only one factor that might save them from self-destruction—they both reviled Sir John McPhee.

Mr. Dunbar felt that as a team sponsor Sir John should financially support the team and leave the coaching to him. He hated when the arrogant philanderer came to practices, insinuating to him that they should do this and that; it was unsportsmanlike conduct and his strategies were grossly outdated. But just as Mum couldn't openly rebuff Sir John's lecherous overtures without jeopardizing her job, so it was with Mr. Dunbar—the position of Head Gardener guaranteed his family's security and he had no other vocation to turn to. He had kept his wits about him thus far; I wondered what might happen if Sir John meddled during the championships.

The reason behind Roddie's disdain for Sir John is painful to tell. Since I was a little boy I'd sensed something contemptible had happened to my uncle. Dad refused to talk about it and I never dared to ask my mother. I was seventeen when Roddie spilled the beans himself.

As soon as I received my driver's license, Uncle Roddie occasionally asked if I wanted to help on the ferry to and from Ailsa Craig. I was happy to oblige—anything to escape Glenapp Castle and the never-ending torture of seeing Sophie everywhere I went.

One moonlit night, after the last run, Roddie suggested we go for a spin in Girvan Bay. I realized too late he'd been drinking. No surprise, really, but it made me uneasy, not yet having the confidence to navigate home in the dark. Curling was the topic of conversation when, suddenly, Roddie launched into a scathing soliloquy about Sir John.

"The goddamn idiot is a pervert. You know that, Tommy."

I hadn't heard *that* before. "How so?" I asked.

"No one's ever told you, have they?"

"Told me what?"

So, there *was* a story. Now I was to hear the truth.

"I was thirteen when Sir John bought Glenapp Castle," my uncle plunged right in. "My mother, your grandmother, had passed on about four months previous from colon cancer. Same as Doon. Gives me the willies to think about what the hell's in store for me. And you, too, for that matter. Anyway, before she died, she wrote each of us a letter: Dad, me and Doon. I cherished that letter more than any other thing on earth. Dad always favored Doon, but I was closest to Mum. I took her death hard. Real hard."

Roddie took two long, slow swigs of whisky, then reached over to turn off the ferry engine.

"What are you doing?" I asked, nervously.

"The wind's died down a bit, and I like just drifting out to sea. No sounds but the water lapping against the hull." Roddie leaned against the railing of the captain's deck and lit his pipe. It was several minutes before he continued.

"Before the McPhees came, Doon and I and the other staff kids pretty much had the run of the place. For three years the castle was owned by folks from America who were never there. When the McPhees bought Glenapp in 1967, Doon and I still used to play hide-and-seek inside. Dad would have jailed us if he'd known. We pulled it off for weeks, first when Sir John and Lady Sylvia were gone, then we got braver and started playing when they were home. On this particular Sunday in July, however, we actually thought they were out.

"Of course, the riskiest place to play was in the north turret wing because it was brand new and considered dangerous. You're a Believer, Tommy—you know what I'm talking about. Sir John always kept one of the apartments locked, but I was running out of time to hide so I tried it anyway. As luck would have it, the door was ajar, so I snuck in and hid behind a curtain. At first I thought the sounds I heard were of an animal whimpering, then I realized it was a woman. When I heard her muffled cries grow louder and louder, I couldn't make myself leave. They were in the closet. You know, Tommy, how enormous those closets are, shelves all around the periphery for storage and such. You could sleep in there. I peeked around the curtain and saw the fucking bastard McPhee had Fiona, one of the maids, pinned against the wall with her own undergarments stuffed in her mouth. She was only a couple of years older than I was, for God's sake! I swear to you, I'll never forget the frightful expression on Fiona's face as Sir John McPhee thrust himself into her, grunting like a wild pig, and he was hurting her—there was blood all over the place. I must have screamed because they both froze at the sight of me. 'Get out of here, you conniving brat,' McPhee yelled, and he slammed the door shut. No problem for me. I blew out of there so fast I nearly tripped over my own feet. I had no idea where Doon was, but I knew I had to get out of the castle, so I ran into the glen and hid there until dark. You know that gigantic redwood that sits on the bank of the burn, the one with the partially hollowed-out trunk?"

Sure I did. It's where Sophie and I meet.

"I crawled into the heart of that tree," he continued, "and shook until the sun went down. Doon almost got caught, too. He was looking

for me in Sir John's study. Wouldn't you know that's right where Sir
John headed next. Doon had to hide under the desk for over an hour.

"Anyway, I didn't know what to do. Didn't know if anyone would
even believe me. If I exposed Sir John for the monster he was, Fiona
and maybe Dad would lose their jobs. Even at thirteen, I could figure
that out. If I didn't tell, poor Fiona could fall victim to God knows
what. I sat like a dumb mute during supper letting Doon make up
stories about what we did all afternoon.

"The next day I faked a cold and skipped school. I shouldn't say
faked because I felt like hell. Sick to my stomach. Sick at heart, I was. I
never felt so lonely and miserable in my life. If Mum had been alive, I
would have told her everything; she'd have known what to do. I wasn't
so sure about Dad. I was in a heap of trouble either way. Doon was
only eleven and couldn't keep a secret if his life depended on it. So as
soon as Dad left the house the next morning, I retrieved Mum's letter
from under my mattress and headed for the redwood tree. I'd read it a
hundred times, knew it by heart, but it always comforted me to know
she'd actually touched the paper and handwritten every word. Anyway,
I must have fallen asleep.

"All of a sudden I heard footsteps approaching from the other side
of the tree. Panicked, I scrambled to my feet. It was Sir John. I swear to
you, Tommy, I've never been so fucking scared in my life. He towered
over me like a giant, and with a mocking smile on his face, he said,
'What's that you have there? It's Roddie, isn't it? Shouldn't you be in
school?'

"'I'm sick,' I mumbled, quivering like a silly lass. Looking back on
it now, Tommy, I should have run like hell, but my legs were mired in
cement.

"'What's that you're reading, a love letter from a little girlfriend?'
he taunted.

"I gripped Mum's letter so tightly, it tore like rice paper. As I
looked down to see the damage, Sir John grabbed it out of my hand
and started to read it aloud. 'My Dearest Roddie, When I am gone,
no matter what happens in your life, you must always remember how
much I love you.'

"'Give me that,' I demanded. I jumped up to grab it but Sir John
jerked it away, holding it just out of my reach.

"'How tender,' the fucker jibbed, and then he proceeded to tear Mum's letter into tiny pieces.

"'Stop that!' I cried. 'That's not yours!'

"'No, Roddie,' he said. 'It's not. It's yours, and I'm going to give it back to you.'

"Thank God in Heaven! Relief poured over me. Somehow, I could piece it back together and all wouldn't be lost. Then, Sir John commanded, 'OPEN YOUR MOUTH.'

"I knew right then and there that this man was capable of hurting me."

"'OPEN,' he shouted a second time.

"Sir John made me chew and swallow Mum's letter, one piece at a time. Then he threatened, 'If you ever mention what you saw yesterday, I'll make sure your father never works again. Do you understand?'"

Roddie tilted his head to the sky and fixed his gaze on the stars overhead. There were thousands visible that night, and I was grateful to see Orion, my favorite. The ferry gently rocked back and forth with the waning tide. Water and the lulling sway—I understood the womb-like haven it provided for my uncle now.

"There wasn't any way I could go home," Roddie went on, "so I ran away. Not very far, mind you. I ran to Auntie Fay's in Ballantrae and told her everything. I was hysterical by then, and it poured out of me like an uncorked dam. I remember her saying over and over again, 'That swine! Don't you worry, young Roddie, I'll take care of this.' She put the kettle on and promised I could sleep on her couch for as long as I wanted. As soon as I dozed off, she drove to Glenapp Castle and told my Dad everything."

"What about Fiona?" I wondered aloud.

"Auntie Fay got her another job straight away. I worried about Sir John thinking I had something to do with it, but Fiona walked right up to him and quit the next morning, and believe me, Auntie Fay made sure everyone in the place knew what happened. It was Lady Sylvia who didn't understand Fiona's sudden departure. I felt for her. She's a nice woman, never said a nasty word to anyone. How she puts up with that conniving son-of-a-bitch, I'll never know."

Roddie drew hard on his pipe; I sensed the story was over. He turned on the ferry's engine and we followed the moon's path back to Girvan.

I had never heard anything so cruel in my life.

*   *   *

As I lay awake, I could still hear Roddie chastising my mother for her laissez-faire attitude towards Sir John, but images of winning the championships and Sophie's head on my shoulder blended like an anesthetic, and I fell asleep.

The following morning I grabbed a scone and hurried to the walled garden, dressing as I ran. The late March air was biting that Saturday morning, and the dampness from the previous night's rain penetrated through my thin, woolen jacket. Walking through the arched doorway of the walled garden, I noticed a light frost had settled over the plants, muting the colors in a blanket of dusty gray and pale blue.

Mr. Dunbar stood up from his weeding, and with a tilt of his head indicated I was to continue my work in the herb garden. His voiceless directive forebode a foul mood, and I acquiesced with a nod.

The herb garden was my designated testing ground, and I took every opportunity to prove my competence there. The area was approximately forty feet in diameter with a circular path dividing the two round herbal beds. In the center sat a stone birdbath, Celtic in design, around which the seedlings of parsley, lemon thyme, and sage had begun to sprout. Last spring, I had experimented with fennel, planting two very different types, one familiar to most weekend gardeners for its wispy, green silhouette, (Unbelliferae), and the other (Atropureum), bearing a dark purple leaf that added contrasting color and definition to the inner bed. The slightest brush of fennel released the pungent scent of aniseed, and I inhaled deeply as I considered whether or not to divide the prolific herb. Looking around, I took stock of the other perennial herbs starting to peep through the ground: three varieties of thyme, tarragon, chives, oregano, rosemary, and the parsleys I had added last fall. And the mints! How rampant they were! I walked around the circle and decided two things: first, my primary job was to figure out what I was going to say to Sophie that afternoon, and second, it was unsafe to make any important decisions regarding the garden that day; I was too distracted. I divided the fennel, scrubbed the fountain, and weeded until it was time to leave.

"Well, then," I said to Mr. Dunbar. "I'll be off, if it's all right with you."

"Actually, I've another job for you, Thomas. I seem to be driving the Missus a bit crazy with my snoring. She won't admit that she snores as loud as I do but there's no telling her that. We'll just clean out the old boathouse so I can throw down a mattress, and we can both get some sleep."

The old boathouse was used mostly for storing garden tools. With the doors open, you have a fantastic view of the lily pond—I envied him that, but I had more pressing matters that afternoon. Yet what could I say? In ten minutes I'm supposed to meet your daughter, the love of my life? That I had waited for four years to tell her how I truly felt?

"You look pale, boy. What's the matter with you? Come along. I won't keep you but a minute."

My fate sealed, I followed quickly behind, anxious to get on with it. The idea of him sleeping in an old, abandoned hut hit me as strange, even ridiculous. I couldn't understand it, really. The cramped, rectangular structure might have accommodated a mattress and small table, but it wasn't even wired for electricity, and it sat well outside the walled garden, maybe fifty yards from the Gardener's cottage. The notion of anyone actually sleeping there, especially in March, seemed bizarre. Finding my voice, I asked, "Aren't you going to be a bit cold out here, Mr. Dunbar?"

"Aye, perhaps, lad, but the Missus can jolly well give up one of her blankets for my chivalry."

We cleared the shed of its contents and agreed a good sweep and a floor wash would satisfy the task. I offered to clean the windows in the morning.

"You can go Thomas, and thank you. Take pity on me, boy, for this is the price of matrimony." I wondered if perhaps it was the price of spending too much time in my kitchen.

I strode away nonchalantly, then sprinted towards the wooded glen. There Sophie sat, her knees drawn to her chest, her gaze riveted on the rushing waterfall. She had come.

She looked so beautiful. Her coppery hair that she always haphazardly pulled back was free now and fell loosely across her shoulders. If only I could sneak up behind her, wrap my arms around her waist, and smother her neck with kisses, I would never emerge.

"Hi."

"Hi, Soph."

I must have looked shell shocked. "Are you O.K.?" she asked, tilting her head in concern.

"Aye," I laughed, "I'm fine. I'm sorry I was late. Your dad wanted me to clear out the old boat house, of all things. Look, could we take a walk?"

For millennia, the Garleffin Burn has meandered its way through the Stinchar Valley in wide, sweeping turns. A carpet of yellow, pink, and lavender wildflowers skirts the mossy banks all year long. It is a magical forest of fir, birch, and wild fuchsia trees, and huge blossoming rhododendrons over ten feet tall. There are two walking bridges, and within a few minutes, Sophie and I had reached the first.

We sat, side by side, our legs dangling over the edge. The stream, teeming from the previous night's downpour, rushed beneath our feet, thrashing the stones to-and-fro in the riverbed. I begged for time to stop. Do you remember your first love? I recall my moments with Sophie in the most astounding detail, even today.

"What I want to tell you is this," I began. "Whatever I did to make you mad at me, I'm sorry. However I hurt your feelings, I'm sorry for that, too. I must be dumb or something because I just don't get it. The problem is I wouldn't care except that I miss having you to talk to. That's the truth of it. I know we can't play the way we used to, but if we could at least be friends…. I think I could live with that."

"I don't hate you, Tom," Sophie replied, shaking her head in dismay, "and you didn't do anything wrong."

This was a revelation. "What was it, then?"

Sophie looked at me as if I must be joking. "Don't you know?"

"No, I truly don't."

"The night of your thirteenth birthday, Dad saw our eyes lock. When I got home, he lectured me about how you and I were getting too old to play like little kids. 'It's time to get serious about your studies, join clubs at school, and make some girl friends. From now on there would be no more frolicking around with Tom Hutcheson,' he commanded.

"I started to cry, and he thought that was a sign there was already something between us. Later that night, I overheard him through my bedroom wall telling Mum he'd be damned if his daughter was going to get involved with a Catholic boy. The next morning, he threatened to take away your apprenticeship in the walled garden if I didn't stop fooling around with you. I debated telling you, Tom, but what good would it have done? It just would have hurt you more. It was easier to let you think you had done something wrong. I hate myself for it, but I didn't want you to lose your apprenticeship, either. I prayed that you'd just forget about me and fall for someone else."

"No chance of that, Sophie. No chance at all."

"Me, neither."

I shook my head in disbelief. "What kind of bullshit is that? I've never seen your parents go to church, and I'm about as Catholic as this bridge."

"It's not about going to church, Tom. You have to understand, no one in my family has married outside the Protestant religion for centuries. It's inconceivable to my parents."

"How dense I've been," I said.

Sophie leaned into my shoulder. "I'm so sorry. You've no idea how guilty I feel. The only excuse is that Dad frightens me, and I was afraid he'd…you know."

"What? Does he hurt you?" I asked, cringing at the thought.

"No, but I'm careful not to give him any excuses to."

"At least it's out in the open; now we can talk it through."

"Aye, we can talk, but it doesn't change anything, Tom. Dad will still stop us from seeing one another, especially now that we're older. Nothing's changed except you finally know the reason that I've been so awful to you."

"We're seventeen now, Soph. He can't control our lives forever."

"He can until I go away to university, and he can fire you as his apprentice as well."

This was true, but I had a secret weapon of my own and he knew it. There was another reason Sophie's mother was kicking him out, and it had nothing to do with snoring.

We sat quietly for several minutes, until, even surprising myself, I said, "Sophie Dunbar, I love you. I think I always have. I don't know where that puts us, but that's what I came here to tell you."

Sophie threw her arms around my neck dissipating into thin air all the agony and frustration of the four worst years of my life. I knew in that moment what true happiness felt like. I kissed her hair, hot from the afternoon sun. I kissed her forehead, the lobe of her ear, her eyes, and the tip of her nose, until finally, our lips brushed ever so slightly. We both pulled back, ecstatic yet shocked by what we were doing.

"It's okay, Tom," she whispered. "I want you to kiss me."

It was the kiss by which I measure all others.

*　　　*　　　*

Sophie and I strolled home, hand in hand, pondering our future, loving life. We were almost to Glenapp's driveway when we heard Sir John's Jaguar increase in speed instead of slowing down as it approached the curve. William Hobbes's little girl, Lucy, was riding her bike along the driveway's edge. Sir John screeched around the corner, and seeing her too late, overcorrected, nearly hitting the monkey puzzle tree, then swerved too far to the right ramming right into her. Lucy never even saw it coming, never uttered a scream, and I suspect never felt the impact of hitting the ground from ten feet in the air.

Sir John McPhee kept right on accelerating towards Glenapp Castle.

"Oh my God!" Sophie screamed.

"Wait, I'll go help Lucy," I proposed. "You go get Mum and the others. And ring an ambulance."

Cautiously, I started to cradle Lucy's limp body in my arms when I remembered you're not supposed to move victims with possible spinal cord injuries. She was wearing black and white polka-dotted shorts, yellow sandals, and a bright red, hooded sweater. How could Sir John not have seen her? Lucy was notorious for her outlandish, colorful clothing and was much beloved among the staff families for her ready giggle and flamboyant costumes. She was only six years old.

I could tell from her shallow breathing that she was alive, but my hands were trembling so, I couldn't track her pulse. Then, for a second, she opened her eyes. "Tell me where it hurts, Lucy," I implored. But the moment of consciousness was to be her last for Lucy Hobbes started to convulse. Good God in heaven, what a ghastly sight to see! There was nothing I could do but watch her thrash about and pray she didn't bite her tongue. "No, this can't be happening," I bemoaned to the skies. "Not to sweet Lucy." When the seizure was over, she lay, flaccid as a rag doll, frothing at the mouth.

"Lucy, wake up," I begged. "Come back. Lucy!"

At last, Sophie, both her parents, and my mum came running down the hill.

"Did you ring an ambulance?" I yelled, no longer able or willing to hide the tears.

"Aye, it's on the way," Sophie assured me. "Tom, is she…?"

"Oh God, Sophie, she's had a fit. It was horrid."

"Is she conscious?" Mum asked, all out of breath and clearly distraught.

"No, not anymore. Mum, what do we do? We've got to *do* something," I pleaded.

From a distance, we heard the ambulance siren grow louder and louder, then quiet as it drove up Glenapp's driveway. My heart sank as Sophie waved her arms to indicate they should slow down. Two medics jumped out, quickly evaluated Lucy's condition, then deftly rolled her onto a flat board and placed Lucy inside the ambulance. I began to feel sick to my stomach.

"Who's next of kin," one asked.

"Her father's gone for the day—it's his day off. I'll go with you," Mrs. Dunbar offered. "Somebody should call William's brother. I'll wager they're having a pint at Frey's Pub."

Sirens blaring, Lucy Hobbes was taken to Girvan Hospital thirty miles away.

Mum looked at me in anguish, her olive skin a dull hue of marble gray. "Tom, what happened?"

"Sir John came barreling up the driveway and swerved to miss hitting the monkey puzzle tree but drove straight into Lucy instead. She flew…it was awful, Mum. He must have tossed her twenty feet in the air. Look at her bike, it's smashed to bits. Then he just drove on as if nothing had happened. I can't get over it. There's no way he didn't know he'd hit her."

"We need to get the bike out of here," commanded Mr. Dunbar. "Hide it in our garage; I don't want Sir John confiscating it."

"Aye, sir," I acquiesced, stunned at the implication.

"I wish I could follow Victoria to the hospital, but I don't think I can leave," Mum lamented. After a moment, she turned to Mr. Dunbar. "Surely, Colin, you don't think Sir John would deny…?"

"I don't see him here, Judith. He's had plenty of time to return to the scene of the accident. I would imagine he's checking his Jaguar for marks of impact."

I looked at Sophie. Her silence was, I knew, calculated to conceal the fact that we'd both seen the accident as we were coming out of the glen together. I was glad one of us had kept our senses. What had happened was terrible, yet I secretly resented the intrusion on what had been one of the best days of my life. I tried to recapture the afterglow of our long, lingering kiss, but it was gone.

"Colin, what do we do?" Mum asked.

Mr. Dunbar thought for several moments. "Thomas, are you absolutely sure of the facts?"

"Aye, Sir. I saw what I saw."

"Of all the times!" Mr. Dunbar fumed. "As if it isn't enough that an innocent young girl is run over and nearly killed; we've got half of Ayrshire coming for a celebration next weekend, and the goddamn bastard is sponsoring my team. What a disaster!" I truly felt for him, for all of us.

"I've got to get back," Mum said. "Tom, will you wait up for me?"

"Sure, of course. Mum, are you going to be okay?" I asked, loving the exchange, hoping we could talk to one another this caringly for the rest of our lives.

"I'm not sure. My God, the poor child! Shouldn't Lady Sylvia know what happened? Yet, how can I tell her that her husband just ran over Lucy when it looks like he doesn't want anyone to know? I could lose my job if I tell her, and lose my job if I don't."

Mr. Dunbar advised, "Let's not do anything until William gets back. In the meantime, Tom, I want you to get the bike out of here."

We heard the rumbling of a car coming up the driveway. It was William. At first, he veered left in the direction of his cottage, then seeing us all standing in the fading light, he backed up. It was the exact scene we didn't want him to witness.

"Hello, there," he greeted. "Planning traffic patterns for the big celebration, are we?"

Then he saw Lucy's bike lying crushed on the grass.

"Oh, Crevins! What's happened?" he faltered as he climbed out of his car.

"Lucy's in the hospital, William; Victoria is with her. Sir John hit her coming up the driveway," Mr. Dunbar tried to calm his voice. "She's unconscious right now, but I'm sure she's in good hands."

"Sir John was drunk," William spat with a vengeance. "I saw him at Frey's with Marti McPherson, drinking and kissing like young sweethearts."

Marti McPherson was the strikingly beautiful daughter of the President of Bristols of Scotland, the sponsor of Roddie's curling team. She couldn't have been more than twenty-six. Sir John was in his seventies, for goodness sake. What on earth would she see in an old man?

William continued, "The cunning bastard! I've never much liked him, but I never…! Oh my poor Lucy," he wailed. "Is anything broken? I've got to go to the hospital. Where's Sir John now? I'd like to strangle him with my own hands."

No one spoke. Finally, I felt compelled to tell William what I had seen, minus the horrific details of the accident and Lucy's convulsing. There was plenty of time for that.

William asked, "Colin, could you take me to the hospital? I don't trust myself behind the wheel."

As they drove off, a dense, colorless haze settled over Ailsa Craig. I sensed something was strangely awry with our small enclave at Glenapp Castle, and I didn't like the fact that Ailsa Craig thought so, too.

"What about the bike?" Sophie asked.

"Tom, put it behind William's cottage," Mum suggested. "Leave him a note that it's there. He can decide what he wants to do with it in the morning."

CHAPTER TEN

ANDREW

IT IS SAID THAT you're not truly a man until your father dies. I suppose the implication is that while he's alive, no matter what happens, one's father is there for you.

I listen to the rhythmic cadence of Eva's breathing from the winged-backed chair my father gave me for my twenty-first birthday. When I'd rung him up to thank him, he'd replied, "Thank your mother; I've no time for such nonsense."

Ruaridh M. Campbell, Honorary Professor and Dean of Veterinary Medicine, author of nine books, and private consultant to the Royal Family at Balmoral. It is an honorable litany of achievement.

So there is to be no reconciliation. I would have liked to have said goodbye. I wonder if he wished the same.

Mother won't be able to manage alone any longer with her crippling arthritis. Though Eva and I have not yet spoken of this, it is logical for her to come live here with us. The turret apartment adjacent to ours is vacant, though I confess I get the creeps every time I go near the place. Once when my insomnia had me wandering about the castle, I heard what sounded like someone opening and shutting drawers in there. Suddenly, my insides felt as if they'd been doused in the Arctic Sea.

When I tried to open the door, it was locked. Eva later told me we've never had a key to that door.

I saw the ravens yesterday—dozens of them, perched, every one, on the north turret window sill as if there weren't hundreds of other ledges to roost on. I must ask Eva if she saw them. There are lots of things we need to talk about.

Eva sweeps a hand across my side of the bed and, not finding me there, props herself up on one elbow. "You all right? Oh, sweetheart, you couldn't sleep, could you?"

She slips into her brown satin dressing gown and contracts like a turtle in my lap. "Thinking about your dad?"

She is the only one who calls him that. "Among other things."

"What about your mum? Should she come live with us?"

"Do you think we could manage her, too? Not very good timing, is it?"

"You're her only child, and we don't want her going to a nursing home, now do we?" We'll put her in the adjacent apartment, and when her arthritis gets bad enough she can use the lift. It will be fine. And she'll love being around Issie."

"You're an angel," I tell her.

"What else is on your mind?"

"I've been considering the wisdom of delving into Glenapp's past a bit. What do you think?"

She is quickly awakened. "I don't think it's a good idea."

I'm a bit taken aback; it's not like her. "But aren't you curious what went on in our own home? We've been here nearly ten years. It's pitiful how little we know about Glenapp's past, and I could easily do some snooping around without anyone the wiser."

"You certainly have more pressing business," she reminds me, cheekily.

There is no holding it back now. "There's something I have to tell you," I say.

She is suddenly standing. "Likewise," she intones. "You go first—unless you're going to tell me you're guardian of another child."

"In a manner of speaking, yes," I reply, cautiously, "but this one isn't mine, either."

Her arms laced across her chest, she says, "Go on. I'm listening."

"Yesterday, when you and Issie went for a walk in the glen, and just before Mum called to tell me Father had passed on, I was helping Tom revive the irrigation system by the gazebo when I hit something solid with my shovel. When I knelt down, I discovered an old burlap sack—you know, the kind they store potatoes in. I emptied the contents to the ground and human bones fell out. It was a wee baby's skeleton, Eva. The very same, I believe, pictured in the photo Issie found in William's trunk."

"What makes you think so?" she asks, eyes widened with surprise.

"It's too coincidental. How many babies are buried in a burlap bag? And remember the woman standing by the gazebo, staring at the ground the day we bought Glenapp Castle? Same place, exactly."

"This is someone else's story, sweetheart. If it makes you feel better, ring the police."

"No. I don't want them involved. Not yet—not until I've spoken with William."

"Where's the wee thing now?" she wants to know.

"I put it in the kitchen cellar, in one of Kevin's jar trays. Don't worry, I covered it with an old tarp."

"Oh Andrew, what if Kevin stumbles across it? Or even worse, Issie! I think we should find a new..."

"I agree, but where? I can't rebury it by the gazebo. The dogs were both digging right alongside me, or, at least Grimshaw was; Rosie seemed to have the sense to leave it well enough alone. Given the opportunity, he'll certainly unearth it again. He was still digging after I left."

Eva crawls back in my lap. "It's weird," she whispers, shivering a little.

It is with great humility that I pose this next question. "Eva, do you ever feel drafts of frigid air around here?"

"Of course, I do. This is a castle—castles are drafty."

She is avoiding the issue at hand; I know her. "No," I clarify. "I mean in unexpected places."

"Oh, Andrew. I need to tell you what William implied yesterday. You see, he was telling Issie..."

I will not let her divert me, not just yet. "Perhaps with your family having haunted hotels, and all that, you're more used to it." This is a back-handed tactic, but I suspect she knows exactly what I'm talking about.

"We didn't *sleep* in our hotels. And I certainly never *felt* one, but I agree, we may have a slight problem..."

"But you believe in fairy legend?"

"I believe in good will towards others, and anyone who is impertinent enough to build his house on the age-old fairy path is destined to suffer the consequences. One mustn't disregard these things, and that leads precisely to what I wanted to tell you. Yesterday, William..."

We are interrupted by a knock on the door. Issie, rubbing the nap sand from her eyes, is trailed by Grimshaw who forever looks as if he's just emerged from the underworld. On to the lap pile she climbs; Grimshaw is declined.

"I miss my mum," Issie murmurs.

Eva draws her close. "Of course you do. I'm sure she misses you, too."

"Do you love me yet?" Issie asks. It has been two days.

"Of course we do," Eva assures her.

"Grimmey says I need to be patient—that it takes a long time to love someone."

This is too much. "You and Grimshaw talk to one another?" The child bewilders me. By day she enchants everyone she meets, hotel guests and staff alike, while at night she commiserates with her dog concerning the nuance of parental love? At present, her canine companion is incessantly barking at something outside our bedroom window. First Issie, then Eva, clamor to see what has captivated his keen interest.

"Someone's driving away," Issie reports.

"It's frightfully early, don't you think?" Eva comments. "It's just half past six."

"A delivery, perhaps," I surmise.

"In a Mercedes sedan?"

*   *   *

I am second to grace the kitchen. Kevin, in full chef's attire, is already brewing coffee.

"Was someone here? We saw a Mercedes...whatever is the matter with you? You look dreadful."

Kevin reluctantly lifts a business card from his chest pocket.
"Oh Crevins! What did this Vicente Flor look like?"
"Like Issie," he murmurs. "Andrew, he looks just like her."
"Is he coming back?"
"At ten o'clock."
It is but three hours away.

CHAPTER ELEVEN

TOM

LUCY HOBBES STILL HASN'T woken up. To this day, nearly ten years after Sir John smashed into her small body, Lucy inhabits a world of total darkness. She breathes—that is all.

The neurologist said she suffered a severe, traumatic brain injury, and after two unsuccessful surgeries to relieve the pressure on her brain, her team of physicians advised William to disconnect the respirator.

The hallways of the hospital were lined with friends and supporters William had known since he was a wee boy. There wasn't a child in Ballantrae more beloved than Lucy Hobbes. Half the village hoped she would give up the fight; the other half was afraid William would go with her.

But Lucy wasn't ready to die. Not yet. Her young, healthy lungs expanded and contracted, expanded and contracted, as William wondered how he was to survive.

*   *   *

Despite the horrific events of the past twenty-four hours, preparations for the party Saturday night continued in earnest. The upcoming gala affair, inspired to commemorate the winner of the men's curling championship, had Ballantrae and the neighboring villages in a frenetic state of excitement. Even old rumors of Sir John's involvement in some sort of lurid underground activity would not discourage the most cynical speculator from a once in a lifetime visit to Glenapp Castle.

The bustle around the castle, however, was thick with gossip about what had happened to Lucy. As you might imagine, William's recounting that he had seen Sir John with Marti McPherson at Frey's Pub was, unto itself, enough to rankle even the most loyal servants. But the audacity to lie about hitting their beloved Lucy—that was unforgivable.

With William now unavailable, Mr. Dunbar carried the burden of preparing the castle grounds for Saturday's affair. When Sophie and I offered to fix up his new sleeping quarters, he acquiesced without protest. We scrubbed the inside of the musty old boathouse top to bottom with such vigor you'd have thought it was our own first love nest. We thrilled in the irony, touching hands when we could, even stealing kisses when we knew no one was watching. Sophie's mum, a bit overzealous concerning her husband's departure, offered the spare single bed from Sophie's room and escorted us out the door. My mum donated a small pine table. With the addition of an antique kerosene lamp, the old boathouse was more than suitable for Mr. Dunbar's nights turned out. In fact, if you asked me, it was downright cozy. Mr. Dunbar said there was one thing he'd like us to add, if we didn't mind. It was a little treasure titled *A Book of Scotland*, his favorite. Sophie ran to oblige and his new abode was ready for occupancy.

For Mr. Dunbar, worse than the work to be done was the lost opportunity to practice for the curling championships. Day after day, he watched Roddie's team gather at the Stranraer rink, fine-tuning their strategy for the final match just six days away. And I knew, unless I made some excuse, I would be helping him after school so he'd be free to practice with his team. But I was in love, so I lied. I told him I had obligations after school all that week. Sophie did the same. We were free and accounted for.

The following five afternoons spent with Sophie on the shore of the Irish Sea were among the finest hours of my life. We slipped off our shoes, buried our toes in the sand, and talked. Sophie confessed her fear of her father, her guilt in not relating to her mother, and her dream of being the best woman curler in the world. Then, an awkward silence foretold her quandary—she had received an invitation to train in Halifax with Hal Munro, the most renowned curling coach in Canada. So, so far away from me, she said. Dalhousie University had sweetened the offer by reducing her tuition. She had no choice. I laid my head in her lap and told her I had been accepted at Findhorn Gardens for a year-long internship with the possible option of staying on as staff.

How could it be that the love of my life was moving a thousand miles away? I was so tired of missing the people I loved. Our time together became more and more surreal as we plunged headlong into a spiraling whirlpool of unfathomable longing. We explored each other's bodies with utmost reverence surrendering all but our virginity, for Sophie and I agreed, the physical melding of our souls would be celebrated in a private place, undisturbed by fear of discovery. We came so close, so many times; it took all my willful strength to control my wanting of her. She was perfection in the guise of a human goddess, and she loved me. I ached with desire for her, but I could wait.

*   *   *

After Lucy's accident, Sir John disappeared. No surprise, really, but it further fueled the staff's building resentment, not to mention sending Lady Sylvia into a near frenzy over details of the upcoming event. So on Friday afternoon, when I came home from the beach, I assumed Mum would be at the castle working overtime and our cottage empty. Not only did I find her in the kitchen, I saw Mr. Dunbar slip through the back door.

"What was Mr. Dunbar doing here, Mum?" I asked, accusingly. "It's none of his business what I do after school. I'm eighteen tomorrow, not that you seemed to have remembered, and I'm sick and tired of being treated like a child. And why is he hanging about? He acts like he practically lives here."

"Sit down, please, Thomas," my mother replied. "Colin was not here to discuss your comings and goings. He was here because I invited him. And I haven't forgotten your birthday. I'm sorry it's the same day as the party tomorrow, truly I am. What *have* you been doing after school, now that you bring it up?" she asked, worried now that I was in some kind of trouble.

"Meeting Sophie at the beach," I declared, throwing down my schoolbooks.

"Oh my," she sighed. "No, Colin didn't mention anything about you and Sophie, but I'm sure he would have, had he known." She paused for several seconds before continuing. "How long have you two…?"

"Not long enough," I raged. "And had it not been for Mr. Dunbar, it would have happened years ago. We love each other, Mum, and there isn't anything you can do about it."

"I have no intention of doing anything about it. I love Sophie. You know that. I'm happy for you."

"You are?" I'd never considered how she felt about anything. Oh, how in that moment I wished I had shared more with her.

It remains the single greatest regret of my life.

"Of course I am. True love comes so rarely, maybe once in a lifetime if you're lucky," she said.

"Fantastic. I'm sorry, Mum. We were afraid Sophie's dad would find out. We thought…"

"I understand," she tried to console me. "Colin has grandiose plans for Sophie and doesn't want her distracted. It's not about you, Thomas. It's important that you understand that. Colin thinks you're a fine young man. He knows Sophie has extraordinary talent and wants her to take advantage of the opportunity to pursue her goals. That's all."

"That's not all," I said.

"No, it's not."

"Mum, the fact that Sophie comes from a Protestant background and I supposedly come from a Catholic one; it doesn't matter to us. It's archaic."

"I agree," she said. "I think you and Sophie were destined to be together. I've always thought so."

"We *will* be together, except now she's moving to Nova Scotia to train with Hal Munro. It's so far away, Mum."

To that there was nothing to say; I spoke the truth and we both knew it.

"So what was Mr. Dunbar doing here?" I pressed.

"I asked Colin to come talk with me concerning my future. I don't think I can stay at Glenapp Castle much longer."

"What do you mean? Hutchesons have lived and worked here for generations. I'm going to be Head Gardener one day. What are you *talking* about?"

"I understand your feelings, more than you might imagine," Mum empathized, "but I cannot continue to work for a man who nearly killed William's daughter and won't take responsibility for it."

"Where would we go? Are the Dunbars leaving? You can't be serious! Dad's buried here! We can't just leave him," I cried.

"I feel horrid about leaving your father here. I'd always assumed he and I would be buried side by side, like all the Hutchesons, but I can't stay at Glenapp for that reason alone."

"William's already told the police. Why don't we just let William handle this? It's his problem. They'll question Sir John, and then it will all come out. He'll be charged with…"

"At the very least, vehicular homicide," she finished my sentence. "The trial could drag on for months, for years, even. I'd be working for a suspected murderer."

The reality of Mum's situation, and mine, slowly sank in. "What about Lady Sylvia? You like her so much. What will she do?"

"I don't know. I'm truly concerned for her, but my first responsibility is your welfare and my personal integrity. Tomorrow night, after the celebration, I'll tell her the truth. Sir John always asks for his nightly port in his private quarters when he retires for the evening. I'll formally resign then. Sunday, we'll move our things."

Leaving Glenapp Castle! I couldn't imagine such a thing. Brilliant, sun filled images of the walled garden flashed through my mind, and I wondered how it would fare without me. I'd always thought it needed my bloodline to survive, that Colin Dunbar was just an interim Head Gardener until I rightfully came of age. It occurred to me, then, that I would never see the fairies light the garden at night as my great-grandfather had.

"The Dunbars aren't sure what they're going to do," Mum continued, "and you're not to mention *anything* to Sophie until Colin and Victoria decide. I suspect once the castle staff knows I'm leaving, those that haven't already will quit. Poor William hasn't had time to address what he's going to do, but I hope to see him later tonight. I'll help him find a flat close to the hospital in Girvan, if that's what he wants."

"So we're leaving Dad here?"

I couldn't get past the idea that we'd be separated from him. The graveyard lay just outside the walled garden, such a natural part of the landscape. I walked past it daily, sometimes stopping to chat, to share how things were going with Sophie, to complain how I couldn't understand Mum sometimes, so aloof, so emotionally unapproachable, as if we weren't even kin. To leave him was unthinkable.

"I'll request that we be granted permission to visit your father's grave. They owe us that."

We sat silently, immersed in our own thoughts, until my mother leaned forward and took my hand. "Thomas, I know this is an awkward time, but I'd like to give you your birthday present now. Tomorrow's going to be frantic and I won't be home until late."

"Mum, you don't have to…I'm sorry for what I said before."

"You've nothing to apologize for. Eighteen is an important birthday, and there's something I want you to have."

"What is it, Mum? A book?" I queried, attempting to muster some enthusiasm.

"Yes, of a kind," she replied with a smile.

I removed the green and white stripped wrapping and saw a letter she had written, paper-clipped to the front.

"Go on. Read it," she urged.

It was the first letter she'd ever written me.

> *My Dear Thomas,*
>
> *At eighteen, you remind me so much of your father—his looks, his mannerisms, even the way you stare at Ailsa Craig as if it beheld the magic key to eternal happiness. I know you've suffered deeply not having your dad around. After he died, my own grief was so debilitating, I entombed my heart alongside his. Beneath it all, I have loved you everyday of your life, Thomas. Your eighteenth birthday present is a collection of poems your father gave me. Now that you're approaching manhood, he would want you to have them. Of this, I'm sure.*
>
> *With love everlasting,*
> *Mum (and Dad)*

I didn't know what to say. She spoke the truth. So many nights spent together alone, she in her room, me in mine, suffering the same alienation, never talking, never acknowledging the melancholy and utter loneliness. Rarely any physical contact. And now, this!

"I don't understand, Mum. Dad wrote these?"

"No," she laughed. "They're a collection of his favorite poems. He would add one or two every anniversary, or on my birthday if he couldn't wait."

"But they're in his handwriting," I said, recognizing his tall, angular penmanship.

"Aye. He handwrote them for me. Some are love poems, most really. Your Dad was quite the romantic," she confessed, "but there are others about curling, and piping, and several about Mother Scotland. You know what a patriot he was. He used to read them to me at night. He actually used to read poetry to you, too, Thomas, if you remember."

I ran my hands over the soft leather cover, deep scarlet and worn smooth by years of tender handling. "Mum, are you sure you want to give these away?"

"The best way I know to convey how much I love you is to give you my most precious possession."

"Thank you, Mum. I promise to take care of it. If you ever want to…"

"No, you're kind, Thomas, but I've read and reread them so often I can recite them by heart. It's time for me to pass these on, and honestly, Thomas, I think it's a good thing for us to leave this place. It's too steeped in memories of the past. Sometimes I think I live under some kind of a spell here."

"Are you worried about tomorrow night?" I asked.

"No, not really. Why?"

"I mean, so much could go wrong," I said, stating what I thought was the obvious.

"Well, as far as the preparations are concerned, we're as ready as we're going to be. If you're talking about the rivalry between Roddie and Colin, with hundreds of people here, I'm hoping they'll behave themselves. One of them will lose; the other will win. That's that."

"When is Sir John coming back?" I asked.

"I don't know. I simply don't understand it, Tom. Is he thinking he can get away with this?"

"Sophie and I thought we'd drive to Stranraer to watch the curling practice. Maybe he'll show up there," I speculated.

She reached for her coat. "I've got to go," she said.

"Thank you, Mum. Dad's book is the best present you could have given me. I'll treasure it forever."

"You're a good boy, Thomas, and I'm proud to be your mother."

I opened the door and watched my mother walk up the hill to the house she has worked at six days a week for over twenty-two years. Just before she rounded the bend she turned around, hesitated, then said, "You and Sophie be careful, Thomas. Don't give Colin Dunbar any reason to question your discretion."

"I won't Mum. Don't worry."

I hated to see her go—such exchanges were so rare.

*   *   *

The Stranraer ice rink, home to the 1997 District Curling Championships the following night, was part of the North West Castle Hotel. It was originally the home of Sir John Ross, one of the first explorers of the North West Passage. His expeditions of 1818 and 1829 both failed, and it was, as history has recorded, William Parry who finally navigated the Pass. But in 1825, between expeditions, Sir Ross returned to his hometown of Stranraer and built his stately home facing Loch Ryan naming it *The North West Castle* in tribute to his passion and nemesis. The hotel was, and is today, managed by Mr. Hammy McMillan, five-time European, and one-time World Curling Champion.

The curling rink houses four playing fields, or sheets, with a glassed-in observatory called the Alpine Room at one end. The coziest feeling in the world came over me when I walked in there. Paneled in rich, butterscotch-hued wood, the room accommodated up to two hundred fans. On the wooden soffits, tributes to the season's champions were noted in gold lettering. Above the mirrored bar was written, "Moderation, sir, aye. Moderation is my rule. Nine or ten is reasonable refreshment, but after that it's apt to degenerate into drinking."

That evening, the Alpine Room was packed with local fans

uproariously waging bets on which team would win the District Championships the next night. On the rink, Mr. Dunbar's and Roddie's teams practiced side by side. The Royal Caledonian Curling Club anticipated the largest crowd ever to assemble for a curling match in southwest Scotland. I smiled as I saw my Uncle Roddie standing guard over his team's red-handled curling stones. His team had yet to lose a curling match throwing red. Roddie's mother had written her letter to him in red ink the color of rubies.

Sophie and I were standing on our toes to see who was there when I felt a hand press on my shoulder. It was Officer Gavin Gillespie, Ballantrae's only policeman. Like everyone else in town, he was an avid curling fan. Tonight, however, he was in uniform, and I knew full well what he wanted.

"Hello, Thomas. Have a moment?" he asked, never taking his hand off my shoulder.

"Aye," I answered, squeezing Sophie's hand.

"I'm coming, too," Sophie announced.

"No, Soph. There's no reason…" I objected.

"I want to, Tom. I was there, too," she stated with that familiar stubbornness I knew left no room for negotiation.

"Mr. McMillan has been nice enough to lend us his office. Come along, this won't take a minute," Gavin promised.

"Sorry about this, you two," he began, "but I need to ask you about Lucy's accident. William and the Dunbars have told me everything they know, but I wouldn't be doing my job if I didn't ask the witnesses, now would I? I will say, I didn't know you were there, Miss Sophie."

"Aye, sir, I was," she says. "Tom and I were returning from a walk, and we both saw the whole thing. I didn't come forward sooner because I didn't want to be in trouble with my dad." Her candor took my breath away. "There you have it."

"Aye, I understand," Gavin replied, a bit taken back. "I admire your verve, young lady. Won't be anybody telling you what to do, now will there?" Gavin cleared his throat and removed a notepad and pen from his uniform pocket, craned his neck once to the left, once to the right and seemed ready to begin. "All right, then, let's take it one step at a time. What exactly was it that you two saw?"

Sophie started before I could even collect my thoughts. She conveyed how she ran to the castle for help because we knew William was gone for the day, and how she kept wondering why Sir John didn't stop, or at the very least, return to the scene of the accident. Gavin asked me if I had anything to add, and I described being alone with Lucy, how I'd agonized over her convulsions, feeling so helplessly inept, praying the ambulance would hurry up.

Gavin wrote it all down, and without even looking up, asked, "Tell me about the bike, Tom."

"Well," I began, trying to calm my thumping heartbeat. "We really weren't sure what to do with it, but since it appeared Sir John wasn't coming back, we all began to worry he'd take it, destroying any evidence of the accident. Mum thought it best to return it to William's cottage. So after the ambulance took Lucy, and Mr. Dunbar and William left for the hospital, I carried it to William's cottage and leaned it against the porch. I put a note on the front door so he wouldn't miss it. Then, early the next morning when I brought William some of Mum's scones, he asked me where Lucy's bike was. I couldn't believe it! Someone had taken it before he'd even gotten home from the hospital. Looking back on it, it was stupid to just leave it unguarded like that, wasn't it? Anyway, I guess we shouldn't assume Sir John took it, but then he disappeared, too…"

Gavin was no longer taking notes. "Sorry," I apologized. "I suppose you know all this."

"That's all right, lad. But let's stick to the facts. What time did you return the bike to William's cottage?"

"I don't know, exactly," I waffled. "I suppose around half-past five." I couldn't see what difference it made. It was gone. "What I don't understand is why no one's questioned Sir John? How is it he can just escape and avoid the consequences of what he's done? It doesn't seem fair," I protested.

"I agree," Gavin lowered his gaze.

"So you've arrested him? Thank God!" Sophie exclaimed, relieved something was finally being done.

"Well, no, not exactly," Gavin admitted. "The fact is, we've temporarily misplaced him. But he'll be back for the championships tomorrow night, mark my word. And once he's here, we'll watch him like a hawk until after the celebration. Sunday morning we'll press charges based on your testimony, and then his fate will be in the hands of the courts." Gavin squared his shoulders and returned his pen and pad to his breast pocket.

"What if he runs away again?" I asked.

"Sir John won't miss this match," Gavin speculated. "He's the sole sponsor of one of the best curling teams in the world. No, he'll be here tomorrow night, I assure you. This is his day of glory, and revenge. You're old enough now, Tom—you know what I'm referring to."

I knew. My Uncle Roddie's story of Sir John forcing him to eat his mother's letter just months after she died was legendary in Ballantrae, still. The defeat of Roddie's team would taste very sweet to Sir John after all these years. But I also knew if Mr. Dunbar's team won Saturday night, Sir John as sponsor would accompany his team to the Nationals, and maybe to the World Cup. Gavin Gillespie was right—he wouldn't miss this for the world.

"I'm sorry to add," Gavin continued, "that Sir John completely denies hitting Lucy. That's a second reason he'll be here, to reinforce his innocence."

"What! You've spoken with him?" Sophie cried. "He denies it? Gavin, he's lying, I swear. You can't let him get away with it. Can't you trace the call?"

"I caught him on his mobile which he apparently turned off soon after I called. I've no intention of letting him get away with anything, young lady. I will remind you that William Hobbes is one of us, and a personal friend. We've known each other since primary school, but one has to use discretion in these matters. You leave this to me," he said. "Now, I understand you're going to Nova Scotia to train with Hal Munro. Congratulations, my girl. We're all very proud to have someone from these parts going so far away, and to curl, no less. My, my…"

"Thanks," Sophie answered. "It's a long way away, for sure, but I'll do my best."

"Good girl. I'm sure your mum and dad are very proud of you," Gavin beamed, all cheerful and friendly now. "Off you go, then. If I need to question you further, I know where to find you."

Officer Gillespie left through the hotel lobby. Sophie turned to me and asked, "Tom, do you really want to watch the practices?"

"What do you have in mind?"

"Come with me." As we walked to my pickup, I remember glancing at Ailsa Craig thinking it odd her lighthouse beacon was flashing on such a beautiful night.

"Dad told me there's a big storm coming," Sophie said. "Look, Tom, there's Orion, your favorite. You can almost reach out and touch him."

I had to laugh. My own dad's never ending lectures on the constellations had bored me silly when I was younger. "Soph, do you know the story of Orion?" I asked.

"Not really, other than he's a hunter and you can identify him by his three-starred belt. But I bet you're going to tell me." She leaned her back against my chest and intertwined our arms.

"Well, Orion, a mere mortal, was killed by a scorpion," I began, "and Asklepios, the Greek god of medicine, tried to revive him. As the myth goes, Hades, God of the Dead, always anxious to populate his underworld, tried to persuade his brother, Zeus, to knock out Asklepios with a thunderbolt. But Zeus admired Asklepios and instead made him into the constellation known as *The Serpent Holder* with the *Scorpion* just below, then he placed *Orion* safely on the opposite side of the sky." I took Sophie's left hand and pointed her finger to the constellation. "See the bright star to the right, below Orion's belt? That's Rigel. It's 20,000 times brighter than the sun. Amazing the details one remembers. Anyway, Orion was Dad's favorite because he believed in the importance of threes, and Orion's belt is the only constellation with three stars in a row."

"What's so great about threes?" Sophie asked.

"Three is a significant number in Celtic mythology. It represented the layers of the universe: heaven, earth, and the underworld. And like the Greeks, the Celtic mystics believed there were three types of beings: deities, mortals, and the dead."

"Let's each make a wish upon a star and see if it comes true," Sophie suggested.

"What kind of wish?" I asked, hugging her more tightly.

"For something we want more than anything in the world," she crooned.

"How many wishes do I get?" I pondered aloud, feeling I was due more than my share.

Sophie whispered, "All you want."

There were three things I wished for: to spend the rest of my life with the girl in my arms, to have a closer bond with my mother, and last, that one day I would be Head Gardener at Glenapp Castle, a prospect that no longer seemed a possibility. When I opened my eyes, Sophie was wishing upon her own star.

"Are you done?" she asked. I nodded. "Let's go home."

"Wouldn't you rather go to Girvan and see who's at McGregor's Pub?"

"Everyone will either be at the castle preparing for tomorrow or here at the rink. We'd have the whole place to ourselves," she speculated.

"What whole place? We can't go to your cottage, or mine for that matter. It's not worth the risk, Soph…really," but she was already climbing in my pickup.

"What's up your sleeve? I don't trust you," I uttered, hopping into the driver's seat.

"It's a surprise and I'm not telling you, so don't badger me."

We drove along the coast road towards Ballantrae, past Sawney Bean's cave to the only home either of us had ever known.

"Just drop me off, then we'll meet outside the walled garden," she instructed.

"Outside the garden? Why?"

"You'll see."

I realized I had a surprise for her as well—Dad's book of love poems. I detached my mother's letter and walked towards the garden, carrying my birthday present under my arm. I found Sophie on the path that led directly to the boathouse.

"Oooooo, Sophie Dunbar," I cautioned. "I know what you're thinking and it's a rotten idea."

"Why not?" she replied, brazenly. "It's only nine o'clock. Everyone will be tied up for hours yet. And…" she pulled a large candle from her coat pocket, "I brought illumination."

Clever girl.

Sophie swung open the wide boathouse doors and lit the candle. The fractured light bathed the interior in a soft, honeycomb luster. She was right. At the very least, her dad wouldn't be home until every last fan had left the Stranraer rink—well after midnight. We shut the doors.

"What's that you have?" she asked, seeing my book.

"It's my birthday present from Mum. It's a book of poems Dad gave her, favorite ones he'd collected through the years. Love poems," I whispered in her ear.

"Are you sure you don't want to read them yourself first?" she asked, deftly placing the candle on the bedside table. The whiffs of vanilla and juniper were intoxicating.

"I thought about it for maybe…two seconds."

We crawled onto the single bed and brought the candle close enough for us to see the slanted penmanship so remarkably my father's. The first poem was titled *My Luve Is Like A Red, Red Rose*.

"Are you ready?" I asked.

"No. Wait," she said, crawling off the bed. Sophie puffed up the pillow, then lay down with her back against my chest. I opened my legs and wrapped them around hers, placing my chin on the crown of her head. This time, when I opened the soft, leather bound book, a pressed White Rose of Scotland fell out. I placed it strategically between Sophie's breasts. "Are you settled now, lassie?"

"Aye, I'm settled."

My Luve Is Like A Red, Red Rose

O, my luve is like a red, red rose,
    That's newly sprung in June.
O, my luve is like the melodie,
    That's sweetly play'd in tune.

As fair art thou, my bonie lass,
    So deep in luve am I,
And I will luve thee still, my dear,
    Till a' the seas gang dry.

Till a' the seas gang dry, my dear,
    And the rocks melt wi' the sun!
And I will luve thee still, my dear,
    While the sands o' life shall run.

And fare thee weel, my only luve!
    And fare thee weel a while!
And I will come again, my luve,
    Though it were ten thousand mile!

"It's beautiful," Sophie whispered. "What a romantic your dad was."

"Aye…even Mum says so."

We lay motionless watching the lemony candlelight flicker across the page. I'd never thought much about my parent's relationship. Were they first loves like Sophie and me? My all-consuming grief had overridden any sentiments beyond a deep resentment that the parent I loved the most abandoned me before my eleventh birthday. I understood then that my mother had suffered equally. The additional revelation that I was conceived in love filled me with indescribable pride.

Sophie slipped the poems from my grasp, and, with astonishing composure, placed my hands on her breasts. Sensing my arousal, she lifted herself up, turned over, and with painstaking accuracy, sat squarely on my crotch.

"Soph…that's not a good position unless you want…"

"Tom, there is only one person I'm going to lose my virginity to and that's you. I can't imagine it any other way. It's perfect. It's perfect because we love each other, and that's what making love is supposed to be. I won't say I'm not scared, but I don't want to do it the night before I leave for Nova Scotia, either. I've loved you, Tom Hutcheson, long before you even thought about it."

"I doubt that," I protested.

"When did you first think you loved me?"

"On my thirteenth birthday, but listen…" I said, squeezing both her shoulders, "are you sure you want to do this, because if not, you need to move."

"I do want this. Just be gentle. Go slow."

"Maybe you should stay on top where you can control things." Surely, I was dreaming this conversation.

Sophie unbuttoned her russet colored cardigan revealing a lace-trimmed camisole that sculpted her breasts so tightly, even in candlelight I could see the outline of her nipples. When she saw my riveted stare, she slipped the camisole over her head. I closed my eyes in reverence of all things born of perfection, pledging never to forget the plump softness cupped in the palm of my hands. When I opened my eyes, Sophie's smile was so unabashed, I wanted to envelop her whole.

"I love the way you touch me," she said, and she started to

unbutton my shirt while rubbing herself against me. I was paralyzed. When she'd exposed my chest, she leaned over and kissed my nipples, first one, then the other. "Equal treatment," she said.

"Sophie, I hadn't planned this. I don't have any means of..."

"No, you wouldn't. You're too much the gentleman. I bought some condoms in Stranraer. Lubricated ones. And they're ribbed. I hope that's a good thing," she grinned.

I burst out laughing. "You are amazing! Traditionally, the guy's supposed to take care of that."

"You can take care of it next time."

I knew I wasn't going to last long in this position and gently moved Sophie off me. We stood in the flickering candlelight and kissed while time stood still and everything not of us dissolved, and the pressure of her warm breasts against my chest nearly buckled my legs.

She undid my zipper, and I hers, and we slid off our trousers, standing naked at last, kindred spirits so tightly bound, our surrender inevitable, perfect.

I lay on my back and Sophie on top of me, her body radiant with heat, her most sacred place touching mine. "Soph, wait a bit," I moaned, and she rolled off me as I felt between her thighs, so slippery and warm. "Can I kiss her?" She jumped when I first touched her there. "My God, that feels incredible," and she lowered herself again and I ran my tongue slowly along, watching her expression of giddy amazement. "Tom, what about you?" but I shook my head. Not yet. Not until she was ready. She breathed in wondrous gasps, sweeping herself across my tongue until she couldn't take it anymore, and she put on the condom then mounted me and guided me inside. She looked into my eyes and said, "Tom Hutcheson, I love you," and slowly slid down. Oh my God in heaven, she was soaked and her nipples were brushing against my chest and I was further in, back out, in deeper and I cried, "Sweet Jesus," and she was dripping on me and the candlelight made her body sparkle, and she said, "Come to me," and I plunged in deeper and my body shivered and jerked and sprung forth a lifetime of pent up frustration and love while she muffled my groans with still urgent kisses. After I was done she was still sliding me in and out, faster and faster, and I hated that I came too soon. But she was rapturous, smiling, tears of joy streaming down her face when she murmured, "Happy birthday, Tom."

Chapter Twelve

Eva

ZIPPING UP MY DRESS, ANDREW REASONS, "Money, I suspect, is his motive. That's simply enough handled. Kitty's estate was left to Issie in a trust administered by the Royal Bank of Scotland. It's a dead end for him; he has absolutely no legal recourse. If he wants Issie back, we will just say he abandoned her and that we are now her legal guardians—period."

"What if she wants to go with him?" I ask. "She might actually know him, Andrew. Why wouldn't she? Kitty only died two weeks ago. Who knows how often he's been around the last five years."

"That's true, I hadn't thought of that. Well, then, while he's here let's be certain Issie's kept busy in the kitchen until we sort things out. We should welcome him as we would any guest and listen to what he has to say."

"But he's not taking her under any circumstances!" I state, emphatically.

"Agreed."

"I really do love her. I can't explain it, but I do. It's as if she was meant to be ours all along and now some wayward, fly-by-night lover of Kitty's is attempting to steal her away."

Andrew tenderly wraps me in his arms. "We'll get through this, sweetheart. We've been through worse."

"Have we?" I cry. "To lose Issie now would be devastating. Vicente Flor is Issie's biological father, Andrew. What on earth could he possibly want other than to reclaim her?"

*   *   *

When I ask Kevin if he would entertain Issie for the morning, he pulls me aside. "Eva, I'm dreadfully sorry about this nasty business. If there is anything I can do?"

"Such as..."

He is stroking his goatee. "I could poison him."

"Arsenic, perhaps?"

"Nightshade tea might do the trick. Or the fruit of a Koenig tree? Makes you vomit for hours," Kevin enlightens me.

We are halted by the heavy brass knocker resounding through the entry hall. "Buck up, old girl, I can guarantee you're taller than he is, and Andrew at six-feet four will seem an absolute monster. It will be fine."

"Would you bring coffee?" I ask.

"Of course. There in a jiffy. Arsenic?"

"Not yet. I'll cough three times if I change my mind. Thank you, my friend. I actually believe you'd do it."

Bit of a frightening thought.

*   *   *

I stand outside the library listening to Andrew and Vicente Flor exchange formal introductions. Through the crack in the door, I study our guest. Kevin was right, the resemblance to Issie is unmistakable. A man of medium stature, he is wearing a three-piece linen suit the color of dry summer sand, his cobalt blue shirt perfectly matched by his checkered, silk tie. There is no denying it—he is strikingly handsome.

My throat is parched, my breath fusty from too many cups of coffee, but there is no retreating now. When I enter the library, Vicente Flor slowly turns around. "*Buenos dias, Señora Campbell.* It is an honor to meet you," he says in a soft, Spanish accent. His iridescent black hair, worn slightly long, falls over his face as he bends to kiss my hand. Reminding myself to breathe, I catch the musky essence of sandalwood.

"Good morning," I reply, bowing in kind.

Andrew has built a fire. The crackling sparks spew and pop like firecrackers in the awkward silence. Ten times the grandfather clock chimes—ten more torturous seconds to await the fate of Isobel Flor Campbell.

"Please Señor Flor, sit down." Andrew and I settle on the facing sofa when Kevin arrives with a silver tray of coffee, winking to get my attention. I cough once. "Thank you," I say too formally.

"What can we do for you?" Andrew asks. His tone is accommodating, frosty.

Our guest crosses his legs and, taking time to collect his thoughts, lingers over a long, leisurely sip of coffee. His dark complexion is smooth and hairless like a woman's making it difficult to approximate his age. Late thirties, I surmise. "Kitty's age," a voice reminds me. My age.

With distinguished ease, he swishes the steaming brew round and round his Spode china cup as if every second he delays isn't tearing my heart to pieces. When he returns his cup to the saucer, a solid gold watch peeks out from beneath his French-cut sleeve. The sun catches its sheen, throwing a pinpoint spectrum of light to the oak-paneled wall.

"I apologize for the intrusion," he says. "I am sure my sudden appearance has caused you unrest, but I am not here for the reason you may think. It is not my habit, I assure you, to discuss *mis asuntos privados*—my private affairs; I find such exchanges vulgar. If you will tolerate my indulgence, I think when I am finished you will understand my reason for coming."

With every word my resolve to dislike him deepens. He'd best get to the point.

"I am originally from the port town of Guayaquil, in Ecuador. It is still my home, though *mi señora's* illness has brought us to London for the present. I must confess, however, that I am not unfamiliar with your great country."

His wife? He is married. Perhaps she, too, is infertile, and in her own desperation he has come to claim what is biologically his.

"In my early twenties, I got into some trouble at home," he says, "a matter of infinitely poor judgment on my part and of great embarrassment to my *familia*. My *papá*, a pious man of high principle, exiled me to Scotland for a time. As I had disgraced myself, I had no choice in the matter. I was flown to Glasgow to work for a colleague of my father's by the name of Sir John McPhee."

I hadn't expected this!

"I was met at Glasgow Airport by Kitty Campbell, your cousin, I believe," he says, glancing at Andrew.

"Kitty and Sir John met at a Robert Burns festival in Alloway and soon became social acquaintances. Sir John could be exceedingly charming and witty and, at the start, Kitty found the old man engaging. But he soon became *obsesionado*, asking her to dinner every night, sending her flowers every day. Exasperated, and looking for ways to appease him, she agreed to pick me up at the airport. I will confess to you, I thought she was *la mujer mas hermosa*, the most beautiful woman I had ever seen.

"Because I spoke fluent English," our guest explains, "Sir John utilized me in various ways: as chauffeur, to run his errands, to make excuses to his *señora*, Lady Sylvia, why he couldn't return home, and the like. Among other things, he charged me with watching over his friend, Kitty, when he wasn't in Glasgow. When I revealed to her my assignment, she became frightened and resolved to end her friendship with him at once. She claimed she had repeatedly refused invitations to have intimate relations with him. Fair enough that he persisted, but having someone watch her like a criminal was unconscionable. Sadly, she didn't end the relationship soon enough.

"For months at a time I did not see Kitty," he went on. "Sir John sent me to Edinburgh, to Liverpool, to Manchester, all over the U.K., delivering and retrieving packages of one sort or another. I found myself meeting strange fellows in dark alleyways at all hours of the night and day. Instead of sporting Sir John's Jaguar, I was now driving a dilapidated Fiat. Then one day, Sir John personally handed me a package addressed to Kitty. Suspecting the worst, I opened it. It was cocaine. I threw the contents in the trash, resealed the box, and delivered it to her empty. Her reaction confirmed my suspicion; Sir John had her strung out on drugs. It was shocking to see her. When

I pointed out what Sir John was doing, we had a terrible row and she refused to see me again.

"When I first met Kitty, nine or so months earlier, she was not on drugs—*estoy seguro*, of this I am certain. Her heart was pure and her fun-loving spirit admired by everyone who knew her. She played the piano exquisitely, loved the outdoors, and had many friends with whom she socialized. Now she was moody and disheveled in her appearance. It was shocking to see her, and I loathed Sir John for what he was doing to her. Twice she was charged with possession of cocaine. In both cases, Sir John had been at the very same nightclub, had left just before the authorities arrived, and did nothing to come to her aid. Instead, he sent me to bail her out. On the drive home the second time, she told me she'd refused to have sex with him and he'd slipped something in her cocktail."

Judge Sinclair was right, then, I thought to myself. Kitty was vulnerable, though not to the antics of Issie's father but to those of an old lecher.

"I made up my mind to tell Sir John I would no longer work for him—being in trouble at home and abroad seemed foolhardy," Vicente noted. "I made an appointment to meet him at his Glasgow office the following day. Because I came and went so frequently, he had entrusted me with a key. I arrived first and went to the men's room. Sir John entered the office while I was indisposed. His mobile rang. The bathroom door was slightly ajar. I remained hidden and listened.

"The call was from an Officer Gillespie," Vicente discloses. "I had no interest in the affair, so paid little attention. I will only say that Sir John was abrupt in his manner, apparently denying involvement in some accident. He called the officer an incompetent *imbécil*, saying that he had been in Glasgow until late and wasn't anywhere near Glenapp Castle the previous evening. 'Yes,' he'd said, he would agree to further questioning Sunday morning. It had better be quick; he was a busy man.

"Then, Sir John made a call from the office phone."

Vicente suddenly stands up and strolls to the bay window overlooking the sea. His once strapping voice dims to a hushed murmur.

"It took several minutes for the call to go through, and I realized with interest that he was calling overseas. Once connected, Sir John began discussing the importation of boys and girls to London. He wanted them as young as possible, ages eleven to fifteen. 'I have an employee, a woman named Judith, dedicated to the children's safety upon arrival,' Sir John said. 'Vicente will manage from there. How many can I expect?' Sir John inquired.

"I listened in horror. ¡*Dios mio*! What had I gotten myself into? Sir John hung up the office line and picked up his mobile. My own mobile started to ring in my pocket. I stood in the bathroom, paralyzed, until I realized our rings were synchronized and decided I'd be better off not to answer. He left a curt message demanding to know my whereabouts and to contact him at once. My insides burned with revulsion and hatred for the man, for I knew what he was about.

"Finally, *gracias a Dios*, Sir John left. My heart was pounding so violently it took me several minutes to think clearly. It occurred to me, then, that I could press the recall button and perhaps discover with whom Sir John had been speaking. I did so. I recognized the phone number. It was *la oficina de mi papá*—my father's office in Guayaquil.

"It was clear to me then that my *papá* and Sir John were transporting impoverished street children from Guayaquil to London as part of an international prostitution ring."

Andrew and I sit, transfixed. "How appalling!" I cry out.

"Good Lord!" Andrew exclaims, shaking his head in disgust.

"I drove straight to Kitty's flat and told her everything—that Sir John was involved in the juvenile sex trade, that he had intentionally hooked her on drugs to seduce her. She didn't believe me at first. When I told her my father was Sir John's partner, her skepticism waned, and she broke down saying she wanted to move to London, to start a new life. Would I go with her? Help her pull herself together? Be her lover? I told her I would follow her to the ends of the earth.

"But it was not to be. Two days later, my *papá* called for my return to Ecuador."

"When was this?" Andrew asks.

"This was in late March, 1997.

"So…" Vicente continues, "I told Sir John that my father had arranged for my return to Guayaquil. He was furious, insisting it was very poor timing. Very poor. I owed him one last favor, he claimed, to accompany him to the District Curling Championships in Stranraer. It was a silly affair in my view, but to protest seemed senseless. We were to leave the next afternoon.

"I will not bore you with the details of my last few days except to confess that my parting with Kitty was soul-wrenching. She loved me, she said. Why couldn't I stay and on and on? She tortured my heart from start to finish."

Vicente sinks back in his chair with a ballooning sigh. "When I got home, I confronted my *papá*. What else was I to do? As it turns out, I had misjudged him.

"You may recall, in the late 1970's, all over the world but in England and South America most tragically, fundamentalist Christian groups accused Catholics of satanic child abuse—of sacrificing innocent children as part of a cult. Ecuador is an impoverished country and susceptible to such fanaticism. Nightly raids of Catholic homes became routine; children were kidnapped and christened into the Christian faith to save their souls. Many children disappeared forever, never to see their families again.

"My *papá* thought that twice a year he was shipping Catholic children to the safety of foster homes in Great Britain. When I told him that Sir John McPhee was transporting them to the red light district to be sold as child prostitutes, it literally killed him. He died two months later."

Andrew asks our guest, "And what has all this to do with Issie?"

"Ah, *sí*...to the reason I have come."

Only now do I realize I am hardly breathing at all.

"In January of 2000, I returned to London on business. I was not yet married at the time, and as you might imagine I was anxious to see Kitty. Not a day had gone by that I had not thought of her. It didn't take me long, and I found her doing well. She was free of Sir John, at last, and had sorted out her life. Most importantly she was glad to see me, and I extended my stay for several days."

So, this is the story! The calculations speak for themselves—Issie was conceived in January and born nine months later on the tenth of September.

"*Mi señora*, Maria, and I came to London last month for a rather complicated surgical procedure," Vicente resumes. "As her recovery has been extensive, I became restless and thought I might ask Kitty to lunch. Please do not think me unfaithful; I love my wife dearly. I suppose I justified my pursuit of Kitty with the fact that I *am* happily married now. *No importa.* The young man who lives in her flat now told me she had been killed in a car accident. When I said I had been a friend, he gave me Helen Campbell's phone number. Ms. Campbell informed me that Kitty has a daughter, a five-and-a-half year old who is living in Ballantrae with her legal guardians."

Here it comes, then. Eleven times the grandfather clock chimes; we've been here an hour. Finally, Andrew remarks, "Your story is indeed remarkable, but what is it we can do for you?"

"I have come with only one request: to know if Kitty and I conceived a child born of our love for one another. *Eso es todo,* that is all. I do not think I can live without knowing. My intentions stop there."

"You only want to know if you are her birth father?" Andrew repeats, incredulous.

"*Sí, palabra de honor,*" Vicente vows, placing his right hand over his heart.

"We believe you are, yes," Andrew confirms. "Issie's middle name is Flor and she resembles you remarkably. She will be six in September. We assumed legal guardianship after Kitty's death and we are adopting her."

Vicente nods several times, then rises and walks to the fireplace. "*¿Cómo es ella?*" he whispers to the fire.

It is my turn. "Issie is bright, clever, and the most affectionate child I have ever known. Everyone here loves her."

For the first time Vicente smiles. "Ah, like her *mamá,*" he reflects with tenderness in his eyes.

Just then, we hear whining outside the door.

"That's Grimshaw. If you don't mind, I'll let him in or he'll scratch a hole in the door," Andrew warns.

"I had not imagined this," Vicente rejoices, dropping to one knee. "I gave Grimshaw to Kitty as a going away present."

"Sorry?"

"*Sí,* I bought him at a pet store in Stranraer two days before I returned to Guayaquil," he says, rubbing Grimshaw's belly.

Seconds later, we hear footsteps thunder down the hallway. Before we know it, Issie is standing in the middle of our conversation.

Kevin arrives next, exasperated. "Oh dear! Awfully sorry. She snuck out after Grimshaw."

Issie is grasping Grimshaw's collar when she notices Vicente. She stares at him, mesmerized. At all costs, this is the meeting we had hoped to avoid.

"Hello," says Vicente. "You must be Issie."

"My name is Isobel Flor Campbell. 'Flor' means flower in Spanish, in case you didn't know," she greets him, politely shaking his hand.

"Is that so? I'll have to remember that," Vicente replies, suddenly jovial and light-hearted.

"What's *your* name?" she asks.

"My name is Vicente Flor."

Issie pauses for but a second. "But that's my middle name."

"He's your birth father, sweetheart," Andrew tells her. Oh my, here it comes…

"What's a birth father? I thought you were my dad now."

Vicente gently holds Issie by the shoulders. "Andrew is your father, now. You're a lucky girl to have so many parents. Some day you'll understand this. For now, just know that I loved your mother very much, and you are the consequence of that love. That's all you'll ever need to know."

"You knew my mum?" Issie gasps, a little unsure of herself now.

"*Sí*, I knew her well."

"I don't believe you because I've never met you before. What did she like to eat?"

"Curry. And chocolate mint wafers, and orange pekoe tea, and cashews. Greek salad, no dressing. And milk. She loved milk. And she was a vegetarian which made eating curry almost every night very challenging." The effort has drained him of color.

"What else?" Issie demands to know.

"What else what?"

"What else did she like?"

"Well, she loved poetry, and classical music, to play the piano. She liked to take long walks in the park, to see romantic movies at the cinema."

"Why didn't you marry her?" An extraordinary question for a five-year-old!

"Because I live in Ecuador," Vicente explains.

"Are you married now?"

"Yes, I am."

"What's your wife's name?"

"Maria."

"Why isn't she here, then?" Issie wants to know.

This is getting uncomfortably intrusive. Time to conclude...

"She's in the hospital, in London. She's been given a new heart."

"Oh my...I hope she's recovering well," I say, genuinely surprised.

Vicente stands up. "Thank you for your kindness. She is gaining strength every day."

"What did they do with the old heart?" Issie asks.

Vicente pauses. "Well, I'm not actually sure. It's no good, so I imagine they threw it out."

"They shouldn't do that," Issie empathically replies.

"No?" he laughs. "And why not?"

"Because the heart is where you keep all the things you love. If they throw away her heart, how is she going to know what to love?"

"She's got a point," pipes in Kevin. I'd completely forgotten he was there. "Right..." he trails, embarrassed. "I'll just tidy up."

"This has been a most unusual morning," Vicente concedes. "*Muchas gracias.* I never dreamed I would actually... Well, suffice it to say, it's been an unexpected pleasure."

"Tell your wife we wish her a speedy recovery."

"Thank you," he replies. "I am only sorry she was not here to meet you."

"Perhaps another time—I don't see any reason why you shouldn't come visit sometimes. Don't you agree?" Andrew asks me.

I am dumbstruck that Andrew would suggest such a thing. "Of course," I say, not wanting Issie to guess the truth.

We escort Vicente to his car. "I must compliment you on your renovation of Glenapp Castle. It had gotten terribly run down," he comments.

"You've been here before, then?" Andrew asks.

"Just once," he replies.

*   *   *

Arm in arm, we watch Vicente Flor's Mercedes weave its way down Glenapp's driveway until it disappears in the forest of tall spruce.

"I liked the fellow," Andrew opines.

"Me, too," I say, hoping never to see him again.

"Me, three," Issie echoes.

CHAPTER THIRTEEN

TOM

I SNUGGLED UNDER MY comforter, listening to the rain splash and skate against my window, reliving every luscious detail of being with Sophie the previous night. Lost in my reverie an hour went by before I decided I'd best offer some help to Mr. Dunbar, so I dressed and headed for the boathouse. I knew he wouldn't be there—not on the day of the biggest curling match of his lifetime and with so much to do for the party afterwards, but I couldn't resist. The shed was quiet but for the deafening drum of rain on the tin roof. Mr. Dunbar had slept there; I could tell by the haphazard making of his bed. I drew closed the doors. Resting on the bedside table was his favorite, scotch plaid *Book of Scotland*. I had an irresistible fancy to see what literary insights presaged my boss's dream life and choosing randomly, I opened to the poem, *My Luve Is Like A Red, Red Rose* by Robert Burns—the exact verse I had read to Sophie the night before from *my* dad's book. Even more shocked was I to discover that Mr. Dunbar had inscribed, *To J.H.*, next to the title.

J.H. could be none other than Judith Hutcheson—my mother. What the devil was Mr. Dunbar doing with the same poem my dad had given her? And why had he written her initials at the start as if she were *his* lover?

The boathouse doors flew open. There stood Mr. Dunbar, clad in his soaked oilskins, glaring at me suspiciously as if I were a gun-wielding vandal. "What are you doing in here, lad?"

Terrified, my throat folded on itself, leaving me mute.

"What's the matter, boy—cat got your tongue?"

"What is your relationship with my mother?" I demanded to know, gripping his wee book so tight the soft cover bowed in my hands.

"What do you mean exactly?" he hissed.

"It's a simple question," I pointed out. "What's your relationship with my mother?" I had challenged the most renowned temper in all of Ayrshire, but I don't remember caring.

"Your mother is a good friend," he replied.

"So it seems. Were you in love with her first, too? Do you love her still? Aren't you ashamed of carrying on with your best friend's widow?" I was crazed, relentless, wild with rage.

"What's that in your hand?"

"Don't change the subject," I railed. "You still haven't answered my question."

"I've never had any designs on your mum. Now your Uncle Roddie, that's another matter."

"Leave my Uncle Roddie out of this! Why would you have written my mother's initials next to this poem if you weren't in love with her?"

"What poem?"

Bloody good actor, I thought to myself.

"You know perfectly well which poem," I said, disgusted with the whole mess.

"Sit down, son," Mr. Dunbar said, using his fatherly voice. I refused to budge.

"*Sit down, Thomas*," he commanded.

"I'll stand, thank you very much," I replied, my insides ready to explode.

"All right, then, stand if you must. But put your youthful theories aside and listen to me. Your father and I were best friends; you know this. He was a learned man, much more than I, and I envied him that. I was always asking him to teach me things. The *Book of Scotland* was his, Thomas. He gave it to me just before he died in hopes I would keep up my interest in learning. I try to read something in it every night. It was he who wrote your Mum's initials next to that poem. Not me."

If the bed hadn't been there to catch me, I would have fallen to the floor, I was so ashamed.

"It's all right," Mr. Dunbar tried to console me. "I don't wonder you suspect something's going on with all the time I spend at your cottage. Truthfully, I've always been able to talk to your mum more easily than to my missus. I don't exactly know why. Victoria's jealous of Judith, but she needn't be. It's just that Judith is easy with things and not so judgmental. I'm sorry you thought there was more. It must have been terrible for you."

He had no idea! But I was well bred and I owed him an apology, if for no other reason than because he was my Sophie's dad. "I'm sorry, Mr. Dunbar. I don't even know what to say."

"Apology accepted. Now listen, Tom, I came looking for you to ask if you'd play your pipes at the opening match tonight. The Royal Caledonian Curling Club approves. What do you think?"

I had no interest in playing in public, and he knew it. "I'm too out of practice," I tried to beg off.

"Well, I thought we'd dedicate the match to your father, being my best friend and Roddie's younger brother, and the best curler of us all. We'd all surely appreciate it. Something that wouldn't take much practice…*Scotland the Brave*, perhaps?"

My due repentance for making rash assumptions! "For Dad…" I said, loathing myself for the betrayal.

I placed Mr. Dunbar's book back on the bedside table and brushed by him on my way out. He budged not an inch to let me pass.

I retreated to my room, yanked my pipes off the shelf, warmed up the drones for thirty seconds, and played the most pitiful rendition of *Scotland the Brave* any Scot ever heard. I could sense Dad hovering in the corner chastising my effortless performance. "Slow down, son. You're not going to the races." But I was. I was racing against guilt and remorse and shame, and losing miserably. And worse yet, I hadn't even offered to help Mum with the biggest party Glenapp Castle had ever hosted. Braced against the wind, I trudged through sheets of stinging rain to the castle, and upon arrival, could not believe the transformation before my eyes. There were tables running the full length of the drawing room, all draped with salmon-colored tablecloths, set and ready to go.

Silver candelabras with tall white candles graced the center of each table on either side of enormous vases filled with yellow scotch broom. The aroma of homemade breads, sweet meats, and puddings drifted in from the kitchen. Mum told me the desserts, all shipped in from Stranraer, were beyond the imagination. There was to be a band, and dancing, and merriment all through the night. Indeed, a gala worthy of the 1997 District Curling Championships.

"Mum, may I help?" I asked. Impeccably dressed in her freshly ironed black and white uniform, she leaned over and kissed me on the cheek. "Good morning and Happy Birthday, Thomas." Soon all the staff, including hired help I'd never met before, were patting me on the back with hearty congratulations. When I followed her into the kitchen I noticed a tall wisp of a woman with a long gray braid cascading down her back. "Who's that lady, Mum?" I whispered.

She looked nonchalantly over her shoulder. "That's Fiona McCarrick," she said. "She used to work here. She's just helping out for the party."

I wasn't sure Uncle Roddie was going to be happy to see Fiona, victory or not. Wasn't she the one Sir John cornered in his big closet?

We hadn't been in the kitchen but a minute when none other than Sir John McPhee burst in. His hair was mussed and steely-gray half circles cradled his puffy, black eyes. There was sand in his pant cuffs and on the soles of his shoes. His manner was agitated, impatient. Several staff members turned their backs to him as he demanded to know, "Where's Colin Dunbar? I need to speak with him straight away."

It was the first time anyone had seen Sir John since Lucy's accident. I supposed he wanted to review the strategy for the curling match that evening. No one muttered a word; I certainly wasn't going out of my way to find Mr. Dunbar. But, wouldn't you know, he walked right in.

"I've been looking for you," Sir John chastised. "I need to know which stones you'll be playing with tonight, red or yellow?"

"The stones were allocated a week ago," Mr. Dunbar said, mockingly. "We're yellow. It doesn't much matter to me except I hate that Roddie gets his bloody red stones every time."

Sir John smiled coyly. "Not to worry, Colin. I have every confidence we'll win tonight. I've already made plans for the Nationals."

"That's a bit cocky, don't you think? Roddie's got a super team.

I'm not near as confident as that. And it's bad luck to plan ahead," Mr. Dunbar protested.

"Mark my word. We'll win." Then, Sir John abruptly turned to Mum. "Judith, what's that woman doing here?" he curtly asked, tilting his head towards Fiona.

Mum, her eyes icy cold, replied, "I needed extra help, and Lady Sylvia said I could hire outside staff for the party. She's as good as they come."

Sir John's expression hardened. "I don't want her here after tonight, is that understood?" And turning back to Mr. Dunbar, he complained, "I bought Lady Sylvia a new Mercedes and the imbeciles delivered it practically empty. As usual, the petrol station in the village is out of diesel. It's a mystery to me how Marsden Frew stays in business. I want two, five-gallon cans on the property at all times. We'll drive her new car to the championships tonight."

"If it could wait until Monday, I'd be much obliged, Sir John," my boss replied. "If the village is out of diesel, I'll have to go to Girvan, and with all there is to do to prepare for the party afterwards…"

Sir John ignored him and walked upstairs to his private quarters. Once outside, swearing under his breath, I overheard Mr. Dunbar pass the chore to William who was headed to Girvan to visit Lucy.

"Can you help me out, William?" he asked. "See if Tom will let you borrow his pickup. I need mine." As I hadn't any transportation needs until the championships, I was happy to comply.

Next, I called Officer Gillespie to tell him Sir John was back.

"Aye," he said, "I saw him myself driving home late last evening, racing down Main Street. I had a mind to give him a speeding fine, but I thought it best not to compound matters. Thank you, my boy, for the call."

"Are you coming to the party tonight?" I asked.

"Aye, I'm on duty. I suppose it's as good a place to be as any. Hope they're ready for this crowd. I know people from Glasgow to Port Patrick planning to come."

Changing the subject, I inquired, "What about the bike?"

At first, Officer Gillespie didn't answer.

"You found it, didn't you?" I pressed.

"Aye, we found it washed up on the beach this morning."

"Just as I thought," I congratulated myself. "Sir John threw it in

Ballantrae Bay. If you come now, you'll find sand in his trouser cuffs and on his shoes."

"That's not substantial evidence," Gavin said, cautiously. "Going to the beach isn't a crime."

It was too depressing.

"Bye, Mr. Gillespie," I said. "I'll see you tonight."

The rest of the day was quiet, except when Sophie came by, and we kissed for so long we found ourselves giggling and short of air all over again. I loved her more every minute.

Finally it was time to go to the championships in Stranraer. I wanted to arrive early to warm up my pipes before the opening ceremony. The Alpine Room overlooking the curling rink was already packed with well over a hundred fans and smelled of wet wool and smoke—aromas certain to make a Scotsman feel right at home. Two barmen kept pints of Tennants lager lined up along the polished, oak bar. I ordered two shanties for Sophie and myself. On the rink, the officials were pebbling the ice, showering the surface with sprinkled water to rough it up a bit so the curling stones wouldn't slide too fast. Roddie's team stood on the right, dressed in their traditional red athletic suits; Mr. Dunbar's team stood on the left, clad in black. On either side of the *hack,* the foot brace from which each player pushes off to deliver the stone, sat eight red-handled stones, and eight yellow.

Curling is, above all else, a gentlemen's sport. Because this was the District Championships officials were present, but up to that point in the season's competition, fairness and honesty were the inherent responsibility of each player. For example, if a player *burned* a stone, meaning he or she mistakenly touched it with their foot during play, they were expected to call it on themselves. Honor and fairness runs deep in the embattled souls of Scots and the sport of curling best represents those characteristics of which we are most proud. Accuse someone of cheating? You'd better be certain.

Without warning, an awkward hush settled over the Alpine Room. Sir John had arrived, formally kilted in the McPhee tartan. "Glenlivits, please, Michael," he barked to the barman. No one moved. The sorrowful image of little Lucy Hobbes, still lying in a coma, flashed through the mind of every person there. Most had made an effort to visit her at the hospital or, at the very least, knew the story of how Sir John drove home stinking drunk and recklessly crashed into William's only daughter like a misguided torpedo. And Gavin Gillespie had made sure everyone knew that Sir John denied it!

To my horror, Sir John then turned to me. "Hello, young Thomas," he said. "I understand you're going to play your father's pipes. Pity he can't be here with us tonight." If his intention was to ignite a fire in my belly, he was burningly successful.

Sophie gently unclenched my fist and announced to the crowd, "There isn't a better piper in all of Ayrshire," which wasn't true and everyone knew it, but it broke the tension, freeing the crowd to resume speculation as to which team might represent Great Britain in the upcoming World Cup.

It was time to go to the changing room to tune up my pipes. When I returned to the rink, the Royal Caledonian Curling Club official pleaded for quiet. Over five hundred Scottish fans from all up and down the west coast and inland, hushed.

"We're here on 29 March, 1997, to play the District Curling Championships. The winning team will go to the Scottish Nationals and hopefully on to the World Cup, and it's no secret that the winning *skip*, Colin Dunbar or Roddie Hutcheson, will likely be chosen to compete in the Olympics in Nagano, Japan next winter." The crowd whooped and hollered, some waved their Scottish national flags while others raucously chanted "Rod-die, Rod-die," or "Co-lin, Co-lin" at the top of their lungs.

"You all know, I'm sure," the official continued over the loud speaker, "that this is the first Olympics in which curling will be properly recognized as a medaled sport, and I've no doubt that the Scots will bring home the Gold."

The fans shrieked with delight, but he raised his hand to indicate he wasn't finished. "Before we begin, in honor of the late Doon Hutcheson, one of the best curlers to ever grace Scottish ice, his son, Thomas, is going to play *Scotland the Brave*."

So there I stood in front of a full house, all rigged up in my Dad's kilt and woolen stockings, in full Highland gear, stark naked underneath, and a bit breezy, thank you very much, as the frigid air worked its way up my legs. I was shaking so fiercely the blood pooled in my fingertips making them heavy and stiff. "Breathe deeply," Dad whispered in my ear, "and imagine it's the two of us. Now close your eyes and play from your heart, son. It will come." And that I did, except for a split second when I opened one eye to see Sophie thumping her heart thrice with her fist—I love you.

While the Master of Ceremonies was announcing the start of the games, I'd filled my sheepskin bag with air, tuned the three drones, and was ready to begin. I breathed in my father, letting my body relax, forcing circulation into my fingers as they swept over the chanter, the resonance filling my whole being with a prideful joy only a native piper can know. So lost was I in the cadence, I hardly noticed the crowd erupting before I'd even finished. When I bowed deeply to each quarter, it ignited their fervor to a deafening pitch. The Royal Caledonian official, arms raised in a plea for calm, had to shout several times over the mayhem. "We wish both teams gentleman's luck and may the best team win! Good curling!"

I ran to the changing room to lay down my pipes on top of the lockers as I didn't want them harmed beneath my feet. Just in time did I return to my seat to see the two teams shake hands all around, and Roddie wince as Mr. Dunbar squeezed his with some extra vigor. To hearty laughter, my uncle, ever the clown, puckered his lips, then shook his hand in the air as if to ease the sting.

Curlers consider the first stone a sacrifice because the ice is rough and the stones cold, but the first red rock barely came close enough to the target to even help as a guard. Mr. Dunbar's team threw then, sliding a yellow stone right into the house just a few inches from the center button. Perfect start. Roddie's team was next, but again, the forty two pound stone seemed sluggishly slow and curled more than it should have. Roddie called his team together along the side within earshot.

"I don't like the way our stones are behaving," my uncle complained. "They're too heavy and swinging too much. Turn your stones over, every time, and check the running band beneath for pits. If you find a chip in the bottom, you know the trick, fill it with pebbled ice. Sweeps, be sharp and brush hard. We need all the help we can get." With that, they resumed play, but it only got worse, and by the fifth end break, Roddie's team was down by nine, an insurmountable deficit. I felt sick to my stomach. Something wasn't right, but this was the championships and nothing could be done.

Moments prior to the fifth end break, I turned to Sophie. "I'm going to the loo, then I want to put my pipes in my truck—they'll be safer there. I'll be right back."

Just as I finished my business two men walked in. I immediately recognized the voices to be those of Sir John McPhee and Mr. Dunbar.

"Are we alone?" Sir John asked.

I quickly sat down on the toilet seat and pulled my legs to my chest.

"What's this about, Sir John? The break's almost over and I'm needed back on the ice," Mr. Dunbar complained, irritably.

"Calm down, Colin. I'd think you'd be very pleased with the way the first half is going. We're up by nine."

"True enough, but something's awry with Roddie's rocks, and I can't figure it out. They're too heavy and landing too short and swinging all over the place."

"Well, they're going to stay that way," Sir John laughed.

"What's your meaning?" Mr. Dunbar demanded to know.

"Lower your voice, Colin, and don't act like an idiot. I simply had the stones roughed up a bit, that's all. The problem is they're even slower than I expected so you're going to have to adjust your game so there's less discrepancy in the score."

"Roughed them up!? Bloody Hell! What the fuck have you done this time?"

At this juncture, an official walked in. "Break's over, Colin. Play resumes in one minute."

As soon as he was gone, Mr. Dunbar decried, "I'm trapped, do you bloody realize that? If we win, I'll always know we cheated. How can I tell my team? I couldn't. But if I fess up now, we'll all be banned from the game forever and Ballantrae disgraced as well, with no one going to the Nationals. You're going to burn in hell for this, Sir John, and I'll likely hang by my own noose," and he left, slamming the door behind him.

Sir John stepped to within five feet of my toilet stall to relieve himself at the urinal, and I swear to you, upon my honor as an Ayrshire Scot, the cheating bastard started to whistle. And if you don't think that my heart didn't plummet when I heard it to be *Scotland The Brave*, the very tune I'd played in honor of my father, in public, against my will.

After Sir John left I waited several minutes, then scrambled to my seat. I had to get out of there. "Soph," I whispered, "I'm going home."

"What! In the middle of the match? Why?"

"I can't tell you now, but I promise to later, really I do."

"Tom, I can't leave Dad, and I don't want to, anyway. What's gotten into you? I don't understand."

"I'm sorry, Soph. You'll understand when I tell you, but not here," and I crawled back over the row of fans, ran through the rain and sat in my pickup, paralyzed, trying to grasp the consequences of what had happened. And what was I to do? Keep this dreadful scam to myself and let Mr. Dunbar represent Ballantrae in the Scots Nationals, and potentially Great Britain at the World Cup? What if he was chosen to play on the 1998 Olympic team? That would never do! I couldn't live with that. On the other hand, if I squealed, Mr. Dunbar would be banished from the Royal Caledonian Curling Club *and* from competing. That would hurt Sophie's future as well. Bloody hell! What a disaster!

I decided to go home and tell Mum what had happened. I found her at the castle putting the finishing touches on the buffet. "Mum, I need to talk to you."

"Thomas," she said, clearly surprised to see me. "Home already? They can't be done yet, can they? Or have you come all the way home just to tell me the fifth-end score?"

"Alone, Mum," I insisted.

She led me through the kitchen to the pantry. "What is it, then?"

"I overheard Sir John admitting to Mr. Dunbar that he had Roddie's curling stones roughed up, and they're going to lose by a heap it looks like. The worst of it is, Mr. Dunbar knows, and he's kept on competing!" I exclaimed.

"What do you mean roughed up?" Mum wanted to know.

"Someone messed with the bottom of Roddie's stones and they don't glide right. There's no way to control them, and they're all coming up short. It's a fucking disaster, I tell you."

"Thomas! Mind your tongue," she reprimanded.

"And you realize, I'm the only other one who knows? Well…you, now. What the hell am I to do'?

"I think we should tell Roddie. It's his loss, and he can do whatever he thinks is right."

"He'll kill Mr. Dunbar," I predicted.

"I doubt that. Let it go for tonight, Thomas," she counseled. "We'll get through the party and tell Roddie tomorrow. By then we'll be off the property and the appropriate authorities can deal with the consequences. You could help me by starting to pack us up. I've got boxes stacked in the garage so they don't get soaked in this rain. Try to think about what we'll need short term; we'll sort the rest out later. Auntie Fay said she'd love to have us, God love her." Mum turned to look out the window. "I don't look forward to saying good-bye to m' lady; she's been a good mistress, but it will be easier if she doesn't know about her husband's cheating when I do. I'll manage Sir John. A quick trip to take his nightcap, I'll resign and that will be the end of it."

Two hours later, packing up my things, I was distracted by the glare of headlights streaming through the cottage window. Uncle Roddie careened through the door without even knocking and precariously leaned against the door jamb, drenched from the rain and looking rotten.

"Where's your mother, Tommy?" he asked in a whisky slur.

"Uncle Roddie!" I exclaimed.

"Hell of a night, isn't it? Hell of a fucking, bloody hell and fire night if ever I saw one. Do you know what the final score was, lad? Seventeen to five! Seventeen to fucking five! Worst performance in the history of the championships."

Roddie fell in the nearest chair with a thud. "What in St. Andrew's name happened?" he rambled on. "You might have thought someone added twenty extra pounds of lead to our stones. In all my days, I've never seen anything like it. Did you leave early? Is that why you're home?" Roddie surveyed the room. "Why all the boxes?" he asked. "Packing for Findhorn already?"

"Aye," I said, trying to stick to the job at hand so I didn't have to look at his pitiful face.

"Bit over anxious, aren't you? There's plenty of time for that."

"Mum wanted me to start clearing out my stuff, so I thought I'd get a head start," I lied.

Roddie was silent for several minutes and I prayed he might doze off. Then, his head jerked up and he asked me again, "Where's your Mum?"

"She's up at the castle." I finally stood up from packing. "Listen,

Roddie. You might as well know—Fiona McCarrick is here. Mum's hired her as extra help for the party."

Roddie slowly turned his head in my direction. "Is that right? Well, well…I'll be damned. I'll just go say hello," he said, laughing heartily as if he saw great humor in the matter.

I couldn't take it anymore. I needed him out of my cottage or I was going to burst. "Listen, Uncle Roddie, how about I give you a lift to the castle? The party's started, surely."

"No thanks, lad. The walk will clear my head," and he gathered himself up and stumbled into the storm.

Moments later, Sophie peered in the window. She too marched right in.

"Tom, are you all right? What's gotten into you?" Then she saw the boxes strewn about and stopped short. "Are you leaving me? I mean, are you going somewhere?"

"Soph, sit down," I said, gathering my nerve.

"I don't think I want to. What in God's name is going on here? First, you leave the rink in the middle of the most important curling match of our lifetime, with both your uncle and my dad playing, and now you're packing to leave? I don't understand it." I could tell she was about to cry and I couldn't stand to see it, for all the love I had for her flooded my heart with such longing, I felt like crying myself.

"Sophie. I need you to sit down. I swear I'll tell you everything. But you've got to let me finish before you jump in—promise me."

She sat in the same chair Roddie had occupied just moments before. "It's wet," she said.

"Aye, Roddie's just been here, but as you can see he didn't stay long enough to take off his oilskins, and he wasn't sober enough to try, anyway."

"Poor Roddie! I can't imagine his state. Did he tell you the final score?"

"Aye, but before we talk about the match, there's something I need to tell you first." I pulled up a kitchen chair and sat opposite her so our knees touched; then I took both of her hands in mine and told her of Mum's decision to leave Glenapp Castle.

"Why didn't you tell me sooner? I thought we promised there wouldn't be secrets between us," she protested, more hurt than annoyed.

"Try to understand, Soph," I defended myself. "Mum asked me not to tell you until your parents decided whether or not they were going to stay."

"What do you mean, stay? Here at Glenapp? Where else would we go? This is where Dad works! There's something you're not telling me, Tom, isn't there?"

Painstakingly, step by step, I shared the conversation I'd overheard between Sir John and her dad in the changing room. She let me finish, then the tears of disbelief streamed down her beautiful face like a monsoon. I tried to keep up with a tissue, wiping her eyes, her cheeks, her chin. The public shame, the indignity, the loss of respect for one's father, the possible ruination of her own curling career, and like me, possibly leaving Glenapp forever—she saw it all laid out before her like a horror flick in slow motion.

With a bang, Uncle Roddie burst through the door slamming it so hard it knocked down a photograph of my Dad, shattering glass all over the floor. Sophie screamed and threw her arms around my waist, weeping openly now. For a moment, we all stared at Dad's smiling expression, the jagged chards of glass tearing through his handsome face.

"So that's it, is it?" Roddie bellowed. "Colin Dunbar cheated me out of the championship! I'd have thought he had some pride left in him, but apparently not."

His oilskin was plastered with dirt and grass from hiding in the bushes. Turning to me, he derided, "Why didn't you tell me, Tom? Am I too pitiful for the truth? I sat here while you made polite conversation, never uttering a word of Colin's cheating! Packing for Findhorn, are you? Who's the stinking liar now?" Then to Sophie, his voice cracked and deranged, "Tell me, pretty lass, where's your daddy now? Still at the rink having his picture taken?"

"For heaven's sake, Roddie, calm yourself!" I entreated. "If you need to be angry, be so with Sir John. He's the one who orchestrated it all, not Sophie's dad."

"From the sound of it, Colin Dunbar knew full well what was going on and the pathetic cheat kept right on competing. No self-respecting Scot would do such a thing and you know it, Tom."

I pried Sophie's arms loose so I could think, but my uncle stomped out, kicking the splinters of shattered glass as he went.

I turned to Sophie, "We'd better find your dad because he won't see this one coming."

We piled in my pickup and sped to the castle as fast as it would take us. Bypassing the designated public parking, I pulled up close to the kitchen entrance amongst all the catering trucks, allowing us to sneak into the drawing room unnoticed. We'd been there not two seconds when we heard Roddie's drunken, brash voice thunder through the crowd.

"Colin Dunbar, you're a goddamn cheat. Do you deny it?"

The band stopped. The accused stood perfectly still, stunned. There he was in front of hundreds of fans, snared like a trapped hare! He scanned the crowd for Sir John, but the master-of-the-castle was simultaneously sneaking upstairs, three steps at a time, leaving Mr. Dunbar to fend for himself. I feared Mr. Dunbar was waiting too long to respond, confirming his guilt, but just then, he turned his back on Roddie and started to walk right out of the room.

Roddie would have none of it. "Colin Dunbar," he roared again over the growing murmurs, "I asked you a question. Are you too much of a coward to answer a simple question? I'll ask you again. Are you, or are you not, a cheater?"

When Mr. Dunbar still didn't answer, Roddie addressed the crowd. "Do you know what he and Sir John did? They had my stones roughed up! Aye, that's right! Roughed up! And do you know how I know? Because I heard my nephew, Tom here, telling his sweetheart that he was in the loo when he overheard Sir John informing Colin at the fifth-end break that the reason for their big lead was that he'd tampered with my team's red stones."

Oh Lord! Now Mr. Dunbar knew about Sophie and me! I imagined he might smite me right then and there, but another storm had been brewing this night. Lightning flashed through drawing room like a swirling strobe extinguishing the lights, then an ear-splitting clap of thunder boomed overhead, sending several guests to the floor as if the great Glenapp Castle might implode before their eyes. When the lights came back on, my mother, the only woman who could reason with these two hotheaded rivals, was standing between them with her arms extended, one hand on each heaving chest.

"That's enough!" she announced. "I'll not have fighting in this house! Not tonight nor any other!" Then she turned to Sophie, "Escort your dad home, Sophie." And, to me, "Thomas, drive Roddie home as well. If you two are going to fight, it won't be on this property and it won't be on this occasion." Roddie and Mr. Dunbar glared at one another, then reluctantly acquiesced.

"Come on, Dad," Sophie coaxed. "Let's go home."

"You'll find your wife at home waiting for you, Colin," Roddie taunted. "After I told her what a cheat you are, she's too mortified to show her face."

With that, I shoved Roddie out the door. As soon as Mr. Dunbar cleared the threshold himself, Roddie, a featherweight compared to his rival, recklessly pounced on his back, sending him face first to the gravel. I heard a dreadful, bestial moan as Sophie's dad heaved himself up and grabbed Roddie by the neck. I thought it was all over for my uncle. "Get Officer Gillespie," I shouted to the mounting crowd. I jumped on Mr. Dunbar's back to distract him, but he just tossed me off with a shrug. "This has nothing to do with you, Tom," he growled. Gavin Gillespie finally came rushing out and with one swift, practiced stroke, whacked Sophie's dad on the back of his head with his baton. Colin Dunbar crumpled to the ground in a heap as Roddie clutched his throat, gasping for life.

"I've had enough of this," Gavin said, disgusted. "You've ruined my evening and everyone else's as well. Go home, both of you, and if I see your faces again tonight or hear of any more trouble, you're both going to jail. Now, clear off!"

"I'll get myself home, Gavin," Roddie said, still massaging his neck.

Gavin nodded. "Sleep it off, Roddie. We'll sort this out in the morning."

"There's nothing to sort out," Roddie pointed out. "We'll both be disqualified, sure enough. The Royal Caledonian has no other choice. That's all there is to it. All there is to it..." his voice trailed.

Gavin turned to Mr. Dunbar. "Will you go home now, Colin, or do I have to take you there myself?" Mr. Dunbar silently accepted the arm of his only child and strode home to the Head Gardener's cottage.

*   *   *

As there was no delight in celebrating a curling championship marred by dishonesty, everyone started to leave. I was glad of it for Mum could start tidying up, then inform Sir John and Lady Sylvia of her plans to resign. I walked back into the castle to help her, and this time she conceded.

Lady Sylvia wandered into the kitchen looking terribly shaken—the news of her husband's cheating must have come as a shock. Mum led her upstairs with a tray of tea.

I was cleaning up the serving dishes when Sir John snuck up behind me. "Tell your mother I'll have my port now," he ordered.

"She's just taken Lady Sylvia up a tray of tea, Sir John," I responded just as curtly. "I'll tell her as soon as she comes back."

It was only ten minutes later that Mum returned, wiping her tears with her apron.

"It's for the best, Mum. Even I can see that now," I assured her. "Sir John says he wants his port."

"All right, I might as well get this over with. Wish me luck," and she placed a crystal decanter and a single port glass on the silver tray. Without another word, my mother headed for the north turret wing, clear at the other end of Glenapp Castle, to inform Sir John McPhee that she was leaving his employment—forever.

While she was gone, the staff gossiped about everything that had gone on that incredible night—who was there, who wasn't, and how their Judith had, at the very least, heroically prevented Roddie and Colin Dunbar from bludgeoning one another. I listened, drying dishes, when Fiona McCarrick echoed my very thought.

"Judith is taking too long," she worried. I knew, of course, that Mum had an additional task to perform, and that Sir John would certainly try to talk her out of leaving. I let my mind drift to the bizarre events of the night when I thought I heard someone scream. I stood, dead still, listening. Just the sharp wind blowing away the foul weather, I decided. Then I heard it again; this time I was sure of it.

"Did anyone hear that?" I asked the staff, all sitting around the kitchen table enjoying a well earned cup of tea. William had joined them, presumably having just returned from visiting Lucy at the hospital; the staff was filling him in on what had transpired that evening.

They all pressed their ears to the task. "No," they replied.

Then, we all heard it.

It's vivid to me still—the image of my mother hanging perilously out the second floor turret window, screaming for help over the squawking of ravens as the flames closed in behind her. The entire north turret wing was on fire.

"I'm coming, Mum. For God sakes, don't jump," I yelled. "We'll call the fire brigade straight away," but then Sir John brusquely shoved her aside and pleaded for his own life.

"You," he commanded. "Get me out of here!"

There were two entrances to Sir John's suite—one inside the castle and a second from the outside turret stairwell. I was so close I chose the latter, but the turret entry was already engulfed in flames. The pungent odor of diesel was everywhere. Holy Jesus! I ran through the darkness to the kitchen. "Call 999. The north turret wing's on fire!"

There was no choice but to go back inside the castle and up the main staircase, but I was met by a billowing mountain of black smoke at the landing, mocking me, warning me to turn back, to give up this heroic charade. Smoke inhalation! Isn't that what people die of? They suffocate then they burn. I stumbled down the corridor, gasping for breath I didn't have, the image of Sir John mercilessly pushing Mum away from the window driving me forward, infusing my mind, body, and soul with a loathing vengeance. When I finally reached the door to Sir John's suite, I placed my right hand on the brass door knob. Within seconds, like tendrils of liquid acid, a searing pain surged up my arm as the flesh on my palm sizzled to the nerve. The agony was unbearable. I kicked at the door with my foot. Voices. Who were they? Fire Brigade. Someone hoisted me over his shoulder. "*No, wait!*! *I can't leave her. No…*" Kicking and struggling, I freed myself and ran back up the stairs and pounded and pounded on Sir John McPhee's bedchamber door…

From that point on, all I remember were Sophie's screams when she saw my body lying supine on the stretcher, and that it was she who shielded my eyes when they brought out the charred bodies of my mother and her employer.

Before I passed out, knawing pangs of remorse pressed mightily on my heart, not from having failed to save my mother, for I had done my best. The keener lashing came from never having told her that I loved her. Not once.

CHAPTER FOURTEEN

ANDREW

IT IS A STUNNING June day with a caressing zephyr blowing in from the sea. I find William weeding the kitchen garden, his handkerchief dangling from his hind pocket, his herringbone cap tipped back just enough for the cooling breeze to brush his balding scalp.

"May I have a word?" I ask.

He painstakingly climbs to his feet, wipes the dirt from his hands, and waits to see what it is I require.

"I thought perhaps you might help me sort out a mystery," I begin. "I found what I think is the skeleton of a child by the gazebo, and I'm not sure if I should call the police. You've been here longer than anyone. I thought you might know of its origin."

William falls back a step, then reaches for his soiled kerchief and wipes his dry brow. He is stalling for time. "I don't see any reason to be calling the police," he intones, defiantly.

"I agree. The thing is…there's this photograph we found that compounds my confusion on the matter." I hand him the picture of the dead infant.

"Where'd you find this?" he demands to know.

"Issie discovered it in the bottom of the trunk you left her, which was very kind of you, by the way," I add, softening the inquest. "You see, I'm not clear if there's a connection between the two. Either way, knowing would help me determine whether or not I should ring up Officer Gillespie to help me sort it all out."

For several moments William blankly stares at the photo, then offhandedly slips it into his shirt pocket.

"If you can help me," I press on, "it would save both me, and Mr. Gillespie, the trouble."

"The trouble of what?"

"The trouble of investigating whose child this was. I cannot have unmarked skeletons hanging about, now can I? It's unethical not to assign a proper marker to a grave, don't you think, William?" He is visibly uncomfortable now. "If you'll just tell me what you know, we might avoid the police altogether."

"Aye…" he capitulates. "I see what you're getting at."

I suggest we sit on the garden bench. Thankfully, Tom is occupied elsewhere, and we should remain undisturbed.

"Many years back," he divulges, "your predecessor, Sir John McPhee, raped a young servant girl. Nine months later in the middle of the night, out of spite, she deposited his stillborn bastard son on the outside steps of the north turret wing. I had no business nosing around," William admits, "but my wife had just passed away giving birth to Lucy and I wasn't sleeping. The truth is, I stored a lot of alcohol in my body in those days and wasn't feeling well enough to lie down.

"When the poor girl left, all weepy and distraught, I looked up and saw Lady Sylvia standing in her window watching the whole gruesome scene. Next thing I knew, she'd walked outside to see what the girl had left and upon recognizing it for what it was, pounded on her husband's turret door. When it registered what Lady Sylvia had in her arms, Sir John slapped her so hard she was knocked to the ground. I was sick with worry for her, but for obvious reasons, I stayed out of sight. Soon after, I watched Sir John dig a wee grave by the gazebo. I can't believe you found it, Mr. Campbell, and I'm mighty sorry for it."

"I was trying to resurrect the old irrigation system," I tell him.

William nods. "Well, there you have it. I don't want the police to know because the woman still lives nearby, and I see no reason to…"

"And the photograph?" I interrupt.

William's head sinks between his knees. "I was the only other living person, save Lady Sylvia, who saw what happened that night. Once I was sure Sir John had gone back to bed, I exhumed the child and took a photo in case Sir John ever denied the young girl's story. That old trunk belonged to my grandmother. I hid the photo behind the paper lining and forgot all about it."

Bloody gruesome! Rape, an illegitimate stillborn, assault, and a gardener digging up a dead baby to snap a photo!

"Think of me what you like," William said. "You didn't know Sir John McPhee. He was the devil himself and I have no regrets."

I am thinking the interview is over when he adds, "He should have a proper burial as I don't much fancy having his wee spirit hanging about."

I couldn't agree more. "Where do you suggest we bury him? Not in the same place; I'm afraid the dogs will dig it up again."

"If you don't mind, I'd like to get in touch with the mother. She's a good lady, Mr. Campbell, and it won't take me but a day to contact her. Perhaps the District Council will let us have a plot in the new graveyard just outside the castle gates."

"I leave it your hands, then. And thank you, William. I know this can't have been easy."

"It's no bother," he replies, but I can see he is shaken by the exchange.

I have one more question to ask. "I'm ashamed to say I know very little of Glenapp's past. I've quite a passion for local history," I fib. "Might you know where the village archives are kept?"

"My cousin, Nessie Brown, has been the village librarian for nearly thirty years now. She'll help you out."

"I'm obliged," I reply.

*　　　*　　　*

Ballantrae's library is housed in a small, red brick building no more than twenty feet square on the main street of town. It is late afternoon and, as luck would have it, the door is open. Buried amongst piles of returned books, Nessie Brown is seated at her desk with her back to the entrance. Without even turning around, she says, "I wondered when you were coming."

"And why is that?" I ask, amused.

Turning in her swivel chair, she replies, "Because rumor has it you're an educated man, and I have the best source of books in town."

She is a handsome woman in her mid-fifties, with short, smartly styled, blond hair, and a warm countenance that immediately puts me at ease.

"Well, here I am."

"It's nice to meet you, Andrew Campbell," she says, shaking my hand. "I suspect you're not here to take out a book."

How did she know this? "Actually, since we've been here over eight years now, I thought it about time I read up on Ballantrae's history." It sounds disingenuous but she is gracious, obliging.

"Interested in the Kennedy feuds or Sawney Bean, perhaps?"

I laugh, relieved she has spared me the embarrassment of deception. "I grew up hearing the legend of Sawney Bean, but tell me about the Kennedys."

"Well, you may take out S.R. Crockett's novel, *The Grey Man*, an extremely loose representation of the facts or you can read my far more accurate account, whichever you'd prefer."

"The latter," I reply.

She pulls up a stepping stool to retrieve an oversized, linen scrapbook from the top of one of the bookshelves. "Here it is, then. There are other items that might interest you as well," she says.

When I'm sure she has returned to her book ledger, I nonchalantly browse for any facts about Glenapp Castle, skipping to the end to see if she's included our purchase in 1998.

"You're not in there, yet," she says to the wall.

"And why is that?" I ask.

"You have to die first."

"There's just a small chance I might outlive you," I point out. "What then?"

"Then you can have my job and write what you like," she retorts.

Nessie Brown's handwritten account of Ballantrae's history is intriguing reading, all thirty pages of it. I discover that Ardstinchar Castle, now a ruin on the hill just outside the village, was built in the fifteenth century by Sir Hew Kennedy, a Scottish captain to Joan of Arc. The castle remained the stronghold of the Bargany branch of the Kennedys for over two hundred and fifty years. Eventually, in a decisive final battle against the neighboring Kennedys of Cassillis, the castle burned to the ground. Nessie added an editorial commentary about the placement of the watch tower directly on the ancient route of the fairy processional.

In the eighteenth and nineteenth centuries, Ballantrae was best known for its smuggling operations. Large logger-rigged vessels called *buckers* anchored in the bay just long enough for mounted middlemen to hide, or distribute, the contraband (mostly tobacco, lace, spirits, tea and brandy) throughout the United Kingdom and Europe. And I knew, of course, that until the 1930's Ballantrae Bay was a busy fishing hub with over one hundred boats moored in the harbor. I was searching for an account of Glenapp's fire when Nessie says, "It's closing time; I hope you found what you're looking for."

"Actually, no…" I chance.

She is fussing about, rearranging piles of books, giving herself time. I hear her keys jingle and fear I am out of luck.

"It's time for my tea," she intones, smiling.

"I never get time for tea these days," I say, "but I'd like to make today an exception. May I buy you a cup?"

"I'd like that," she replies, cheerfully. "I'll just tell my Jonathan that I'll not be back for a bit. Going to Thistles Tea Room, are we?"

"I'll wait for you there."

Just past the Royal Bank of Scotland and the village post office, a sign for Thistles directs me through a narrow alleyway to the cozy teahouse. A delightful pebbled patio, radiant with sunshine, offers outdoor seating. I promptly order tea and shortbread for two.

Nessie and the tea arrive simultaneously. "Well then," she begins, pouring us each a cup. "What's the real reason you've come to see me?"

I plunge right in. "Tell me about the fire."

She is not the least startled. "How much do you know?"

"Very little," I confess. "Only what tidbits the police would tell us when we bought Glenapp in 1998. I'm not even certain who perished."

"Sir John McPhee and Judith Hutcheson."

"I knew about Sir John, of course, but who's Judith Hutcheson—a distant relation to our Head Gardener?"

"His mother."

"His mother? Tom's mother died in the fire?"

"Aye, and a horrible death it was, not the least for having to perish in the same room with John McPhee," she decries.

I must say I am genuinely taken aback and need a moment to gather my bearings. "The stupidity of us not to know when we hired young Tom," I lament. "I'm mighty sorry for it. I took him for a bit of an odd chap, but goodness me, this explains a great deal. What caused the fire?"

"The fire brigade detected traces of diesel outside the north turret entrance to Sir John's quarters. It was arson. Murder—plain and simple."

"Who were they trying to murder?"

"Sir John McPhee, certainly. Whoever did it could not have known Judith was in there."

"What was she doing in Sir John's bedroom suite in the first place?"

"She was Head of Staff and was taking Sir John his nightly port. Tom told Gavin Gillespie she was planning to resign that night."

"Did they ever convict anyone?" I query.

Nessie shakes her head. "Gavin Gillespie held a four month investigation, even brought in the Criminal Investigation Department, but everyone had a credible alibi. The fact is, it's still an open case."

"Lord!" I declare. "Who were the prime suspects?"

"There were five: Lady Sylvia, Colin Dunbar, Roddie Hutcheson, Fiona McCarrick, and William Hobbes."

"William?" This is unsettling news.

"He's the least likely to have done it," she assures me, "though he would have been justified if he had. You needn't worry; my cousin hasn't the constitution for murder."

"Who were the others?" I ask, not convinced. "I don't know them."

For the next hour, Nessie relays the whole incredible saga leading up to the fire. I doubt she misses a detail, as she seems privy to the intimate goings-on of all involved.

"After the fire, what happened then?" I ask.

"Lady Sylvia wanted her husband buried at Glenapp, but Tom refused to have either of his parents laid to rest on the same property as Sir John, so he appealed to the District Council to have his father's body exhumed, then he buried them side by side in the new cemetery just outside the castle gate. It was quite an emotional day, I tell you. We all cried our hearts out."

"What about the others?" I dare to ask.

"Lady Sylvia shut down Glenapp at once and moved to her brother's estate in Aberdeen. As a consequence, the staff was forced to leave. Roddie already lived in Girvan, so no change for him. Tom moved in with his Auntie Fay until he left for his internship at Findhorn Gardens. Colin and Victoria Dunbar remained in the Head Gardener's cottage until they moved to Halifax, Nova Scotia with their daughter, Sophie, who was going to university there."

It was a lot to absorb!

"There's more," Nessie warns me. "You might as well know all of it because you're going to hear it eventually, and I'd rather it be from me, so it's accurate.

"The Criminal Investigation Department let Colin Dunbar move to Nova Scotia on probationary conditions, meaning he had to report in to the authorities every fortnight. During Sophie's second year at university, Colin hanged himself from the attic rafters. Victoria is one of my best friends and she wrote me the whole terrible truth. The disgrace of being banned from the Royal Caledonian Curling Club was a terrible blow and followed him to Halifax where they refused him membership to the local curling club. Worse yet, he couldn't find proper gardening work—the only vocation he'd ever known. There, now, you have the most of it."

"Most of it?" I say, watching the sun slip behind Ailsa Craig. Eva will be wondering where the devil I am, but I cannot leave, not yet.

Nessie pours us a second cup of tea. "After the disastrous party at Glenapp, pretty much everyone went home. Before long, we heard one fire brigade come from Girvan, then another from Colmonell. The whole of Ballantrae spilled into the streets. God help us all, Glenapp Castle was on fire! The flames lit up the whole hillside. My Jonathan and I worried for them all, but especially for Colin and Victoria. As I mentioned, they were good friends—Victoria being Godmother to our daughter, Jenny. We knew we wouldn't get past the monitored gate, so we had no choice but to wait and watch.

"Within the hour, the ambulances brought the remains of Sir John McPhee and Judith Hutcheson to Samuel McCreadie's funeral parlor in the south end of the village. You may not believe what I'm about to tell you," she warns me. "If I hadn't seen it with my own eyes, I wouldn't either."

"I'm listening," I assure her.

"It was past ten when the two ambulances drove down from the castle, quietly, so not to wake everyone. Of course, we were all up, still mulling around, horrified about the fire and all. There was little sleeping in Ballantrae that night, I can tell you. Anyway, I swear to you on my Scottish heritage, the roof of the ambulance carrying Sir John's body was covered, every inch, with nasty black ravens, and *huge* they were. You could see their shiny ebony coats in the moonlight, and despite the strong gale still bending the trees nearly to the ground, not one raven was blown off that roof. By the time the ambulance reached the car park, you could hear their haunting *craws-craw's*, and their pecking on the ambulance windows halfway across the village. The ambulance, directly behind, carrying Judith, had not a one."

"How could that be, Nessie?" I object. *And ravens are harbingers of death.*

"Wait, I'm not finished, Mr. Campbell. Hear me to the end, then you can choose whether to believe it—it matters not to me.

"Lady Sylvia waited the traditional three days to bury Sir John. Day and night, the ravens hovered around the funeral parlor, perched on the roof, in the gutters, on the wheelie bins. You couldn't see the top of the hearse for all the black scavengers sitting there, waiting, waiting. Samuel McCreadie couldn't leave the place for fear of being pecked to death, which meant he had to sleep with the dead bodies."

Nessie, helping herself to a piece of shortbread, checks my reaction.

"Go on," I say.

"Sir John was buried first as Tom had to wait another two days for permission from the District Council to move his father. On the morning of Sir John's service, and a blustery morning it was, they managed to get his coffin into the hearse, but the ravens immediately swarmed it again. Samuel could hardly see through the windshield to drive. When they arrived at Glenapp Castle, with the entire village trailing behind, the enormous flock of ravens flew directly to the gravesite. Now, mind you, this was a new site, and one has to ask how the creatures knew where it was. As we all gathered round, the ravens hovered in the trees, the branches bowing with the weight of so many.

It was the eeriest thing I ever saw. When they lowered the casket in the ground, the sinister, black beasts swooped down and perched on the lid as if to push it deeper into the earth, screeching all the while. Quickly as they could, Samuel and the minister covered the coffin with dirt, ending the whole affair as graciously as possible."

Here, Nessie takes a lingering sip of tea. I sit, stupefied, trying to take it all in.

"The next morning," she continues, "Lady Sylvia went to visit her husband's grave only to discover that in the night someone had unearthed the coffin and raised the lid of the casket. There were black raven feathers everywhere, floating through the air, blanketing the ground, stuck to Sir John's bloodied corpse. They had plucked out his eyes and mutilated his body beyond recognition. Lady Sylvia's screams could be heard all the way to the village. Colin and Victoria were the first to arrive; they found her huddled on the ground in the fetal position, in shock, no doubt.

"Two days later, we all attended Judith Hutcheson's funeral. It was a stunner of a morning, filled with a chorus of joyful chirping birds and not a raven in sight.

"That's the end of it, Mr. Campbell. You wanted the history of Glenapp; I'm afraid you have it."

I shift awkwardly in my chair; so fantastical a tale surely isn't plausible. Such ghoulish fables were commonplace in medieval times, but in contemporary life?

"Sounds like a good piece of fiction," I comment.

"The nuance between fantasy and reality is oftentimes illusionary," she replies, delicately dabbing her mouth with her napkin. "But I would not worry—you're doing all the right things.

One must never underestimate the power of good intentions, Mr. Campbell. It is one's thoughts, words, and deeds that determine the unfolding of events. You've hired Tom Hutcheson to revive the walled garden, and you have a child living at Glenapp now. I sense she is a gifted, perceptive little girl. Together…" she pauses, "Well, I strongly suggest you not allow conventional thinking to muddy the waters, as they say."

What *ever* is she talking about?

"My husband will think I've run off," she declares, standing up to leave.

"One last question, if I may. Why was Sir John McPhee knighted by the Queen?"

"For civil service. He owned a shipping company that exported various goods to South America; Guayaquil was the main port-of-call, I believe. Through the years he donated medical supplies and dry foods worth millions of pounds to the impoverished children there. All in the name of the Crown, of course. He was knighted in 1964, three years before he bought Glenapp Castle."

And then he enslaved the poor things, shipped them to London, and sold them for sex.

"Let me walk you home," I offer.

"That won't be necessary," she declines. "I live just a block away on the Shore Road."

"Thank you, Mrs. Brown. You have been more than kind," I say.

"Good day, Andrew Campbell," she bids me farewell. "Come back sometime, and we'll talk about your ghosts."

CHAPTER FIFTEEN

EVA

ON DAYS WHEN I simply must get outside, it is the terraced garden at the rear of the castle I retreat to. In May, though William and Henry have yet to plant the summer annuals, the mossy retaining walls are dripping with fuchsia and sweet white clematis. There is a square of grassed lawn bordered by red barbarous hedge, and in the center stands a lichen-covered stone statue of the Celtic Mother Goddess, loosely gowned and leaning over a sundial as if to escort nature's course through the season's solstice. In my early years at Glenapp, I prayed to this mythical icon of fertility that I, too, might be blessed, but it was not to be. I have often wondered if the *Genii Cucullati*, the three hooded saints adorning her pedestal, counseled against it.

The truth is, I have just received a call from Vicente Flor and needed some air.

"We're leaving London tomorrow," he informed me, "and I wanted to thank you again for your gracious hospitality the other day. I talked for much too long. I apologize."

"Nonsense," I replied. "We've just heard more gruesome tales of Sir John's escapades. It seems you were lucky to have survived his employment."

"*¿Cómo qué?*" he asked. "I am sorry, I forget myself. Such as what, may I ask?"

"Such as rape, infidelity, nearly killing a little girl, cheating during the District Curling Championships—the latter resulting in the eventual suicide of one man—the list goes on and on."

"*¡Qué horror!* Who would that be?"

"You wouldn't know him," I said. "He was Head Gardener at the time. We also discovered we unknowingly hired the son of the woman killed in the fire." I stopped, reticent to say more.

"Vicente, are you there?"

"*Sí*. How dreadful," he replied, genuinely dismayed. "I'm just surprised someone else perished in the fire. I knew about Sir John, of course, but I returned to Ecuador and just assumed…"

"How is your wife?" I inquired, anxious to change the subject.

"Maria is better, *gracias*. We're leaving for Ecuador tomorrow, but will be returning to London in eight weeks time for a follow-up with the heart surgeon. We're tired," he admitted.

"Well, please come see us when you return. Issie would love to see you and we'd like to meet Maria. That's in mid-July, then?"

"I think it's the third week, actually. I'll call when we return, and *sí*, we'd love to visit your beautiful hotel. As hotel guests, though, I insist."

"I'm afraid that won't be possible," I protested. "We're completely booked, but we've plenty of room in our private quarters. By the time you return, Andrew's mother, Mary, will be living here as well. It's a virtual circus, Vicente. You and Maria will be a welcome addition."

"*Muchas gracias*, Eva. Please give my best to Issie and Andrew, and to Grimshaw," he laughed. "*Ciao*."

Only nature can forgive such naked hypocrisy; I want Vicente and Maria Flor to visit about as much as I want a virulent outbreak of salmonella in the kitchen.

"There you are!" Andrew bellows across the garden. "I have good news. William has made arrangements for the burial in the new cemetery just outside the castle gates. You don't look very relieved," he observes.

"Vicente's coming back, in mid-July," I tell him.

"He doesn't have to, sweetheart. We don't ever need to see him again if you don't want to."

"I know. I invited him. I didn't mean to, it just happened, and now he's bringing his wife. Doesn't it bother you at all?"

"I haven't really thought about it, honestly. I just assume he'll be here for a short period of time and then return to Ecuador. What is it about him that bothers you?"

"It's not him, per se, it's his presence, and all this talk about Kitty makes it difficult for me to establish myself as Issie's mother. And it has to be confusing for her."

"I suspect it's more than that," he perceives. "I think it's hard to share Issie with everyone—Vicente, Kevin, Tom, William, and all the guests crooning over her—and now with Maria coming. You haven't had a chance to get your foot in the door, have you?"

How well he knows me. "It isn't that I don't want to share her, it's that I've never had the chance to be her primary caretaker, her number one Mum. And she's so independent, Andrew. I marvel at the way she runs around making friends everywhere she goes. Selfishly, I wish she needed me more, yet if she were a demanding child, I couldn't manage that, either."

"As I said before, we don't have to invite Vicente back, Eva."

Andrew shoves his hands deep into his pockets, clearly changing the subject. "Nessie thinks we have ghosts here." He surprises me, for he has not mentioned this before. "Tell me, did you know Glenapp Castle was haunted before we looked at it?"

I am certain, though he is addressing Ailsa Craig, that the question is intended for me. "Before we looked at it? No," I carefully reply. Before we *bought* it, that's another issue all together.

"That bone chilling cold I feel—considering all that I have told you, in your opinion, is it Sir John McPhee?"

"Yes, I believe so, and there is another," I confess, taking a deep breath, for I will not lie to him. "It's Judith Hutcheson, I suspect. But there's no reason to panic; we can have them cleared out. In fact, your new friend, Nessie Brown, does it."

"Does what?"

"Clears old houses of bad spirits."

"Tell me you're not serious."

"Quite serious," I say.

"How do you know this?"

"For all the time you spent with Nessie, did you not sense that she communicates with the spirit world? She's an intuitive—a psychic."

"What? Nessie, a psychic? Rubbish!"

"Kevin and half the staff go to her for readings," I disclose.

"Oh, well then," he shakes his head in disbelief. "Now I'm *really* convinced!"

"A psychic is merely someone who reads your thought energy," I reply. "You needn't scoff so."

"There's no scientific evidence proving one person can read another person's thoughts," he protests.

"There's no scientific explanation for ghosts, either," I point out. "If you and I honestly think we have ghosts here, then we're already defying scientific logic. It may make you uncomfortable, but if we want Sir John McPhee rid of you need to broaden your thinking a wee bit, sweetheart. We're talking about lingering spirits who have chosen, for whatever reason, to remain here. But first you have to admit they exist, and then we'll have to find someone who can communicate with them. However, I object to banishing Judith. She's harmless—helpful, in fact. You can do what you like with nasty Sir John, but leave her well alone, if you please."

"You're being ridiculous, Eva," he chastises. "You've let your father's obsession with the supernatural taint your sense of reason."

Once again, it is Issie who saves the day, for I was just about to reveal that it is Glenapp's north turret wing that infringes on the route of the traditional fairy path and thus is the source of all our problems. Perhaps we should clear out Sir John McPhee first—he is, after all, the real problem.

"I can't do anything about it now," Andrew whispers as Issie approaches. "I've just received a call from Judge Sinclair that the adoption papers are ready, and I need to go to Glasgow tomorrow—then we've the wedding. Then we're booked solid for the British Open at Turnberry, then mother arrives…"

"You needn't worry," I try to allay his fears. "They're not going anywhere."

Issie is upon us. "You've *got* to come to the kitchen," she exclaims, clearly distraught.

"What happened?" we ask.

Her cheeks are stained with the residue of tears. "Kevin says he's going to chop Grimmey up into little pieces because he ate all the haggis for the wedding, and then Grimmey got scared and threw up all over the floor. It's a disaster! Come *on*…!" she pleads, tugging us each by an arm.

CHAPTER SIXTEEN

TOM

FOR TWO MISERABLE DAYS they kept me in the hospital for treatment of my burned right hand. The doctor informed me, though I might regain marginal use of it, the nerves had been badly damaged and, with the eventual buildup of scar tissue, it was unlikely I would ever have feeling in my palm.

I never saw Sophie. Colin Dunbar, watching his own life plummet to the depths of hell, vice gripped his daughter's instead and forbid her to leave the house without his permission.

For the next three months I navigated life through an anesthetic fog, receiving condolences from friends and family, yet feeling nothing but an all consuming, crushing sadness. I'd return from school to my Auntie Fay's and sleep until breakfast the next morning. Sophie talked to me when she could between classes, but I had no recollection of what she said. Dad dead. Mum dead. Sophie leaving me for at least four years. Life seemed pointless. I knew that somehow we needed to say good-bye, to decide what our commitment was, but inertia stood firm and I kept telling myself I'd sleep on it.

A week before the Dunbars moved to Halifax and I to Findhorn Gardens, Sophie caught my arm as I was getting into my pickup after school. She said her mum and dad had one last round of questioning with Gavin Gillespie that afternoon.

"I'll have about two hours," she said, excitedly. "Let's go to the redwood."

"No, Soph," I declined. "Not today."

"Wrong answer," she replied, climbing into the front seat.

We said nothing to one another on the way to the glen. For weeks I'd considered what I could ask of Sophie. She was beautiful and vivacious and warm, and above all, she possessed a heart of gold that extended to everyone around her, especially to those kids who never found their way to popularity at school. People loved her. Wasn't it more courageous, more loving to set her free to love someone else? She'd be furious and hurt at first, but she'd get over me. But I'd envisioned writing a letter, maybe slipping it into her suitcase, then slithering away like a coward in the night. Not this.

When we reached the car park, she leaned over and took the keys out of the ignition. "Let's go," she said.

Sophie took my hand as the trail led us through the ferns and bamboo patches and florescent moss-covered roots along the banks of the Garleffin. I loved her so much it hurt.

"Did you think I was going to run away without saying good-bye?" I asked.

"I considered it a possibility, aye."

"I hate good-byes," I confessed.

"No one's saying good-bye."

"Soph, you're free," I said.

She stopped in her tracks. "Free to do what?"

"Free to love someone else. We can't pretend that you're coming back here, Soph. You'll be gone for four years, and with your folks moving there what would possibly bring you back to Ballantrae?"

"You."

"It's not going to happen," I said. "Besides, you'll likely be curling all over the world by then. You're good and training with Hal Munro will make you even better. I wouldn't be surprised if your parents applied for Canadian citizenship which means you could join the Canadian Women's Curling Team, travel all over the world…"

"You said that already. Have you no faith in love, Tom Hutcheson?" she challenged.

"Not really. Everyone I've ever loved has left me."

"Well, I'm not leaving you. I'm going away for four years, but I'm not leaving you."

We followed the path across the kissing bridge and through the dense pine forest until we came to the steep trail that led to our secret redwood. Here, the rushing water cascaded down a waterfall forming three-tiered, sandy-bottomed pools of crystal clear water. Until we turned thirteen, Sophie and I swam there every day in the summertime.

"Here's how I see it," Sophie began. "You and I are destined to be together, but fate keeps pulling us apart. I've thought a lot about this, Tom. Sometimes you have to be torn apart to realize how much you love someone."

"That's bullshit, Sophie. I don't need you to be gone for four years to know how much I love you."

"Maybe not, but when we can finally be together, it's going to be all the more amazing."

I couldn't have disagreed more, but what was the point of arguing? I simply said, "I will wait, but I'll understand if you…want to be with anyone else."

The biggest lie of my life.

"You sound a wee bit touched in the head, do you know that? It's not going to happen," she assured me. "Let's make a pledge, right here and now. Repeat after me, 'I love you, Tom Hutcheson, and I will wait for you.'"

"I love you, Tom Hutcheson, and I will wait for you," I repeated, faking a smile.

"Do it right—this is important," she scolded.

"I love you, Sophie Dunbar, and I will wait for you," I pledged, meaning every word.

I cupped her face in my hands and drew her to me for what I knew would be our last kiss for four unbearable years.

The day Sophie left, William asked if he could borrow my pickup to take the Dunbars to Glasgow Airport. I hid among the beach dunes until I thought they'd be out of sight, but alas, I mistimed their departure, and as I stepped back onto Main Street they were driving through the middle of Ballantrae. Sophie flung her head out the window to steal a last glance of the village when she saw me. She practically stood up, crazy girl—her golden, red hair blowing every which way—and blew me a kiss. When she was almost out of sight, she pounded her heart three times with her fist, then threw open her arms to the skies…I will love you…forever.

*   *   *

Findhorn Garden, on the northeast coast of Scotland, where I was to intern, was founded by three individuals, two of whom were said to have the gift of communicating with the nature spirits. The results were astounding, and Findhorn became famous throughout the world for the legendary enormity and vibrancy of the vegetables grown in the sandy, dry dirt. There really were forty-pound cabbages, and brilliant orange carrots too big to put in your mouth, and raspberries the size of walnuts. I ate them every day.

I spent nine years at Findhorn, first as an intern, then as a staff gardener. Blundering my way through a labyrinth of grief and depression as best I could, the years seamlessly coalesced into a churning cesspool of misery and self-pity. The truth of the matter is that the kind people at Findhorn saved my life by leaving me alone.

In my sorry state, one might ask if I pondered who set Glenapp Castle on fire. I obsessed over it. William had written me about Colin Dunbar's suicide, a shock to be sure, but an admission of guilt? Maybe. Maybe not. He had reason enough to hang himself without the additional burden of murder. On the other hand, if he were guilty he bore the cross of two souls and his suicide was just retribution. The fire was clearly premeditated. Could he have orchestrated such a feat after reportedly leaving Glenapp Castle? Possibly, yet Sophie and her mum swore he was home at the time the fire was set. I believed them. So did the police.

What about my Uncle Roddie? He despised Sir John, for sure, but enough to murder him? And between discovering the cheating and making such a fuss at the party, he didn't have enough time to pour ten gallons of fuel down the turret staircase of Sir John's quarters. Roddie swore he went right home as Gavin Gillespie had ordered him to and fell asleep. He was lucky to get home at all.

Though William Hobbes is a man for whom I have deep respect, he merits serious consideration. William was supposedly gone most the evening visiting his daughter, Lucy, in the hospital in Girvan. If my memory serves me correctly, I didn't see him until the party was over and Mum was already in Sir John's quarters delivering his port. Everyone says William was the one who alerted the fire brigades. Could a man, so quiet, so diminutive in stature, plan and execute a murder? My heart tells me…no. He hasn't what it takes. Sir John almost killed Lucy, William's pride and joy, and had the audacity to deny it, but was that motive enough to burn him to death? Perhaps, but I cannot bear the thought as he is one of the few friends I have left in the world.

Lady Sylvia McPhee—sweet, demure, and seemingly so devoted to Sir John—what did she know of his infidelities? She knew that her drunken husband drove into Lucy and denied doing so. And she was standing right there when Roddie revealed to all of Ayrshire that Colin Dunbar and her husband had cheated during the District Curling Championships. But why would she set her own castle on fire? If she wanted to be rid of her husband, why not poison him?

That leaves Fiona McCarrick. Rape certainly qualifies as a motive, and she was at the castle all day and night with time to plan anything she pleased. Gavin said it was difficult to break her alibi as one staff member or another accounted for her every move. Unfortunately, my mum isn't alive to testify on her behalf. And who would implicate her, anyway? Every staff member there knew Sir John raped Fiona years ago, and most wouldn't mind seeing him dead for their own reasons. Could it have been a conspiracy?

And round and round I went until, eventually, I wore myself out. If Gavin Gillespie and the Criminal Investigation Department couldn't figure it out, neither could I. It may be hard to believe, but after a while I stopped caring.

Then, the final blow.

Weather permitting, the garden staff at Findhorn ate together, community style, around a picnic table at lunchtime. Someone had received a copy of *Curling Magazine* from home and was reading the gossip column aloud.

"Listen to this," he read. "Sophie Dunbar, now residing in Halifax, married her curling coach, Hal Munro, last week. 'She's World Class,' says Munro of his bride. 'This is the happiest day of my life.'

"Sophie Dunbar is originally from Ballantrae, Scotland," our reader continued, "where she led her high school team to the Girls District

Championships. She is presently captain of the undefeated Dalhousie University Women's curling team. Sadly, at least for now, Scotland has lost one of its best woman curlers."

Staggering away from the table, I ran aimlessly for miles along the shore of Findhorn Bay until finally, dizzy and disoriented, I vomited until the gastric juices singed my throat. Any torture was preferable to this. Any torture at all. To the vast oceans I bellowed aloud my solemn pledge never to embrace a god, for no divine being would take away the only salvation left to me. Such cruelty was surely reserved for the forsaken.

My isolation at Findhorn had served me well in many respects, but this? Why hadn't Sophie told me? It explained why I hadn't received a letter from her in…had it been several months? At the very least she owed me an explanation. At the very least, she should get on her knees and beg forgiveness for breaking her vow to love and wait for me.

Drugs and alcohol were forbidden at Findhorn so for the next two years, sometimes out of grief, sometimes out of anger, sometimes apathy, but never for love, I shagged anyone who was interested. Names, faces, innuendos whispered at climax—I remember none of these. Then, one chilly winter morning, I peered down on my latest conquest and wept, for I didn't even know her name.

I requested a meeting with Iain Henry, coordinator of the gardening staff. When I entered his office, he smiled. My reputation preceded me.

"You can wipe that grin off your face," I said, not jesting.

"Why?"

"Because I want to talk with you, seriously, about my job."

"You do good work here, Tom. Are you unhappy?" he asked.

"Yes. No. I'd like to take on more responsibility, something that will more fully occupy my mind."

"I see…"

Iain settled deep in his tattered swivel chair, pondering my request. "Do you want to be just busy or are you interested in doing more mindful work?"

"Both," I professed, unconvincingly.

He swung his unlaced muddy boots onto his desk. "You can't have both, Tom, they're mutually exclusive. Incessant work, being busy all the time, isn't conducive to mindfulness. Your need to be frenetically overactive is rooted in trying to forget the past, and justifiably so, but you'll have to be more attentive to the present to achieve enduring peace of mind. You've a gift, but as long as you see yourself as separate from Divine Spirit, or in a larger sense a cosmic order, it will remain unrealized. You're still biting off the hand that feeds you."

"I've no faith in any higher power," I confessed.

"I know. You blame God for your misfortunes. It's understandable, but don't you think you're here for a reason? What do you think that is, Tom? I think you have a great opportunity to heal here at Findhorn, not by intensified manual labor, but by opening up to the quiet wisdom the gardens have to offer you. That's where your salvation lies, with nature—communing with the magnificent beauty around you. You have to stop seeing yourself as a separate entity and a victim of circumstance, my friend. As humans we're not disconnected from the world around us; life's an intricate web of interactions between all life forms. Until you understand that, you're just another gardener. To partner with a higher source is a leap of faith sometimes, but the heights it will take you to are limitless."

I said nothing. What nonsense!

"Your request is denied," Iain said. "I want you to go back to what you were doing. Try to clear your mind as you work, meditate on the unique beauty of each plant you touch, and be grateful for each moment. In six months, we'll talk again."

What do they say? You have to commiserate with the devil before seeing the light? Nice guy though he was, Iain didn't understand. You can't just slough off being fatherless at ten, an orphan at eighteen, and having the love of your life run off and marry someone else without even telling you!

Stubborn, ignorant fool that I was, against Iain's advice, I started working back to back shifts in both the perennial and vegetable gardens thinking it would increase my chances of seeing the plant fairies if I were physically present more hours of the day. It was easy as plenty of people were happy to forfeit their shifts. When my reserves failed me I slept standing up, leaning against a tree, hoe still in hand. At night, bizarre, contorted dreams terrorized my sleep and I became an insomniac. As if on a death wish, I stopped attending meals so I didn't have to speak with anyone. Then one day, my head ached so badly I fell forward with the crippling pain and slammed my head hard against the manure spreader resulting in a concussion and a deep gash over my left eye.

Iain came to see me in the infirmary. "So?" he asked.

"So, what?"

"So, are you ready to look at alternatives to slave labor?"

"Do I have any other choice?"

"Sure you do," he said. "You can continue to self-destruct."

"I'm out of resources," I pointed out.

"There's always drugs and alcohol," Iain grinned.

"Damn hard to get around here," I reminded him.

My boss chuckled out loud. "Good thing or you'd be dead by now."

The truth of his statement stung my pride. How pathetic I was. I looked out the window at the beauty of Findhorn's pastoral landscape and knew I had grossly abused my privilege of residing there and I felt ashamed.

Iain cleared his throat. "If you want to stay at Findhorn, Tom, you may work eight hours a day in the perennial garden. That's it! You're to eat three meals a day with the community. The rest of the time I want you to relax, read, and be grateful you're alive. If that isn't acceptable to you, I'm going to ask you to leave."

My Good Samaritan didn't know it, but that day, March 29, 2004, was my twenty-fifth birthday. When Iain left I closed my eyes, and for the first time since the night of my eighteenth birthday, standing alone on the curling ice, I implored my father for help. His deep, raspy voice solemnly counseled that it was time to relinquish my addiction to grief. The problem was... I had no idea where to begin.

Not a minute later, Iain returned leading what I mistook to be a white coyote. The lanky, blue-eyed dog hopped on my bed and started licking my wounded eye.

"I found her along the road, but she doesn't seem to like me much," Iain said with honest remorse. "Clearly, she's found her mate."

"Thank you, Iain. I could use a friend. I'll call her Rosie, for the White Rose of Scotland. It was my mum's favorite."

"It fits her."

When I'd regained enough strength to work, Rosie and I met Iain in the perennial garden one evening after supper. It had once been a walled garden, but only one side of the old stone enclosure remained standing. The tradition at Findhorn was to enter through the facade door in the wall, anyway, in honor of the woman who, along with the nature spirits, designed and cultivated the original garden. Before entering, I noticed an old ladder leaning against the outside of the crumbling wall.

"Climb up and have a look," Iain called through the open door. I slowly ascended, one rung at a time, wondering what folly Iain had up his sleeve. When I observed the garden from above, I realized for the first time that the flowerbeds reflected the shape of a butterfly.

"My God, I've been here seven years, and I never realized…" I said, aghast.

"You've been very busy," Iain commented from below. "Findhorn's founder didn't realize it herself at the time. She just let the plant spirits guide her. Then one night when she couldn't sleep, she strolled into the garden and, illuminated by the moon, climbed that very same ladder and saw what she had created. It's a well known tale here at Findhorn, Tom. I'm surprised you haven't heard it."

"I've been living underground," I admitted.

"I want you to work in this particular garden because the energetic vibrations are extraordinarily strong here. It's an honor to manage this garden, Tom Hutcheson. Handle each plant with loving care and trust your intuition. You'll have a staff of three to help you."

"Thank you, Iain. I don't deserve this."

"You're welcome, and I don't agree. You've suffered gravely and you're a hard worker. Maybe you'll even be lucky enough to see the nature spirits."

"How does it work? I mean, who are the nature spirits, exactly?"

"Come on down and I'll explain the best I can," Iain offered.

Iain stood in the middle of the garden and swept his hands across the sky. "All across the planet are leylines, broad bands of energy that crisscross the earth's surface. Like gravity, we can't see them but they're there. Where leylines intersect, the potential for dynamic creativity is magnified, and those attuned enough can manifest the physicality of spirit. The founders of Findhorn Gardens were able to do just that, to communicate with the energy of the plant spirits brought here by the leylines. Those who have actually seen them claim the fairies have wings of the red admiral butterfly."

I struggle to calm myself, to concentrate. "So then, Findhorn is at the heart of intersecting leylines?"

"That's right. It's no different than at the spiritual sites of the great standing stones here in Great Britain or in France. Our ancestors were more sensitive than we are and intuitively built their spiritual temples where the energy was strongest. Findhorn is at one of those intersecting vortexes. We're standing in the middle of it right now. More importantly, the shape of this garden is telling us that the guiding vibrations were those of the nature spirits. Pretty amazing."

"What if the founders had never come here?" I asked.

"Well, obviously Findhorn's famous gardens wouldn't exist," Iain explained. "On the other hand, if someone of mal intent had built something here, the opposite would be true; the damage to the earth or to any inhabitants who lived here would be greater because the leylines augment the potential for good *or* bad energy. It's no different than anywhere else. Negative thoughts and actions produce negative results, and loving thoughts produce positive results. It's just that if it occurs in a place where the leylines intersect, the impact is exaggerated."

"You're a Believer, then?" I chanced.

"A believer that attention to the laws of nature should guide everything we do? Absolutely."

"Can leylines connect different places?" I asked.

"Of course. Why do you think the devoted make pilgrimages from one place to another? There are mystical trails all over the world, Tom. Leylines are just traditional routes for navigating a life imbued with spirit. That's why I want you to work here, in this perennial garden. It's loaded with spirit, and you could use some."

"Iain, do you ever...hear them or see them?" I asked with hesitancy.

"No," he laughed. "I'm too left brained. I leave that to the likes of you."

For the next two years, I steadfastly devoted myself to cultivating the perennial garden, each day replenishing my faith that I could learn to live without Sophie, after all. On my twenty-seventh birthday, I received a letter from the only friend I had left outside of Findhorn—William Hobbes. In it he included an advert for a new Head Gardener at Glenapp Castle, dated March 2006.

It was the perfect job in the wrong place! Maybe the wrong job in the perfect place! Maybe I should just forget it. Maybe I should stop running away. Maybe it was time to go home to Ballantrae, to the salty sea and sweet smelling banks of the Garleffin. Home to where my only kin were buried. I'd known for months I needed to move on from Findhorn. It seemed as good a time as any.

When Iain Henry saw my changed expression, he dropped his handful of thyme and escorted me to his office to conclude my business.

"Where are you off to, Tom?"

"Home."

Iain looked up, surprised. "Do you have work?" he asked with concern in his voice.

"No."

"Well, then, I wish you luck, my friend. Findhorn was lucky to have you these nine years."

And that's the end of my story, really. Rosie and I have lived in the gardener's cottage at Glenapp Castle for nearly a month now. I hadn't planned on working here, and as hard as I've tried to conjure up reasons not to stay, the truth is I love this estate and I like the Campbells. I like their little girl, Issie, too. The child seems to float through the gardens like a butterfly, randomly flitting from one flower to the next, so drawn by the magnificent, rich colors she's unable to decide where to settle. Time and time again I've watched her pick up the marker, memorize the name, then bury her nose in the newly discovered blossom so as to imprint the sweet, pungent fragrance in her mind. The following day, she'll recite the name to me, then flutter away to check on its progress. I've taught her that if she's still and listens carefully, the plants will send her messages from the nature spirits. The butterfly quiets, then tiptoes to the flower with the widest open petals and bends her ear. I pray the fairies don't disappoint me. Not this time.

There's something haunting about this lonesome child. Perhaps it's her insistence in wearing the outdated, brightly patterned clothing that reminds me so much of Lucy Hobbes at her age. Perhaps she symbolizes the little sister I never had or the child I may never be blessed with. It matters not; I'm tired of analyzing my life. She's a kindred spirit and one of the reasons I've chosen to stay at Glenapp Castle.

I would, however, be foolhardy to think the past is altogether dead and buried. Each Sunday morning I go to the graveyard just outside the castle gates to visit Mum and Dad, and yesterday, whom should I see but Fiona McCarrick, her once gray braid now a frosty snow white, standing with her back to me, watching two men install a wee baby's tombstone. When she followed them out, I wandered over to see who it might be. The engraving read:

William McPhee
Born and died
October 14, 1971

CHAPTER SEVENTEEN

ANDREW

B Y THE FIRST OF July, scandal concerning the new McPhee tombstone has simmered down, at least enough for the staff to speak of other things. Unlike Eva, who speculates long into the night if William is the child's father, I have put that whole affair to rest. No more unidentified bones lying about is a good thing, besides which, I have others matters of greater import, for today we are celebrating the formal adoption of Isobel Flor Campbell.

Eva has planned a tea party for the three of us in the old Victorian conservatory. Flowering vines of yellow begonia and peach tree blossoms parade the full length of the interior walls. As in the walled garden, miniature stone sculptures peek out from behind the wistful, draping leaves—a cherub reading, a classical bust of Mother Nature wreathed in sweet jasmine.

As I stroll alone through the conservatory, it feels as if I've happened on the studio of a great maestro, his canvas sketched and waiting for dawn's first splash of color. Tom has planted hundreds of seedlings, each labeled and categorized for future planting: pink and white peonies, yellow iris, pink honeysuckle, and Star of India clematis, black-eyed Susan's, Jerusalem and Globe artichokes, lemon balm and rhubarb, dill, coriander, thyme, basil, fennel, and on and on.

The three glass houses are spotless. Even the miniature lily pool, once shrouded in scum and algae, boasts pale, chiffon-yellow blossoms. On the conservatory wall facing the castle, between two seedling trays, is a vase of fresh-cut flowers with an envelope addressed to Issie. The largest section of the conservatory is called the Stove House, or Orchid wing, as it was once temperature controlled by heating pipes that ran across the ceiling. On this beautiful day, however, it is to be *The Tea Room*. The round table is adorned with a pink linen tablecloth and matching lace napkins. Kevin, naturally, has outdone himself, preparing an irresistible array of goodies, all Issie's favorites, the handwritten recipes strategically placed under each serving plate, the first to be included in a children's cookbook they hope to publish together one day. Just as I am placing the bouquet in the center of the table, Eva and Issie sneak up behind me.

Issie's elation is contagious. "This is an oriental poppy," she proudly points out, "and this is pink foxglove, I think, and that's a purple iris. This must be from Tom because he taught me these, but wait…I don't know this one. Is it a rose?" Then she notices the light blue envelope and tearing it open with unmitigated delight, she hands it to Eva to read.

> *Dear Issie,*
> *I hope you like the bouquet. It's a gift from the garden. Did you notice I added a new one? Its color is pale ivory, and it usually grows wild on the banks of the seashore among the hazel woods. It's called the White Rose of Scotland.*
>
> > *Your friend,*
> > *Tom*

Issie plucks the delicate rose from the vase and examines it closely. "This makes thirteen flowers that I know," she says, excitedly.

"Congratulations," I commend her.

I consider how the staff's involvement in our private affairs might have seemed intrusive only a few months ago. Eva and I once took great care to separate our public and private lives as nothing is sacrosanct from the gossip-thirsty, insatiably curious minds of hotel employees. But Issie seems to have changed all this. One and all, we delight in her childlike innocence, hoping by osmosis we might rekindle that delirious, fearless wonderment she exudes so effortlessly. Glenapp Castle is different now. We are all different now.

Raising my teacup, I toast, "Isobel Campbell, this is a very special day for us. Your mum and I want you to know that we think we're the luckiest parents in the world."

Addressing me, Issie asks, "What does it mean, exactly, being adopted?"

"It means we're your parents forever, and we will love and protect you for as long as we live," I say.

"But what if you die, like my real mum?" she asks.

"That's extremely unlikely, Issie. We have plans to live until you're well into adulthood and have your own family. I've heard being a grandparent is great fun; I wouldn't miss that for the world."

"Nor would I," echoes Eva, taking Issie's hand.

"Will I ever have brothers and sisters?"

"No, sweetheart," I say. "And who needs more children when we have you?"

Issie contemplates this for several seconds, then asks. "So, you're not going to adopt more kids, ever?"

"No," I reply with finality.

"Then I'll be an only child, always?"

"That's right. Just like me," I smile. "It's not so bad."

"Tom is an only child," Issie mentions out of the blue. "Do you know where he is now?"

Eva plays along. "No, where?"

"You know William, the gardener? Tom is visiting his daughter, Lucy, in the home for people who aren't awake."

"That's very kind of him," Eva replies.

"I met her," Issie says.

I chime in, "William asked me last week if he could bring Lucy to the walled garden at a time guests wouldn't be here and I agreed."

"I'm glad of it. Have you met her?" she asks me.

"Not yet, no."

"She's in a wheelchair," Issie informs us. "Tom says she was in an accident and she can't talk, but I know she wants to. I put on her old clothes so she might remember and maybe wake up, but Tom said she's been like this since she was six. He thinks that being in the garden will help heal her soul, and that's better than nothing. What's a soul?"

"Your soul is that part of you that never dies," Eva says. "It's that which wants the best for you—to be loving and compassionate and forgiving, and nonjudgmental of others. The soul always strives for goodness and kindness, and it represents the best in friendship because it's always with you so you're never alone. It asks us to make good choices so it can be free to return to the spirit world enlightened by this life."

Eva reclines, aware she's gotten a wee bit carried away. But Issie hasn't missed a word. "So is Lucy's soul sad about what happened to her? I mean, is it trapped inside or can it fly around?"

"I'm sure," Eva assures her, "that they are going through this life together. Your soul doesn't abandon you because you've had an accident. It goes through whatever you go through, good *and* bad. I think Tom's right, bringing Lucy to the garden might help her spirit."

As they chat on, half-listening I gaze through the open French doors onto the garden remembering the day I discovered Tom standing on top of the twenty-foot stone wall surveying the fallow two-and-a-half acres from above.

"Hello," I bellowed from the bottom of the ladder. "What are you doing up there?"

"It's quite a different perspective. Would you like to join me?" he asked.

Abhorring heights, I started to decline the offer. "I don't like the climb either," he confessed, offering a hand, "but it's worth it."

He was right. Seeing the entirety of the walled garden from above was magnificent.

"Would you like to hear my plan, Mr. Campbell?"

"Call me Andrew, please."

"Are you sure? I'm not accustomed…"

"Yes, I'm sure, unless you'd like to be addressed as Head Gardener Hutcheson."

"No, thank you," he laughed. I wasn't sure I'd ever seen him smile before. It rearranged the whole configuration of his face, crinkling his crystal-blue eyes almost shut while forging deep crevices on either side of his mouth, and radiating a warmth I would never have thought him capable of. I suddenly felt as if I would trust this man with my life.

"You may not know this," Tom continued, "but I worked in this garden right through high school. That's both a good and bad thing because it makes it harder to visualize my own design without falling back on the old one."

"It's a fantastic view from up here," I commented.

"Aye, the best there is."

"And you've already made such headway," I commended him. "I'd love to hear your plan."

"Well…" he said, "the garden is already defined by the intersecting pathways and the rivulet dividing it into quarters. The herbal garden is in perfect light at the south end, and the fruit orchard is equally well located. You've thriving scarlet oaks and conifers of various kinds here, and look at the Scotch laburnum," he pointed to the far end. "Those are worth keeping, and I've always loved the element of surprise as you round the corner to find the small sculptures here and there, don't you? So far I've cleared out the dead foliage and trimmed the trees, shrubs, and hedges enough to decipher which plantings are worth salvaging. I've drawn a three dimensional design of potentially six tiers in all; three tiers of flowers, shrubs, small trees, then larger trees. Fortunately, I already know which plants are symbiotic with the soil here saving us years of experimentation. I'm going to put William and Henry to work in here, if it's all right with you."

"Of course."

"The Head Gardener at Culzean Castle has offered to give me any perennials I want. For now, as you can see, I've filled the gaps with annuals so your guests can enjoy the garden. But notice," he pointed, "there's more here than meets the eye. Under all those weeds are remnants of flowers just needing sunlight and a little tending to flourish. There are Centurion Sky-Blue larkspur, phlox, foxglove, and over there…Spartacus dahlias growing alongside the zinnias, and the variety of lilies are astounding. By this time next year I believe we'll see real progress. I'd welcome any comments. You needn't feel like a stranger here," he graciously adds.

"Thank you. I haven't wanted to be in your way, disturbing the master, as they say."

"Nonsense, it's your garden, after all. I'll show you my drawings and we can choose the future plantings together, if you'd like. I could use some help, actually. I've not been too successful enticing William or Henry out of the kitchen garden," Tom joked.

"Yes, well, Kevin has us all hopping to his beck and call. I'll tell them."

Tom paused for several seconds. "I'm grateful to you and Mrs. Campbell for hiring me," he said, focusing on the garden. "Growing up I always dreamed of being Head Gardener here, but after the fire I honestly never thought it would happen."

Neither of us said anything for a bit. I finally confessed, "We were mortified when we learned about your mother. And to think we didn't even know when we hired you. I'm frightfully sorry."

"You've nothing to be sorry about. I prefer it that way as you hired me on merit not sympathy."

"We hired you because William said there wasn't a better gardener in all of Ayrshire."

Tom offered his right hand to steady my descent down the ladder. I felt, for the first time, the hardness of his burned palm. Our eyes met.

"Does it hurt?" I asked him.

"Only when I dream about it," he answered.

"Have you feeling? I suppose not."

"No. I've been told not to expect any, ever."

As we returned the ladder to the potting shed, I lost all constraint. "Tom, I don't mean to pry, but have you thoughts about who might have set the fire?"

"Thoughts, surely, but conclusions, no. I've certainly wasted plenty of time speculating. You may not know this, but one of the main suspects is no longer with us."

"Yes, I'd heard that. Colin Dunbar, was it?"

"That's right. He was my boss and my girlfriend's father. He killed himself. That will likely satisfy the authorities."

"Do you think he did it?" I asked.

"No, I don't, but everyone else has credible alibis. In the minds of most people I imagine the case is closed."

"And is it for you?"

"Honestly, I try not to think about it. My mother was in the wrong place at the wrong time. No one meant to kill her. Whoever did it is living in hell knowing her life was sacrificed. Somehow, that's enough."

"You're a better man than I, Tom," I said. "I'd have obsessed over it."

"I did for a long time, but half the suspects are like family to me, with the exception of Fiona McCarrick. She's a strange one but that doesn't make her guilty of murder."

"No, it doesn't."

Tom, eyes to the ground, swept his foot in an arc as I waited. "May I ask you a question?"

"Of course," I said.

"Issie said something about finding a picture of a dead baby in a trunk?"

There are evidently no secrets with Issie around. "Yes, she and Eva found it in a trunk of clothes William gave her the first day we brought her home. When I asked him about it, he admitted he took the photo."

"Was it taken of the child just buried in the cemetery outside the castle gate?" he asked.

"The same. William claims he wanted evidence in case Sir John denied his paternity, or some such thing," I shared. "What I can't figure out is the relationship between William and Fiona. I suppose it doesn't much matter at this point."

"No," Tom agreed.

"Are they both widowed, then?"

"I don't believe Fiona ever married," Tom replied.

*   *   *

Eva gently squeezes my arm bringing me back to the present. "Sorry, I was just recalling..."

"What?" Issie asks, stuffing the recipes into her jumper pocket.

"Well," I say, stalling for time, "I guess I'm just amazed how much Tom has accomplished in two short months. It's miraculous, don't you think?"

"It's because he talks to the plants," Issie says. "He says plants are just as alive as we are and that if we treat them with respect and listen to what they need, they'll grow twice as fast."

"Is that so?" Eva says, pouring us another cup of tea.

Issie can barely contain her excitement. "Tom thinks that plants and animals are here to remind us not to be so hoity-toity."

Eva and I laugh. "He's a smart gardener, isn't he?"

"You bet your britches," Issie agrees. "May I go now?"

"Before you run off, Issie," I say, "I want to tell you that your grandmother Campbell, my mum, is coming to live with us. Her name is Mary and she'll be moving here later this month."

"Your mum?" Issie exclaims with guarded curiosity. "What's she like? How old is she? What if she doesn't like Grimmey? Is she going to die soon?"

"Whoa, slow down! You'll love her. She's sixty-five. She'll adore Grimshaw as we always had dogs of our own. No, I don't think she'll die soon, but she has troublesome arthritis and can't manage on her own. We want her to live out her life with us. Any more questions?"

"Who are her other grandchildren?"

"You're the only one. She can hardly wait to meet you."

"Is she bossy?" Issie worries.

"I don't remember my mother ever bossing me around, actually. Disciplining me, certainly, but never interfering with my life unnecessarily. She's a very wise woman, Issie. She taught Comparative Literature at university until she was fifty-seven years old."

Issie looks unimpressed.

"She's going to live in the second floor turret apartment where she can have some privacy. She'll be eating with us at suppertime, and you'll be expected to be on your best behavior, as usual," I add. "Remember, you'll be starting school soon and I imagine your lessons will keep you busy. Maybe she can help you."

"What does she look like?" Issie asks, trying to envision this new addition to her family.

"Well, she's of medium height now, having shrunken a bit. She has hazel eyes like mine and a great mane of white hair. I've never known it to be any other color and she wears it loose. Always has. Maybe she'll let you brush it; it's quite a chore and one of the tasks that gives her trouble now. Believe it or not, my father used to brush it for her every night before going to bed."

"No! Really?" Eva says, surprised at the tenderness.

Issie's inquisition continues, "What's her favorite animal?"

"Horses. No question. She rode until her joints hurt too much, and I know she misses it every day."

"Then, I'll call her Grand Mare! Maybe then she'll tell me some good horsie stories."

"I think she'd love that," I say.

"What does she do all day?"

"She reads, mostly. And listens to classical music. And she loves to tell local politicians and newspapers what she thinks," I reply.

"And…" Eva whispers in a spooky voice, "she can read your palm and predict the future. She used to read tea leaves, too, does she still?" Eva asks me.

"Unfortunately, yes."

"I bet she'll come sooner than you think," Issie predicts. "I just know she will."

And that she did—two weeks early, in fact. The first night she arrives, Eva plans a quiet dinner in our private dining room. As we sit down, we notice the table setting includes teacups and saucers with dry tea leaves resting in the bottom.

"What's this about?" I inquire, knowing full well.

"I've no idea," Eva admits.

"It looks to me like someone wants their tea leaves read," my mother observes with a tinge of amusement. "I certainly didn't arrange such a thing."

"Kevin!" Eva and I surmise at the same time.

"He wants you to read his fortune, Grand Mare," Issie says.

"Well, as he's not here, we'd best start with you," Mum replies, rubbing her knobby hands together. "Put the kettle on, dear, and we'll give it a go."

I am not amused. As the steaming kettle whistles through the room, I feel the tectonic plates of reason slowly shifting in the wrong direction. There is no hope for me.

"First, we'll pour the steaming water over your leaves and let them steep. When it's cooled, drink all but a sip then swoosh the tea leaves around the cup clockwise three times. There's a girl. Now, turn the cup over onto your saucer and gently tap it. Good. Turn it upright and let's see what we have."

Issie does as she is instructed. Irresistibly, Eva and I press forward.

Mum carefully lifts Issie's cup from her eager hands to examine the contents.

"The art of reading tea leaves is called tasseomancy, Isobel. It was employed by ancient cultures all over the world to prophesy upcoming events. Each person drinks their own tea so their essence is released in the water. The remaining tea leaves form shapes that reveal what the future holds."

Issie glares into her cup and opines, without hesitation, "I think it looks like a chair."

"I agree," my mother says. "You're a clever girl."

"What does it mean?" Eva asks.

"A chair means that you'll soon be expecting a guest, and by the looks of it, fairly soon. The tea leaves reach clear to the top of the rim."

Oh dear! Vicente Flor and his wife, Maria, arrive tomorrow—most unfortunate timing, but there it is. Regretfully, in the bustle of moving, I haven't told my mother anything about him. Issie, all in a dither, manages without me.

"Grand Mare, you're right! My real dad is coming tomorrow to visit. His name is Vicente and he's bringing his wife. We haven't met her yet because she's been sick."

"Andrew, dear," my mother quips, slowly moving back to her seat. "How extraordinary! I'm not quite sure I understand."

"Well, it's rather an unusual situation," I confess. "For now, let's just say he seems nice enough, and, as he has no legal claims on Issie, we seem to have befriended him. He and his wife live in Ecuador and they come to London to tend to her medical needs. They're just stopping for a few days."

"My, what a surprise. You mean he and Kitty…? Well, well," she collects herself, "maybe he'll let me read his tea leaves, or better yet, his palm."

"No, Mum. I think not."

"And why not? I read Kitty's, and though I didn't tell her, her early demise was written all over her hand," she states matter-of-factly.

"You knew my mum?" Issie interrupts, her eyes wide with curiosity.

"Of course, child. Your mother was my niece. I knew her well. It was a miracle she lived as long as she did."

"Mother!" I protest. "Please!"

"Well, Andrew dear, it's true. That girl was born wild. You know it as well as I do." Then she turns to Issie. "Mind you, child, your mother could play the piano like an angel, and we shared a great love of poetry. She could put a room of people into a trance reciting Robert Burns's verse. There's only one thing she loved more."

"What's that?" asks Issie.

"You. She loved you more than anything in the world. Already I can see why. You've an honesty about you that's rare. You've already charmed this old lady's heart."

"Why haven't I met you before?" Issie asks.

"Because your grandfather and I lived in Edinburgh and you and your mother lived in London. This is delicious," she comments, sipping her cock-a-leekie soup. "Obviously prepared by a true Scotsman."

"A Scotsman brought up and trained in Paris," I correct. "We're never sure what we're eating."

Ignoring me, Mum says adamantly, "Well Eva, you're next. Let's see what your tea leaves reveal."

Eva mimics the same procedure—drinking her tea, swirling the remains three times, dumping them on her saucer and, shuttering her eyes with her palm, she hands the cup to my mother.

"First tell me what you see," Mum says.

Eva slowly unveils her eyes and peers into her tea cup. "I see a triangle or is it a bell?"

"The interpretation is the same for both. It means there's to be unexpected news. The fact that the leaves are oddly clinging to the middle of the cup, neither near the rim nor close to the bottom, means the news is neither good nor bad. Just newsworthy."

"That's a relief," I say.

"Now you, Andrew, dear. Drink up! I'm getting tired."

Just to humor her, I finish the last of my tea and follow the routine. "Tap the bottom of the cup, dear. There. Now, let's see what we have." I lean back in my chair and wait for my future to unfold.

"Most unusual," she exclaims. "Marvelous! I've never seen this before. Tell me what you see."

I cannot resist. "It looks like a broom stick."

"Nonsense, it's a rake, plain as day. It means you should be vigilant and watchful for the next few days, Andrew. Pay attention to details!

Something extraordinary is going to happen. But now, my dears, it's time for me to retire. I've reached the end of my tether. Please tell your chef I'll read his tea leaves another time."

"I'm sure he'll be waiting with baited breath," I say.

"Can I come tuck you in, Grand Mare?" Issie asks.

Seeing Mother yawn, I suggest, "Not tonight, sweetheart. Best let your grandmother settle in by herself."

"Nonsense," my mother rebuts. "It's not every day I get to have my pillows puffed up by my only grandchild. But first, Issie dear, you must ask if you may be excused from the table."

"Can I?"

"*May* I? Of course you may. Hurry along, then."

Eva and I eat quietly for several moments for it has been a long day and we are tired. "I wonder what she's like," I muse, thinking out loud, really.

"Who?"

"Maria Flor. I'm curious what type of woman Vicente chose after Kitty. Mum's right—Kitty was a wild, tameless thing. Now that we have Issie, I wish I'd known her better."

"Perhaps your mother can fill you in," she jests.

I am staring at the air bubbles in my water glass, when Eva blurts, "Sweetheart, changing the subject a wee bit, there's something else I have to tell you. I know you disregard fairy legend as poppycock, but William said that Glenapp Castle…"

Suddenly, without any provocation, my glass tips over, spilling water all over the table and soaking the front of my trousers. "How the devil did that happen? I never touched it." Then, before my very eyes, the water glass rights itself and that familiar joint cracking, teeth chattering chill settles in my bones, and I am unwittingly reduced to a blabbering idiot. "Do you fee-feel that?"

Eva is on her own feet. "Feel what? I certainly saw your water glass tip over then right itself. Andrew, what if he starts spooking our guests?"

"He?"

"Judith would never be so clumsy," Eva professes. "I know her."

"I'll call Nessie Brown in the morning."

CHAPTER EIGHTEEN

EVA

I T IS CLOSE TO ten o'clock the following night when I see the headlights of Vicente's silver Mercedes pull into the car park. Collecting myself, I walk outside to extend my welcome when I notice someone lying across the back seat under a white cashmere throw.

"Hello, Eva," he greets me. He is wearing a gossamer-thin, white linen shirt, open just enough for the silver Saint Christopher's pendant around his neck to swing free as he bows to kiss my hand. Seeing my eyes wander to the back seat, he apologizes, "Maria thought she'd take a siesta. I'm afraid this added excursion may have tired her."

"No, Vicente," she corrects him, "*Yo quería venir*—I wanted to come."

Like a Bedouin queen she emerges, her sparkling gold coin necklace and dangling earrings framing a face so lovely, I know at once such beauty could melt the hearts of kings. With a carefree gesture, she brushes free the wrinkles from her fitted silk suit, its copper sheen dancing seductively in the moonlight. When our eyes meet, I think to myself that men have gone to war and died in ecstasy of having loved, just once, so perfect a creature.

As she warmly brushes both my cheeks with a kiss, her luminous black hair fans across her shoulders. It is hair just like Issie's—an entity unto itself, lustrous and thick.

"Vicente tells me you are one of the nicest women he's ever met," she says. "*¿No es verdad, Vicente?*"

"Vicente's flattery knows no bounds," I reply, graciously. "Please, come in. Have you had supper?"

"We have, thank you," Vicente replies. "Perhaps a night cap before we retire."

"Wonderful. Andrew is saying good night to our hotel guests and will be along shortly. Let's get your…" I start to say luggage when Grimshaw appears, and for no explainable reason, starts barking and twisting in midair like a circus bear then concludes his act by standing upright on his hind feet directly in front of Maria.

"Grimshaw! For heaven's sake!" I scold. "Whatever has gotten into you? I'm sorry, Maria," I apologize. "I've never seen him so excited to meet anyone. Usually when guests arrive they're lucky to be graced with a raised eyebrow."

Maria just laughs and bends down to rub Grimshaw's tummy, now fully exposed and milky white in the moon's afterglow. "I didn't used to be very fond of dogs, really. But my, he's charming. Where did you find him?"

Oh dear! I hadn't anticipated this one!

"Actually," I jump in, "he came with our adopted daughter, Issie. They're inseparable, I'm afraid. He follows her around like a lovesick puppy. Come along now, Grimshaw, show them that you can walk, too," and without further ado, Vicente and I carry the bags to their room.

Maria lays on her side on the guest bed and, slipping her prayerful hands beneath her cheek, she falls fast asleep before I leave the room. In the lamplight I can see tiny beads of perspiration frost her forehead, and her eyelids start to quiver as she surrenders to exhaustion. I listen, transfixed, as her breaths brush the pillow in a labored, catlike rhythm. Suddenly, I am aware Vicente is watching me. "I'll leave you two alone," I whisper. "If you'd like coffee or a night cap, Vicente, come join us in the library."

"Thank you for your understanding, Eva. It's been a terribly long week for us both. I'll be just a moment."

"She's lovely," I find myself saying. Vicente acknowledges my compliment with a nod.

Andrew, Vicente and I reconvene in our private quarters, this time with Grimshaw nestling at Vicente's feet. Three months have darkened the shadows beneath Vicente's eyes, and Andrew, sensing something is amiss, offers him a whisky.

"You look like you could use this," Andrew hints at Vicente's haggard appearance.

"What is it?" Vicente politely asks.

"It's Lagavulin, a single malt whisky from the Isle of Islay," Andrew says. "Would you prefer something else?"

"No, gracias, my friend. This will do fine."

"Is everything all right with Maria?" I chance. "I suppose it's only natural for her to be fatigued after the long trip from London."

Vicente shakes his head as if warding off the temptation to divulge too much. "She is…" he stops. "She is doing as well as can be expected, the doctors tell me. Such an enormous ordeal is this heart transplant business—not only the surgery, but taking on someone else's heart is a highly dramatic experience for the recipients and for their families."

I am genuinely curious. "How so, may I ask?"

"I'm not sure I can actually explain it. In subtle ways, Maria's personality has changed since she received her new heart. She has always been of a quiet nature, painfully shy in fact. Now she loves to go into the public square, to meet total strangers, especially children. She rejects traditional Ecuadorian dishes she's enjoyed all her life saying she has lost her taste for meat. Suddenly she favors classical music and drinks milk, of all things. I could go on and on," Vicente says, looking altogether nonplussed. "Maria is the youngest of six children, and when we married she made me promise not to pressure her to have children; now suddenly she wants to adopt. It's impossible, of course," Vicente continues, as my heart drops through the floor. "She hasn't the constitution, nor the stamina. It's difficult to understand the change of heart.

"The worst are the *pesadillas*, the nightmares," he carries on. "Once a week or so, Maria has a recurring dream of driving in a foreign country, where wild ponies graze alongside the road, and just before crashing, seeing the whites of a drunken man's eyes as he loses control of his vehicle. Screaming, she wakes up, insisting the man seems oddly familiar.

"I'm sorry," he apologizes, "there is something about you two that inspires me to reveal too much, and we have more pressing matters to discuss.

"It concerns your home and the history here and something terrible that I have done. There are things I have withheld, bad things about Sir John McPhee that I thought I would never repeat. He is dead now, but so is a woman, Eva tells me. I never knew this. For his death, I do not grieve. But an innocent woman? This comes as a shock to me! And now I understand there is a man who killed himself as a result of the cheating at the curling championships?" Vicente drains his whisky.

Andrew is quickly on his feet. "Another dram?"

"*Por favor.*"

"I'll have a brandy," I say. Andrew raises an eyebrow—I never drink brandy.

"Vicente, whatever it is you have to tell us can't be that earth-shattering," Andrew attempts to lighten the mood. "I, we, have pieced together most of the story, besides which, Sir John and Colin Dunbar have been dead for years now." *Although one of them still lives here.*

"*Eso es verdad,* but there are things you do not know," Vicente divulges. "I've hardly slept since Eva told me that someone else perished in the fire. You see, I was at Glenapp Castle that very day, though not for the reasons you might imagine. Perhaps you recall my sharing with you that before I returned to my home in Guayaquil, Sir John asked me to accompany him to the District Curling Championships."

"Yes, vaguely," Andrew replies.

"Late in the morning of that day, it was the last Saturday in March of 1997, Sir John asked me to meet him in Stranraer, at an ice rink attached to the North West Castle Hotel. We entered through the back entrance, and, as I was accustomed to his obsession for privacy, I thought nothing of it. He pointed to eight round curling rocks with red handles and informed me that his team's curling stones needed to be sanded on the bottom to slide properly across the ice, that I was to 'rough them up a bit'. Handing me several sheets of coarse sand paper, he demonstrated how he wanted it done. 'Rough up the red set of eight curling stones *only*,' he insisted, 'just until the surface is scratchy. It won't take much,' I recall him saying. 'Leave the stones just as you see them now. When you're done, you are to call me on my mobile.' And most emphatically, he stressed, 'You *must* talk to me personally,' and he departed by the same back door.

"*No sabía nada* about the sport of curling. I just wanted to return to Glasgow to help Kitty move to London before I flew home myself, so I performed the task as quickly as possible, spending no more than five minutes on each stone."

Andrew shoots up and proceeds to pace across the room like a caged panther. "Oh Crevins," he exclaims. "Do you know what a huge scandal that was? Ballantrae's teams lost the chance for the winner to compete in the Nationals. They would have certainly represented Great Britain in the World Cup *and* in the Olympics as well! Colin Dunbar was banned for life from The Royal Caledonian Curling Club for his part in the cheating and killed himself over it! You didn't suspect something strange was going on?"

I am astonished at Andrew's accusatory tone. "Obviously Vicente didn't know what he was doing."

"I honestly didn't," Vicente admits, sheepishly. "He told me the red-handled stones belonged to *su equipo*—to *his* team. How was I to know they were his opponent's? And yes, I see that because of my stupidity I am in part responsible for not only sabotaging the championships but also for a man's suicide."

Andrew takes a deep breath. "No, Vicente. You cannot hold yourself responsible for another man's suicide. Our local librarian told me Colin Dunbar knew of the tampering halfway through the championship match and kept right on competing. What's been a mystery is how Sir John managed to rough up the stones without anyone knowing, and, of course, he died before he could be held accountable. Good God…" Andrew shakes his head in dismay. "We'd best let this die right here in this room. People around here would crucify you if they knew," Andrew warns.

"I'm not sure we're making him feel any better," I try again, emboldened by the warm glow of brandy.

"I'm sorry, Vicente," Andrew apologizes. "Eva's right, but my advice still holds. Take this to your grave, and we will do the same."

"*Pero hay mas*—I'm afraid there's more," Vicente nervously tips his glass for one last drop.

"After I finished sanding the stones I tried to call Sir John's mobile, but there was no answer. 'Never leave me messages at home' was one of his edicts, but out of impatience, I dialed his home phone anyway. 'He's not to be disturbed,' a woman's voice informed me over the castle phone. Beside myself with frustration, I walked around Stranraer for an hour or so, trying to decide what to do when I noticed a pet shop. In the window was a basset hound puppy sitting all by himself, looking at me as if he were the loneliest creature on earth. Being only in my late twenties, I lost my senses and bought him, thinking it the perfect going away present for Kitty." Vicente rubs Grimshaw's long, floppy ears and receives multiple licks of gratitude.

"But I still had the problem of how to contact Sir John," he continues. "I drove the twenty miles to Ballantrae, Grimshaw in tow, and found it easily enough. It was late Saturday afternoon by then. There was quite a bustle of activity, supposedly for a big celebration after the curling championships that night. As it was my first visit to Sir John's home I had no idea where to find him, and as there was no answer at the front door, I wandered around the back and indiscreetly asked the first person I saw. I never learned his name. He wore a tattered woolen cap, a gardener perhaps from the looks of the dirt under his nails, and not a particularly friendly character."

William Hobbes!

"We were standing on a croquet lawn where we had full view of the north end of the castle. Just then," Vicente leans forward, "we both saw Sir John looking out from his second floor suite towards that big sea mountain of yours. What do you call it?"

"Ailsa Craig," I answer.

"Yes…well, it was quickly disappearing behind black storm clouds. In any case we temporarily lost sight of Sir John in the window, but then he reappeared in the adjacent turret suite at the front of the castle as if they were connected by an interior door. That was when I noticed the gardener's face twisted in confusion. 'That's odd,' he said. 'That suite's been shut up for years.'"

"They *were* connected," Andrew interjects. "After we bought the castle and were able to more closely determine the fire damage, we realized that particular door between the two suites was the only thing left standing. The bloody thing was made of steel. In fact, when we tried to knock it down to rebuild the floor, we discovered a steel door frame was bolted to a metal beam running the full breadth of the room, otherwise it would have collapsed with the rest of the floor. We thought it peculiar at the time, didn't we, Eva?"

"Indeed we did," I concur. "I wonder what Sir John did in there? Whatever it was, we needn't tell Mary."

"Mary?" Vicente queries.

"My mother," Andrew replies.

"Your mother lives there now?"

"Yes. She moved here yesterday," Andrew ignores Vicente's concerns. "So what happened after you saw Sir John cross to the other suite?"

"He drew the heavy curtains and, before I was aware of what was happening, the gardener shoved me against the castle wall. 'Listen,' I said to him under my breath, irritated now, 'this is absurd.' I started to rid myself of the pest when we both heard what sounded like a recorded woman's voice, then male groans of what could only be of a sexual nature.

"As I mentioned before, it was a dark, stormy afternoon so we were able to see the white light of a video projector flickering around the edges of the heavy, drawn curtains. Sir John was watching something lewd, there was no question. Suddenly it stopped, then after several seconds it began again. I made a move to escape, utterly disgusted by now, when I heard an all too familiar voice say, 'My name is Kitty.' I broke free and started for the turret stairs," Vicente recalls, "but the gardener said, 'Wait. I want to see what's going on as well as you do, but not now. Come back after seven o'clock when he'll be at the District Championships.' Then I lost my nerve. 'No,' I protested. 'I'm leaving this wretched place. You'll have to manage without me,' and I left the premises.

"I drove for many hours trying to calm myself, and finally concluded I couldn't return to Ecuador without confiscating the tape and, at the very least, destroying it. And I had to know if the filming was consensual on Kitty's part.

"To my surprise, the turret stairway door was unlocked to this suite 'that no one uses anymore' as the gardener claimed. In fact, he was in there too, snooping around. When he saw me he quickly grabbed one of the video tapes. 'Lock all the doors when you leave and destroy the key,' he said.

"In his search, the gardener left open one of the drawers to a built-in cabinet. Sir John had categorized his pornographic tapes by the first name of his victims. I looked in the K's but couldn't find Kitty's name, then I remembered it was likely still in the video projector.

"Like a matador my heart raced, and for several moments I stood, immobilized. I finally turned on the projector. There before me, naked except…" Vicente stops. "'My name is Kitty,' she murmured to the camera. Then I heard Sir John in the background give directions, and a strange man, unclothed himself, gagged her with her own underclothing and tied her to the bed. They must have been in a hotel somewhere in Glasgow. Kitty didn't resist. Instead the man had to carry her like a rag doll, she was so doped. Then Sir John gave the man instructions to do things to Kitty that no man or woman should ever have to witness.

"I removed the tape and examined the outside. It read: Kitty—Sent January 1997. Sir John had sold the film on the porn market."

Vicente puts down his glass, stands up, and walks to the window.

"I'm glad Kitty's parents aren't alive to hear this," Andrew exclaims.

I am speechless, for rape seems the worst possible violation of one's body and to be drugged into submission—the ultimate abuse of one's free will to resist. What fortitude it took for Kitty, and Fiona, to carry on, to forge a new life after facing such a hideous ordeal.

"How was he able to conceal the tapes all those years?" Andrew questions.

"I'll tell you how," Vicente turns to face us, relieved to move on with his story. "After I removed Kitty's tape from the video projector, I explored the place. The drawer of porno tapes was concealed behind a paneled wall. With further investigation, I discovered a huge walk-in closet. In the far corner was a camcorder bracketed to the ceiling; it was hardwired to a joystick remote so he could control its direction. And the closet was soundproofed. All he had to do was shut the door and no one could hear a peep. Sir John apparently lured his victims into the closet and filmed them without their knowledge."

"But I still don't see how he kept his activities secret from the entire household," Andrew persists.

"When I had called earlier," Vicente reminds us, "I was told Sir John was not to be disturbed under any circumstances. He was master of the house, after all. And besides, it's unclear what the staff did or didn't know. The gardener was clearly suspicious of some untoward activities."

Andrew is pacing the room again. "Vicente, it all makes sense now. Your partner in crime, as you call him, is William Hobbes, our assistant gardener. I suspect the girl in the video he removed was a young housemaid named Fiona McCarrick. William must have been in love with her all along; I just hadn't put it together."

Vicente's large eyes broaden with the revelation. "*Perdón*, did you say the gardener still works here?"

"Yes," I reply, finding my voice through the glow of brandy. "He's a bit of a recluse but now I can understand why. He lost his wife in childbirth, has a fifteen-year-old daughter in a vegetative coma, and apparently has been in love all along with a woman raped by his previous employer. I'd be in a mental institution."

"What happened to his daughter?" Vicente asks.

"We've heard that about a week before the big curling celebration and the fire, she was hit by Sir John coming home drunk one night," Andrew shares.

"That was the phone conversation I overheard in Sir John's office the day I was to tell him I was returning to Ecuador. Remember the call from a policeman named Gavin Gillespie and Sir John's denial that he was involved in an accident? He lied when he said he was in Glasgow the previous night. He spent the day with a beauty named Marti McPherson in Maybole, then drove home. I know because I arranged the rendezvous. There is no end to my involvement in this mess," Vicente bemoans. "The worst of it is, I am ultimately responsible for the death of your Head Gardener's mother."

"Judith Hutcheson? Good Lord, Vicente! How so?" Andrew responds, astonished.

"Remember, before I left, I locked the steel door between the two turret suites and destroyed the key. Don't you see? I locked them in! Once they realized there was a fire, Judith Hutcheson and Sir John could have escaped through the steel door, but I'd locked it on the other side."

"But why wouldn't they have done the obvious thing and just walked out the door into the main corridor of the castle?" I wonder aloud.

"The investigative report said that when Tom tried to rescue them from inside the castle, he found the door to Sir John's suite locked," Andrew adds.

"Perhaps Sir John locked her in."

Andrew scoots forward, riveted. "Those old bedroom doors could only be locked with a key. If Sir John locked Judith in, then pocketed the key, what would Judith do then?"

"Well," I hypothesize, "if she knew about the steel door between the two suites, she'd avoid it for fear of entrapment. Her only option would be to escape by the turret stairs."

"Exactly," Andrew agrees, excitedly. "And she'd be overcome by fumes because that's where the fire originated. The room would quickly fill with smoke which would force them to open the window for air. Opening the window just sucks air and oxygen into the room causing rapid combustion and eventual explosion."

Vicente adds, "Sir John would have to debate whether or not to try to get out through the secret steel door. But I'd locked it, so they were trapped."

"I can't imagine they would have had time, Vicente," Andrew conjectures. "Once they'd opened the window, they were doomed. By the time Tom managed to reach them from inside the castle, the entire north wing was swallowed up in flames. In fact, the fire had likely spread down the main staircase. It all must have happened too fast. I do think it's a miracle Tom didn't perish himself. To this day, the palm of his right hand is scarred from grabbing the burning-hot door handle."

"So you see, Vicente," I quietly conclude, "your locked door made no difference. They never had time to reach it."

For several moments Vicente sits, stone still.

Andrew tilts his head towards the door indicating that perhaps it is time for bed. "I don't know about you," he softly intones, "but it's past my bedtime."

Transfixed, Vicente whispers, "Does William Hobbes still live on the premises?"

"Yes…in one of the staff cottages."

"Would you mind if I sit here awhile?"

"Of course not," I say. "Feel free to stay up as long as you'd like. We'll see you in the morning, then."

As is our habit, Andrew and I walk through the hotel before retiring, puffing up pillows and generally straightening up. It is our policy that there must be at least one staff member available as long as guests remain in the public rooms. A large group from Germany, celebrating a birthday, will be partying yet for hours, and I gratefully overhear Betty, our most reliable staff member, offering to stay up.

As we ready for bed I comment, "It's an incredible story, but I'm not sure why Vicente is telling us all this."

"I think he's riddled with guilt over the possibility that he trapped them by locking the secret door from the other side. It's possible he's right, but there's no point in making him feel worse. You can see the poor man's miserable enough."

"I wonder how he'd feel if he knew Sir John and Judith's ghosts were still here."

"Hopefully he'll never know. I spoke with Nessie this morning," Andrew informs me as he crawls in, naked as always in the warmer summer months.

"And?"

"She'll come after the Flors leave." Andrew nestles further under the comforter. "Sunday, perhaps. She says she needs two others to help. I am thinking of Mother."

"Mary? Are you sure? Sweetheart, she just got here. I'd hate…"

"And I recommended you," he says, grinning.

"Me? Why me?"

"Because you're intuitive minded and I want nothing to do with it."

"Well, that's fine; I'll do it as long as Judith can stay," I bargain.

"Nessie says they both must be granted the opportunity to join their loved ones in the spirit world." Andrew yawns, clearly closing the subject. "I've never heard such bullshit in my life."

"And what if Mary doesn't want anything to do with clearing ghosts?"

"I've already asked her. She's chomping at the bit. By the way, what do you think of the dream Maria keeps having? Where would there be wild ponies alongside the road? Do you think it's a real place?"

"There are wild ponies in La Camarque in southern France and in southern England in parts of the New Forest area, and I imagine other places around the world," I reply, catching Andrew's yawn.

"What's she like?" Andrew asks.

"Who?"

"Maria. She went to bed before I could meet her."

"She seems nice," I mumble, noncommittally.

"I mean, what does she *look* like?"

There is no mercy. "Well, she has long black hair, huge almond-shaped brown eyes, lovely, flawless skin, the body of a sex goddess. Need I continue?"

"Really?" Andrew says, propping himself up on one elbow. "Then I *will* look forward to meeting her."

"She may be prettier than I am, but she could never do to you what I do," I reproach, gingerly slipping my hand between his legs.

CHAPTER NINETEEN

MARY

I'VE HARDLY HAD TIME to catch my breath. Within a month, I moved in with my son and daughter-in-law, have finally met my adopted granddaughter (who shockingly looks *nothing* like her mother), and I'm about to be introduced to her biological father, Vicente somebody, and his wife, somebody somebody (it starts with an M).

I am housed in a beautifully decorated second floor suite (not ideal, but I can take the lift) that looks out onto the croquet lawn and to the front courtyard of this lovely Victorian castle. Eva chose a pale green and rose floral wallpaper and lime-colored slipcovers giving the room the freshness of springtime—quite suitable, if a bit formal. As with everything she touches, it's done with exquisite taste. I've a writing table (perhaps at Andrew's suggestion), two deliciously soft reading chairs carefully chosen so I can lift myself up easily, and a small mahogany dining table in case I choose to take my meals in private. How strange it is to be residing in the suite where I will likely die. Meanwhile, there's plenty to keep me occupied. Yesterday, my first morning here, Andrew escorted me by the elbow to the library and proceeded to act extremely ill at ease, crossing his left leg over the right, then the right over the left until I finally couldn't bear it any longer.

"What is it, dear boy?"

"Mum," he practically stuttered, "I know this is…is an odd request, but you see…we have a problem."

"All right, then," I said. "What is it?"

"Well, you see…we have these two ghosts," he began.

"Really? How marvelous!" I exclaimed.

"No, not marvelous," he refuted, shaking his head disdainfully. "In fact, I'm trying to get rid of them, you see, and she said I need two people who are intuitive. You're intuitive, aren't you?"

"Who needs two people?" I asked. He knows to use a proper name when introducing someone in the first sentence. What's the matter with him?

"Nessie Brown. She's our local librarian and apparently she knows how to get rid of them."

"Get rid of whom?" I inquired, my attention now fully engaged.

"What?"

"The ghosts, Andrew, dear. Who are they?" I was beginning to wonder if he was hard of hearing.

"Sir John McPhee, the previous owner of the castle, and a woman named Judith Hutcheson."

"Hutcheson. Why does that sound familiar?"

"She is, was, our Head Gardener's mother," Andrew informed me.

"Oh dear! Does the young man know?" I asked.

"No."

"Well, I suppose there's no real reason…"

"I can't seem to find one."

"How is it they've come to reside here?" I asked.

"They both perished in the 1997 fire—murdered, actually, only no one meant to kill Judith. It's rather complicated but the bottom line is they're both still *here*." Andrew started fumbling with his tie. "The fact is, Mum…he, Sir John that is, resides in our rooms, and…"

"Which rooms?"

"Yours and ours. They were adjoined once and Sir John used them for unmentionable activities."

"Unmentionable activities! What on earth does that mean?" I asked, marveling as I always do at young people's vernacular these days.

"Mum, it's difficult to explain. Could you just help out? I know it's a lot to ask; you've only just arrived, but we're really quite desperate, you see. What do you think, Mum? Could you manage?"

"I don't know, really. I suppose I could do some academic research," I offered.

"No, I mean, would you be willing to give it a go?"

"Honestly, Andrew! Give *what* a go?" I can't tell you how surprised I was at Andrew's senseless meandering. He used to be such a direct child.

"Have a clearing or some such thing. Sit with Eva and Nessie, in a séance or whatever you call it, to banish our ghosts, once and for all."

"Well, of course," I agreed, enthusiastically. "I'd be delighted. Why didn't you just say so in the first place? When and where?"

"Our suite first, then yours if necessary, as soon as the Flors leave, which I assume will be tomorrow, between the time guests check out, and before the next round arrives, around half past eleven," he said, watching for my reaction.

"Lovely."

Andrew's shoulders relaxed. "Thank you, Mum," he said, giving me a grateful hug.

Not wanting our time together to end, I reflected, "Let me remind you, Andrew dear, there are lots of ghosts cited in British literature, many of whom resided in castles. Hamlet's father's ghost comes to mind, and surely you remember when Macbeth killed Banquo and was haunted by his ghost at the supper table?"

Andrew smiled. "And the three witches taunted Macbeth, 'Double, double, toil and trouble. Fire burn, and cauldron bubble.'"

"And there was the ghost in *Wuthering Heights*, and in Dickens's *Great Expectations*," I pressed on, enjoying our old game.

"That poor little boy, Pip," Andrew sighed. "I used to have nightmares about that one."

"I remember."

"All fun and fiction, Mum, but this is serious. There's been a double murder here and their ghosts are still hanging about. If word gets out Glenapp Castle is haunted business will decline, and all Eva and I have worked for will be for naught."

"I should think it would enhance business," I say, looking on the bright side.

"Nessie Brown told me there are eight haunted castles in Ayrshire;

the closest one would be Culzean Castle, I suppose," Andrew speculated. "There's a bagpiper there who is said to appear when family members have a celebration. It's true, people flock there hoping to catch a glimpse of him, but it's one thing to visit a haunted castle during the daytime; it's quite another to want to pay our prices to be spooked while snug in bed for the night."

I saw his point. "Why aren't you participating in this clearing yourself, dear?" I asked.

"Nessie says I'm too much the skeptic."

I was surprised. "You don't believe in ghosts?"

"I don't pretend to understand supernatural phenomenon, no," Andrew said, seemingly frustrated by the fact. It made sense. My son was a veterinarian, analytical and scientifically minded like his father, not that I was going to point that out.

"What is it that you don't understand?" I asked. "Ghosts are just spirit energy that, for whatever reason, remains on the earth plane. There is usually a tragic component to their story, murdered as often as not, or they don't want to leave someone behind. I should think someone like Nessie, if she's truly capable, will send them on their way easily enough. The spirit is endowed with free will," I reminded him. "I believe we make choices in life *and* in death. Remember James Allen's wonderful little book, *As A Man Thinketh*?"

Andrew, bless his heart, recited a passage from memory.

> Mind is the master that molds and makes,
> And we are Mind, and evermore we take
> The tool of thought, and shaping what we will,
> Bring forth a thousand joys, a thousand ills.
> We think in secret, and it comes to pass—
> Our environment is but a looking glass.

And I recited another,

> As a being of power, intelligence and love,
> and the lord of your own thoughts, you contain
> within yourself that transforming and
> regenerative agency by which you may make
> yourself what you will.

"When he wrote that in 1904," I surmised, "I'd wager James Allen didn't expect it to become a manifesto on the power of positive thinking that it is today. His whole point was, of course, that we *can* affect our destiny by the nature of our thoughts, though I'm certain he'd find it farfetched to apply it to the manifestation of ghosts. I, however, do not. I made your father *promise* to visit me from the spiritual world and he has, twice, and no one could persuade me otherwise."

"Really?"

"Really."

Andrew's expression changed to one of concern. "Will you be all right here, Mum, without Father, I mean?"

"Yes, dear, I'm going to love it here. Not many aging, arthritic widows get to live out their days in a castle."

"What about Father? Do you miss him?" Andrew asked, avoiding direct eye contact.

"I try to live in the present. Your father is gone and now it's time for me to be with my son and his family. Perhaps I can make up for what your father was never able to give you."

"That's not your responsibility, Mum."

"No, it's not, but I can try, nonetheless."

"Mum…did you love him? I mean…was he good to you?"

Ah, this was what Andrew really wanted to know. "Yes on both counts, but being the love of my life didn't necessarily make him a good father, did it? For one thing he failed to demonstrate the love and approval you deserved, and for that we have all suffered."

Andrew nervously tapped his fingers against the mantel regretting, I suspect, having brought up the matter of his father.

"Andrew, it wasn't that he didn't love you, he was just incapable of showing it."

"Not to you, apparently," he admonished.

"I am a woman. It's different."

"I'll ponder that one," he responded. Changing the subject again he asked, "Well, Grand Mare, what do you think of our Issie?"

"She's precocious, beguiling, headstrong and extraordinarily engaging, just like her mother. One hopes she has more sense," I added.

*   *   *

It was after ten o'clock this morning before I managed to dress myself and mosey downstairs. I found Andrew in the office. "Where is everyone?" I inquire. "I skipped my morning bath hoping not to miss all the excitement."

"I've yet to see Vicente this morning. My goodness," Andrew says, looking surprised at the time. "Well, in any case, Kevin and Eva are headed to the kitchen garden, and Issie has taken Maria to the walled garden to show off all the plants she can identify, some twenty now, I think. They may be there a while."

Maria! That was it. I knew it started with the letter M. "What's she like?"

Andrew ruminated a moment. "I'm not sure what my impression is, really. She seemed cheerful one moment, then solemn the next, game but vulnerable. Fragile, I suppose. One can understand with what she's been through. The curious thing was, Issie barely let Maria out of her sight, a wee difficult for Eva who always seems to be competing for Issie's affection. I don't think Maria got two mouthfuls of breakfast before Issie crawled on her lap, and they started chatting as if they've known one another all their lives. Do you want to venture down to the walled garden and join them?"

"Yes, I'd love to," I say, knowing the exercise would do me good.

"I'm warning you…"

"Warning me about what, dear?"

"Be prepared to be amazed," my son advises.

*   *   *

Despite the cane I borrow from the umbrella stand, it takes me nearly fifteen minutes to cover the several hundred yards from the castle to the walled garden, all downhill! Andrew suggested the shortest route is past the croquet lawn, down the four stone steps, then to enter into the garden through the wrought iron gate. I almost let slip a grimace when he mentions steps. As I confront them now, I contemplate the fact that I've faced far greater trials than the hip pain I am about to endure. I send each leg doggedly forward, determined to reach this beautifully rejuvenated garden I've been hearing so much about. Besides, it's a glorious day, and I'm not about to spend it sitting inside when everyone else is out and about having a jolly time.

This isn't my first visit to Glenapp Castle, of course, but it's been a year since I've seen the walled garden. It was a sadly neglected affair—a two-acre jungle of entangled weeds and untrimmed scrubs and the perennials either dead or strangled in the overgrowth—a monstrous maze of unruliness.

I am within several feet of the iron gate when I catch my first glimpse of the fairyland Tom Hutcheson has divined. The garden seems otherworldly, ethereal, giddy with oceans of color, and lush with a vitality so palpable I wonder if perhaps I've crossed over. I cannot describe how I feel at this moment—joyful, breathless, infallible, pain free, loved to the point of exaltation! Utterly amazed! How has the young man done it? How, in such a short period of time, is his garden teeming with butterflies and bees dancing, hovering wondrously, sucking up a life force so delicious my own mouth tastes of honey?

For several minutes I hold onto the gate, awe flushed, praying I can harness the faculties to take it all in, when I hear trills of girlish laughter barely audible over the canopy of birdsong. There they are, kneeling on the grass, Issie presenting Maria Flor with a handpicked bouquet of freshly cut flowers she's gathered just for her. Maria, delicate as a budding rose, reaches up to hug her, and they embrace heartily for an awkwardly long time. The intimacy of it strikes me as boundless, primal, almost desperate in its fashion. It is Maria who finally loosens Issie's stronghold, sweetly saying, "*Gracias, mi amor.* When the flowers pale, I will press them in my diary and keep them with me always."

Eva is watching from the other end of the walled garden. How long she's been standing there, I do not know. It doesn't matter—I am a mother—I know the tremors of jealousy my daughter-in-law is feeling, for the loving tenderness of the moment was undeniable.

The experience tires me unexpectedly and I return to my room for a nap before lunch. Just as I start to doze off there is a knock on my bedroom door. "Grand Mare, it's Issie. Can I come in? I mean, *may* I?"

"Of course, child," I reply, delighted. "Come in and lay down with your tired grandmother. I can do with a thimble full of your youthful energy right now. I'm fatigued after my walk to the walled garden."

"You were there? Isn't it beautiful? I didn't see you," Issie says, surprised as children are that if they don't see something, it simply doesn't exist.

"I saw you and Maria enjoying the sunshine. She seems very nice," I say, wondering if Issie might want to talk about it. My granddaughter's enormous eyes well with tears and she buries her face in the pillow. Then with a wham, she throws her arm across my midriff and draws me close with an urgency that I surmise must be months of unexpressed grief over the loss of her real mother. I let her cry her little heart out for several minutes until finally, after wiping her tears on my new duvet, she asks, "You're not mad, are you, Grand Mare? You won't tell, will you?"

"Good heavens, child, of course not. The most scrumptious, delectable aspect of life is the secrets we keep. I chomp on them for days at a time. What's your secret, then?"

"Promise not to tell?"

"Promise. Cross my heart," and I do.

"Maria's leaving tomorrow and I don't want her to go," Issie decries through her sniffles. Like all good grannies, I hand her a tissue.

"You seem very attached to Maria. Is it because she looks more like you?"

Issie, at my insistence, blows her nose while thinking it over. "Maria says she can never have children because of her weak heart, but if she could, she'd want a daughter just like me. Why can't I be *her* adopted daughter?"

"Sometimes we can't have the thing we want most, child. You've been granted the love of Eva and Andrew instead."

"I don't *want* Eva and Andrew to be my parents anymore. I want Maria and Vicente. He's my real father," she declares. "Why can't I go live with them?"

The luncheon bell rings, temporarily halting Issie's outburst. "Perhaps you and I could have our lunch in my rooms," I suggest, hoping to spare Eva and Andrew the sting of Issie's new proposition.

"No, we can't, Grand Mare," Issie protests, collecting herself. "We have to go meet Vicente and Maria. She promised me we could sit next to each other at lunch. Come on…" she gently nudges me off the bed. "We've got to *go*."

"It will take me a moment to freshen up. Wash your face so your secret remains with us, and I'll be down shortly. And Issie, mind you, not a word of this at lunch." But my granddaughter doesn't hear me. She is staring at the blank wall.

"There he is."

"*Who* dear?" I ask, following her gaze.

"The old man who used to live here—the one who died in the fire. William told me he's the Son of the Black Fairy."

"Where *is* he exactly?" I casually inquire, as if I saw ghosts every day.

"There…" she points. "He's wearing a kilt, see? He's opening and closing a drawer as if he's looking for something. Don't you see him, Grand Mare?"

"No, I cannot, but I feel him, all right. Could you ask him what he's looking for?"

Just then, the lunch bell rings again and Issie disappears downstairs. So…Sir John McPhee *does* live in my quarters. I will not lie that I'll be exceedingly glad to be rid of him tomorrow. Quite astonishing that Issie saw him. I must remember to speak to Andrew of this.

To my surprise, when I arrive there is no one seated at the luncheon table. I wander outside and overhear Andrew and Eva talking.

"What's going on?" I inquire.

The expression on Andrew's face is one of stark bewilderment. "Vicente and Maria left unexpectedly."

"Perhaps they've gone for a drive or decided to lunch at the King's Arms," I suggest. Then Andrew hands me a note.

> *Please forgive us. Maria is not well, and we are headed back to London.*
>
> *Always,*
> *Vicente*

"How extraordinary!" I comment. "She certainly seemed well enough in the garden this morning."

"Did anyone even *see* Vicente today?" Andrew queries.

Eva, who still hasn't said a word, and I shake our heads. "I think he was afraid he'd meet up with William," Andrew speculates, addressing Eva.

"William? The gardener? How would they know one another?" I ask.

"Long story, Mum. Where's Issie? We might as well get on with lunch. It's starting to rain."

Issie runs towards us from the direction of the walled garden. "I can't find them *anywhere*." As Eva conveys the news that they have departed, Issie refuses to believe it.

"*No! No!*" she screams at Eva. "Maria would never leave without saying good-bye. She loves me. You're lying! You *made* them leave. I wanted to go live with them and you sent them away. I know it. I hate you, Eva! I *hate* you," and Issie races to her room, giving the door a good slam for effect.

No words can describe how I ache for my daughter-in-law at this moment. Andrew reaches over to console her, but she retires to her room, an expression of dejection deeply etched in the lines of her face.

"Mum, could you?" my Andrew requests, looking towards Issie's room, his own expression twisted with anguish.

"Yes, dear, I'll comfort Issie. You go to Eva. But Andrew, I'd like to talk with you later, if I may," I say.

"Come to the office when you can, then."

I find Issie sitting on her window seat alongside Grimshaw, watching the rain and, I can only assume, faithfully awaiting Maria's return. On her bed is a leather suitcase, jam-packed and ready to go. When she turns around to face me, I notice with some amusement she's slipped her toothbrush behind her ear so as not to forget it.

"Taking a trip, are you?" I ask. "You'll need more than that if you're going all the way to Ecuador. And what about Grimshaw? Will you leave him behind?"

"Grimmey!?" she declares. "Oh no…I forgot about him. What do I do?"

"He'll have to stay here," I say, matter-of-factly.

She throws her arms around my waist as if I am the last person on the planet she can trust. "Oh, Grand Mare," she whimpers.

"It's not your fault, child. The human spirit can take just so much, and I believe you recognized something in Maria that spoke to your heart. You mustn't punish yourself," I counsel, stroking her back. "Guilt is a colossal waste of time, in my opinion. There's nothing to do about it now, though I suggest you pay Eva a visit and apologize. No matter whose fault it is, it's always best to say you're sorry. I'll unpack your things. Go along now," I urge. "And Issie…"

"Yes, Grand Mare."

"Try to remember that love comes in different forms—sometimes you just have to work harder to recognize it in those you live with."

"Will I ever see Maria again?" she bravely asks.

"I don't know, child."

*   *   *

Andrew and I arrive at the office simultaneously. "That was nice of you to send Issie to Eva," Andrew says. "It's been like Mt. Vesuvius around here this morning. I'm sorry, Mum."

"How is Eva?"

"Devastated, heartbroken. The last time I saw her cry was tears of joy when she first met Issie. Now this. What on earth happened?"

"I think that it's obvious Issie hasn't had time to grieve the death of her mother," I opine. "Think of it, Andrew. Kitty was killed only three months ago. Within days Issie was picked up by new parents, brought to a castle hotel bustling with strangers, and was expected to fall in without a glitch. This is just a first bump in the road and quite natural, I should think. Difficult for you both, but not altogether unpredictable."

Clearly fatigued, Andrew slumps into the office chair. "I don't understand it, Mum. What was it in Maria that Issie became so attached to?"

"I cannot say. Whatever it was the attraction was irresistible, reminiscent..."

"Reminiscent of what? You're not going to tell me they've been together in a previous life or some such rubbish," Andrew snaps.

"No," I hedge, thinking exactly that, "but I will remind you that your tea leaves predicted that someone would soon visit with unexpected news."

Someone is knocking, and I see through the glass-paned door that it is one of the gardeners. "Hello, William. Come in," Andrew says. "Have you met my mother?"

Hoping he doesn't squeeze too hard, I offer my hand in greeting. "No, I don't think we've met. Hello, William, I'm Mary Campbell."

"Hello, ma'am," the man blurts, failing to remove his cap in the presence of a lady.

It does not take an intuitive to sense from the gardener that he has private business. I still haven't told Andrew about Issie's ghost sighting. It will have to wait.

"I think I'll return to my rooms," I excuse myself.

"Would you like me to have your lunch brought upstairs later, Mum?" Andrew kindly offers.

"Thank you. That would be lovely, dear," I reply. Perhaps Sir John will dine with me.

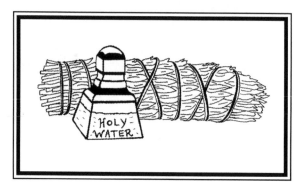

CHAPTER TWENTY

ANDREW

"THAT MAN, WHY WAS he here?" William rudely demands to know.

"What man?" I ask, knowing perfectly well whom he means.

"That man with the black hair. He was driving the silver Mercedes."

"Was he, now?" I sound haughty, but I cannot help myself; William's abrupt demeanor irritates me sometimes.

"What was he doing here?"

"Really, William! I find your questions rather inappropriate. He was a guest."

"I apologize, Mr. Campbell, but I have good reason to inquire."

"Yes, I suppose you do," I concur, softening a bit.

"What's your meaning?"

Ignoring his question, I state simply, "His name is Vicente Flor."

William silently mouths the words.

I sigh. Really, must I further involve the staff in *everything* that goes on here? Before I decide how much to divulge, William says, "Flor... isn't that Issie's middle name?"

"Yes," I capitulate. "He is Issie's biological father."

The flush drains from William's sun-leathered cheeks so quickly, had he not gripped the door frame, I fear he might keel over.

"Biological father?" he stammers.

"Vicente had a relationship with my cousin, Kitty, who was killed in a car accident several months ago. I am Issie's legal guardian. We have since adopted her. Vicente and his wife were just visiting. It's a bit of an odd story but he's gone now, so you needn't worry," I attempt to conclude our business.

"Kitty!" he mumbles several times under his breath.

Then I recall the scene Vicente described last evening—he and William, partners in their shocking discovery of the pornographic tapes, pressed against the castle wall beneath Sir John's window when they heard Kitty's name.

I offer William a chair.

"My God," William bemoans. For several moments, neither of us speak. Then, finally, William asks, "What did he tell you?"

"He told me about the tapes. That's all, really," I lie. I wasn't about to share Vicente's guilt over having locked the steel door between Sir John's adjoining rooms. What was the point? And I certainly have no intention of divulging his involvement in the curling debacle. Enough said! Yet, why William is so afraid to see Vicente, I cannot discern. Does it have to do with the fire? Perhaps the intimate nature of the individual tapes has made them edgy, for neither can be assured of the others involvement in the matter. Perhaps one or both are protecting someone. In William's case, who would it be? In Vicente's case…Kitty, most certainly. Could she have set Glenapp Castle on fire? No, she was in Glasgow packing up her things to move to London, or so Vicente claims. I couldn't blame her if she had.

William raises his eyes to meet mine for the first time. "If you ever hear from him again, tell him I said he should stay away from Glenapp Castle."

"I doubt we'll be seeing him, William, at least not in the near future. He's going back to Ecuador."

"Ecuador?"

"It's in South America."

"I know where Ecuador is," William spews, visibly insulted.

"Then you've no reason to worry."

"You just tell him to stay away," William repeats. "There's no reason he needs to come here."

"Except that he's Issie's biological father," I remind him.

"That's not sufficient reason, Mr. Campbell," William replies, abruptly standing up to leave, then he hesitates.

"Is there something else, William?"

"I've a favor to ask you, if you don't mind?"

"Yes?"

"Tomorrow my daughter, Lucy, will be sixteen, and I wonder if we might spend some time in Tom's garden, weather providing."

Tomorrow? Nessie Brown is coming. I'm not sure I want more people on the property when we finally deal with Sir John's ghost. What will Issie and Eva be doing during that time? Knowing Issie, she'll want to play in the walled garden. That would be fine. Ideal, really.

"All right. Certainly. Between eleven o'clock and two," I suggest.

"I'll pick her up at half past eleven and be here by midday, if that's all right," William promises.

"Fine, then. Sixteen years old. My goodness! Think of it!"

"Aye, sir."

He is halfway out the door when I am suddenly curious. "William, what's it like? I mean, is it tricky transporting Lucy? Issie mentioned she's in a wheelchair."

"It takes two nurses plus me to get her out of bed, into the wheelchair, and into my car. Once I'm here Tom helps me. Sometimes I'm not sure it's worth it, but Tom seems to think the garden does her good."

"I'm sure it does. Well, good luck, then," I say.

"I'm sorry I was short with you before, Mr. Campbell, but I stand by what I said."

"I understand," I reply, not understanding at all.

I start to leave the office when the phone rings. It is Nessie Brown.

"All set for tomorrow morning, are we?" Nessie asks, all business.

"We are. Can you come at half past eleven? All the guests will be gone by then. We'll have about two hours."

"I can, but I have some concerns," she says.

"Not getting cold feet, are we?"

"No, not exactly. I'm not worried about Judith's ghost. We'll send her on her way easily enough, but I'm the only one of the three of us who actually knew Sir John. He's not going to want to leave, and I'm not sure I'll have the strength to do it alone."

"What do you suggest?" I ask, instantly regretting the question.

"I think you need to join us, Andrew," she says. "You've the greatest will to be rid of him."

"No possible way in hell," I mumble under my breath.

"Sorry?"

"Not interested. Besides, I thought you only wanted three participants."

"Aye, three's a sacred number—it's a direct link to the spirit world," Nessie agrees. "Who should we eliminate? Eva, I think," she decides, ignoring my objections.

"I thought you said I was too much the skeptic to be useful," I plead my case.

"You are the one who called," she reminds me. "But I warn you, this isn't going to be easy. He'll ultimately want forgiveness for all the abominable things he did during his lifetime. A heinous monster, he was."

"He transported children from Ecuador under the guise of saving their souls," I add, shivering a little.

"I don't require the details. Where will Issie be during the clearing?" she asks. "The walled garden would be best. She and Lucy will be safe there, and we'll need their young energy on the property to help counter Sir John's resistance."

"That's fine," I concur, thinking her comment the most convoluted, obtuse, cockamamie thing I've ever heard. And how did she know William just asked permission for Lucy to visit the garden—it was but minutes ago?

"Good day, Andrew Campbell. I'll see you tomorrow at eleven, then," she bids me farewell. "I hope this goes well."

"So do I, Nessie Brown. So do I."

*   *   *

The beaming, late July sun shines unimpeded by a single cloud, and I roam aimlessly among the blossoming rhododendron bushes awaiting Nessie's arrival. On the horizon, however, Ailsa Craig remains masked behind a dense curtain of iron gray. On one of our previous phone calls, Nessie shared her theory that Ailsa Craig, the village of Ballantrae and Glenapp Castle, burdened with a violent history they didn't ask for, are helplessly snared in a web of circumstances they can't untangle. For all my cynicism, I do believe inanimate objects, be they huge monoliths, towns, or buildings, are capable of retaining memory. One only has to visit Stonehenge, or the great standing stones in France, or Sawney Bean's cave to feel the stranglehold untoward circumstances can wield over a place. Still, I wasn't as optimistic that clearing our ghosts would break Glenapp's cursed spell, as Nessie put it. We'll see.

Knowing all that I do now, I ponder the wisdom of meddling in Glenapp's past. The suffering Sir John inflicted on so many innocent, unsuspecting people, especially my cousin, Kitty, has deeply saddened me. Vicente's story recycles through my mind often, and I am left wondering how the human psyche survives man monsters like Sir John McPhee, or more to the point, whether some evildoers truly deserve to die.

Nessie's car finally appears through the stone entry gates. Eva and Issie long ago departed for the walled garden and mother is still in her rooms, honing her intuitive skills, I suspect.

Though Nessie Brown and my mother have never met, I knew they will become fast friends. They greet one another like old pals, wasting no time with formalities.

"We'll start with Judith," Nessie announces with schoolteacher authority. "I highly suspect she's worried about Tom's welfare, and she can't get to him since he doesn't live in the castle, so we'll have to help her out. All right, Andrew, lead us to your bedroom, if you will."

"Aren't you going to tell us what we're supposed to do first?" I ask.

"All I need is your genuine desire that Judith be returned to the spirit world. I knew Judith for twenty some odd years. She used to come to me for readings. I've no doubt she'll communicate with me, and when she realizes she's dead, with a little encouragement, she'll happily cross over. Shall we begin?"

As we take the lift to our master bedroom, I wonder what my veterinary colleagues would think of me now!

"No time for cynicism, Andrew," my mother quips. "Those who aren't open to the paranormal wouldn't understand such things."

My God, does she know everything I'm thinking?

"What a lovely room," Nessie comments. "Strange that Judith and Sir John died in here, isn't it?" Nessie lights a bundle of dried herbs, swishing the smoke throughout the room.

"What's that?" I ask. "You'd best be careful or we'll have another fire in here."

"Sage," she says. "It protects the room from other evil spirits interfering." Then she hands Mum a vial of clear liquid.

"And Holy Water," Mum adds, sprinkling it here and there, "imbues the room with the sanctity of the Divine Spirit."

"Who blessed it?"

"Reverend McCrindle," Nessie informs me.

"Who's he?"

"Honestly, Andrew Campbell. Have you not been to your local parish?" Nessie chastises. "Reverend McCrindle has been our pastor for over thirty years."

I close the curtains.

"Right…" Nessie says, wiping her hands clear of the herb. "Let's form a circle. That's right—palms up. Initially I will ask Judith to reveal herself. If she has a message for Tom, please listen carefully because I often don't remember anything afterwards."

"What if it's too lengthy to remember?" I worry.

"Perhaps you'd best have a piece of paper ready, just in case," Nessie agrees.

I remove a large sheet of *Glenapp Castle* stationery from the drawer and lay a pen next to it. When I turn around, Nessie and mother are already standing side by side, palms open with their eyes closed. The noose is hung; I have no choice but to join them.

After what seems an interminably long time, I hear the bathroom linen closet door close. Mum and I both turn toward the noise when Nessie, eyes still shut, surprises us both by saying, "Judith Hutcheson, are you here? Good. I'm Nessie Brown—you used to come to me for psychic readings, remember? We've come to return you to your rightful place in the Spirit World. Your husband, Doon, your parents, and all your loved ones are waiting for you there. You don't realize your spirit is still here on the earth plane. Is there a reason? A message you'd like to give someone? Your son, Tom, perhaps?"

Suddenly I'm freezing. Nessie speaks, not in her normal voice, but in a deep, raspy cadence that belongs to another world. "Sir John locked me in," the strange voice says. "I was so frightened. I tried to escape down the turret stairs, but smoke and flames came shooting out. I ran to the window and shouted for help. My boy was there, standing beneath the window but Sir John shoved me and I crashed into the table. When I came to, I hit Sir John over the head with the decanter of port igniting us both in flames. The last thing I heard was Tom calling my name and kicking, kicking the bedroom door with his foot, but I couldn't breathe any longer… "

Mum and I listen, horrified at the grisly details of Judith's struggle to stay alive. Nessie says nothing for several moments, then it occurs to me that if she is serving as a channel for Judith's ghost, someone else has to ask the questions. I turn to Mother, but she emphatically shakes her head—no!

"Do you have a message for Tom?" I ask, rubbing my arms, bristling against the cold.

Suddenly the lights flicker off and on and the room warms slightly. Nessie, now totally entranced with her eyes rolling to the back of her head, starts mimicking the motion of writing something.

"Quick," Mother orders, "get the paper and put the pen in Nessie's hand. She can auto write Judith's message."

"She can what?"

"Just do as I say."

To my utter amazement, seconds after I place the pen in Nessie's hand, she commences writing, and I realize it is a poem. When my eyes chance over the script my mother's look of reproach reminds me that this message is for Tom Hutcheson, not me. Never in my life have I witnessed such a thing. After she finishes, Mum snaps her fingers, bringing Nessie abruptly out of her trance.

"She's gone," Nessie declares, a little disoriented. "What's this?" she asks, looking down at Judith's poem.

"Marvelous!" my mother chants. "Absolutely *marvelous!*"

"Gone?" I say. "You mean she's…?" I point upwards.

"Yes, she's crossed over. Can't you feel the difference? How much lighter the air feels? Did I write this?" she begs to know, looking down at the poem. "This isn't my handwriting. Oh my, you won't believe this, but this is Judith's penmanship. I've never had *that* happen before. How remarkable. The question is…" Nessie continues, handing me the sheet of paper, "who should deliver this to Tom? I wouldn't mind, though I haven't seen him in months."

"And I've never met him," Mum chimes in.

"I'll take care of it," I offer, laying the poem inside Eva's desk drawer. "But I'm not certain how. I can't exactly just slip it under his door, now can I?"

"I'm sure you'll figure out a nice way to handle it," my mother assures me. "Perhaps it's best to tell him the truth." Then turning to Nessie she marvels, "My, my, wasn't that exciting!"

"Aye…as clearings go, Judith was easy enough. Sir John, on the other hand, may be more of a handful."

"Issie saw him in my bedroom yesterday," Mother says.

"You're joking?" I exclaim. "Mum, why didn't you tell me?"

"Son, I tried several times, but I couldn't seem to get you alone for more than two minutes yesterday."

"She actually *saw* him?"

"Was he wearing a kilt when he died?" Mum inquires.

"Aye," responds Nessie. "Sir John wore his clan's kilt to the curling championships and to the party he and Lady Sylvia hosted the night he died. Judith was just bringing him his port when the fire started. He wouldn't have had time to change into his bedclothes."

"Good lord!" I say, exasperated. "I wish someone had told me about this."

"Issie said he was opening and closing drawers looking for something he'd lost," Mum tells us. "I wonder what it was."

My heart sinks. Neither Mum nor Nessie know about Sir John's pornographic videotapes, and I see no reason to enlighten them. "Let's be done with the bastard," I say.

"Andrew, really! Such language!"

"I'd like to get this over with, if you don't mind," I defend my irrational behavior. "And Nessie… I want to know who murdered him."

Nessie steadies her gaze. "If you have that information, Andrew Campbell, you're going to be responsible for making that person accountable. Are you willing to do that? Asking spirits for that kind of information is risky business. And how do you know that he'll be right? What if he implicates the wrong person? Besides, there isn't a court of law in Scotland that's going to believe a ghost's testimony."

"I'll just feel better if I know whether or not the murderer is still working for me," I declare with false bravado. We both know I'm referring to her cousin, William Hobbes.

"Then, you'll have to ask Sir John yourself. My job is returning lost souls to the spirit world, not dredging up their past."

With that, Nessie inquires as to the direction of my mother's bedroom. "It's just next door."

"I think it odd, quite odd in fact, that Sir John wouldn't still be in the room he died in. Did he have an affinity for your mother's bedroom?" Nessie asks me.

"They used to be connected by a secret door," I say.

"So Sir John would have felt both were his domain?"

"Yes."

"All right, then. Let's go in. Mind you, brace yourselves. And Andrew, stay sharp. You're likely the one he'll be most angry with for trying to banish him. It may be your will against his." But before Mum even touches the brass knob, her bedroom door flies open by itself blasting a tunnel of arctic air at our faces. Several curling stones skate across the floor with no human arm to propel them.

"Oh Crevins! I forgot the sage and blessed water," Nessie frets, retreating down the passageway.

"I think it's a little late for that," I declare, grabbing her by the arm, for I am not going to be left there without her.

"I'll not have him bothering my things," Mother bellows, looking around the room. "John McPhee, we're here to have a civil conversation—mind you don't disturb my valuables." Nessie and I both raises our eyebrows, and without further ado, as any gentleman would, I invite Nessie to step into the frigid room ahead of me. Truth be known, I'm terrified.

Nessie closes the curtains and indicates we should stand in a circle.

"John McPhee, are you here with us?"

The lights don't just flash off and on; they're extinguished altogether. We are standing in total darkness. A heavy wooden drawer slams shut and when I look up—there stands my nemesis, dressed in full Scottish regalia, frenetically rifling through the drawer as if his life depended on finding something. When he turns to face me squarely, his generous smile might have warmed me had I not noticed his coal-black, dead eyes.

Nessie, entranced again, says, "He says there are two videotapes missing. Are you the imbecile who stole them? If so, you have no goddamn business pilfering his private property."

The words freeze in the air. "If he tells me who murdered him, I'll reveal who stole his tapes," I bargain.

"He says you reveal first who stole his tapes."

The cunning bastard. "Vicente Flor and William Hobbes."

Nessie, now jolted out of her trance, looks at me as if I'd accused her cousin of manslaughter. Mother simply looks bewildered. But I have bigger concerns, for as I witness John McPhee's ghost fade, my very insides feel as if I've plunged into the Norwegian Sea.

"God," I gasp.

"What's wrong, dear?" Mother worries.

"I feel so heavy and cold; I don't think I can stand it any longer."

"Buck up, Andrew," Nessie demands, gripping my arm. "He's using your body to make it harder for you to will him away. Steady yourself. Remember, you must be the stronger one."

"I want to know who murdered him," is the last thing I remember saying.

Later, when my shaking subsides, Nessie tells me that I grinned maliciously and said in what she recognized as Sir John's voice, *"Really, you're all mistaken about me. I never did anything to anyone that wasn't consensual to both parties. And those dirty Ecuadorian urchins—they should be thankful I saved them from the clasp of Satan. Sex was their payback, that's all. And the delicious girls like Kitty Campbell…so easily seduced…"*

"Kitty! What on earth?" My mother's infuriated voice sounds galaxies away. "Well, I never in all my life…"

"What's she to you, old lady?" the voice demands to know.

"She's my niece! How DARE you! For God's sake!" and mother slaps me across the face.

And with a final seismic tremor, John McPhee slithers from my body like a venomous serpent.

"Who murdered you?" I demand to know.

"He doesn't know," Nessie replies. "He says he truly doesn't know."

Mother is suddenly hugging me. "Andrew dear, are you all right? I'm so sorry, darling."

"I want him GONE," I shout.

"John McPhee," Nessie intones with her eyes closed again. "There is no future for you here at Glenapp Castle. Redemption is yours in the afterlife. You are free to go to the Spirit World now."

Nothing. Nessie tries again and again as my bones splinter into a thousand fractured icicles. Sighing with exasperation, she finally surrenders in defeat.

It is my turn. "Your existence as a ghost is a living hell here. You'll never find your tapes. They're gone. And this is not your home anymore, John McPhee, because I'm master-of-the-castle now and I'm not leaving this room until you vanish and never return."

We wait. Like the aftermath of a cyclone, the atmospheric pressure begins to lift and ever so slowly my insides unknot as blood returns to my fingers and toes and stinging cheek.

"He's gone; I can feel it," Mother rejoices. "Andrew, by God, you did it!"

Just then the lights come back on, and the grandmother clock strikes one.

"Something's happened to Lucy," Nessie blurts, surprisingly cheerful.

"Should I ring an ambulance?" I call after her, fighting the urge to lie down.

"Not necessary," she shouts over her shoulder. This can't be happening! The last thing I need is for Lucy Hobbes to expire in the walled garden.

"Who's Lucy? Goodness me, what's all the fuss about?" Mum asks as Nessie bustles down the stairs.

"She's William's daughter. I'd better go to the walled garden, Mum. I've no idea what's going on, but I don't imagine that it's good news."

"Andrew, I'm so terribly sorry I slapped you. Whatever got into me?"

"I think that's the first time you've ever hit me," I reply, rubbing the sting from my cheek. "I'm glad I had to wait until I was thirty-six."

I have forgotten Judith's Hutcheson's poem. Perhaps I should take it with me. When I return to the master bedroom and open Eva's desk drawer, it is gone.

CHAPTER TWENTY-ONE

WILLIAM

I DON'T BELIEVE IN coincidences. I used to but my cousin Nessie convinced me that everything that happens is part of a divine plan we design for ourselves. She may be right; I certainly want to believe her. She's the closest thing I have to a sister, and she's been like a mother to my Lucy. Not even Nessie, however, can persuade me that I preordained the return of Vicente Flor.

By some confounded twist of events, ten years later, the foreigner shows up as Andrew Campbell's dead cousin's lover, and Issie's biological father. I should have put it together before—they look just alike. I knew he had worked for Sir John McPhee, and I can only guess he came to Glenapp Castle that fateful Saturday in March of 1997 to report on some dirty work he'd done for him and discovered, as I did, the pornographic tape of someone he cared for.

There are two reasons I don't want to see Vicente Flor again. The first is he (and now, unfortunately, Andrew Campbell) are the only other living beings who know about Fiona's tape, and I want it to remain that way. My Fiona doesn't even know Sir John videotaped his assault on her. Hopefully, she never will. For God's sake, we just reburied the offspring.

The second reason is more complicated. Vicente Flor saw the two five-gallon cans of diesel sitting outside the turret stairs that the arsonist used to set the fire that burned down the north wing of Glenapp Castle, and I don't want Gavin Gillespie reopening the investigation. I have my reasons. With closer scrutiny, Gavin might start asking more questions. There were at least three sets of fingerprints on those two diesel cans that day; mine, Roddie Hutcheson's, and Colin Dunbar's. Thank God in heaven they never found the cans, but I'm not taking any chances.

March 29, 1997 was the Saturday of the District Curling Championships and a festive celebration that was to follow at the castle. It was also the sixth day Lucy had been in a coma as a result of Sir John driving his Jaguar right into her. As you might imagine, I hadn't been to work for a week, but on Saturday morning, knowing Colin would need help, I asked if there was anything I could do.

"William, are you going back to Girvan?" he asked, all worked up.

"I am," said I.

"Could you do me a favor and find two five-gallon cans and fill them with diesel?" Colin asked. "See if Tom will let you borrow his pickup. I need mine."

"Diesel? Whatever for?" I remember asking. "None of the mowers run on diesel."

"Sir John's gone and bought a Mercedes for Lady Sylvia and can't seem to find any diesel fuel. Marsden Frew's station's out in the village, and I don't have time to go gallivanting all over Ayrshire looking for some," Colin replied, winded with frustration.

As it so happened, I was going to Girvan later to check on Lucy and told him so.

"Thank you, William. I'm much obliged," Colin said.

Young Tom Hutcheson walked by and said I could borrow his pickup if he could have it back in time to go to the District Curling Championships around five thirty that afternoon. It was Tom's eighteenth, and I wished him a happy birthday. He looked downright gleeful about something, I didn't know what.

I drove to Girvan Hospital to check on Lucy and to confer with the endless stream of doctors. Who do you think was there? Roddie Hutcheson, of all people.

"I know I should have come sooner, William," he bemoaned,

blowing his nose and shaking his head in disbelief. "I just couldn't get myself to do it."

"I understand, Roddie. It's not a pretty sight," I conceded.

"That bastard McPhee, I'd like to kick his ass to kingdom come," he fumed.

"Then beat his team at the championships tonight," I patted him on the back. "That's what you can do. In the meantime, tell me where I can find diesel for his new Mercedes."

"What? Can't the idiot fill up his own car?" Roddie looked disgusted.

"Apparently they delivered it almost empty and Ballantrae's out of diesel."

"I've got two five-gallon cans in my pickup," Roddie offered. "I always keep extra ferry diesel around in the summer. All the bloody stations seem to run out on Sundays, and it's my busiest day now. Take them; I'll get more on my way back to the marina."

"Are you sure?" I asked, thinking it was mighty kind of him.

"Aye, you've got better things to do then drive around doing Sir John's bidding with your daughter lying here."

"Thank you, Roddie. I'm grateful," I said, meaning it.

"Where do you want them? I'm on my way out."

"Tom's pickup is in the car park. Mind you wedge them against the side, it's blowing up a gale out there," I warned. "And good luck tonight, Roddie. Don't tell Colin, but I hope you win the championships just so Sir John's team loses. It would warm my heart to see you curling in the World Cup. By God, it would!"

"Thank you, William. I'll do my best," and Roddie took one last look at Lucy, nodded, and left.

Hence…the transfer of the diesel cans to Tom's pickup with Roddie's fingerprints all over them.

When I returned to Glenapp Castle around two o'clock, it was starting to thunder. As I wasn't sure where Sir John wanted the diesel cans, I was glad to see Colin raking the front walk.

"I'll take them," he said, grabbing both handles.

"Never mind, Colin," I shouted as the wind nearly blew off my cap. "Just tell me where you want them. You've got enough to do."

He released his grip. He didn't have gardening gloves on, hence

Colin's fingerprints on both cans. "Best put them outside the north turret stairs. We've done enough. And thank you, William."

"Thank Roddie Hutcheson—it's his diesel." I could see Colin Dunbar wasn't in the mood to be grateful to his old rival, so I let it go.

When I pulled Tom's pickup close to the turret stairs, there was a strange man snooping around. I got out, picked up the two cans of diesel (hence, my own fingerprints) and placed them outside the north turret stairs. The intruder, agitated and fidgety, asked me in a thick foreign accent where he could find Sir John McPhee. I wasn't sure where he was from, but it wasn't Scotland. He had black hair the color of fresh tar and skin designed for warmer climates.

"Most folks knock on the front door," I informed him and turned to leave.

Yet I didn't leave right then, and the reason why isn't anyone's business. I'll only say it involved something terrible that once happened to someone I love, something I've been trying to forget for many years. Nessie says when you think bad thoughts they take on a life of their own so I don't let myself think about it. The point here is that the two five-gallon diesel cans had three sets of fingerprints on them, each of us with good reason to want Sir John McPhee dead. Vicente Flor saw me place the cans outside the turret staircase where the arsonist later poured the highly flammable material down those very same stairs, igniting the biggest fire in Ayrshire since the Kennedy feuds in the 1500's. It was arson, all right, and it's still an unsolved case. I will say one thing—I've enjoyed watching Andrew Campbell try to solve the mystery. Every now and then he gets an idea in his head, and he comes around to ask me what I think. What I think is…he suspects I'm the culprit. I keep to myself.

There are lots of things Andrew Campbell doesn't know. He doesn't know, for instance, that Nessie has the whole village of Ballantrae in a tizzy over this ghost clearing business. She's been working this theory of hers that ridding Glenapp Castle of Sir John's ghost will bring the fairies home, so to speak. She thinks that all the bad things that happen to us are the consequence of accumulated bad karma in the region—*imprints* she calls them. I'll be frank with you—there isn't one villager who doesn't wholeheartedly believe her. Our history is so rampant with gruesome deeds of ill renown it's downright shameful.

When those black ravens swarmed Sir John's casket for three days, we knew she was right.

First, Nessie got hold of Roddie Hutcheson and firmly instructed him not to tell his usual stories about Ailsa Craig and the eight thousand rats that used to scamper all over the island, and certainly not about the smuggling and murders for which it is well known. No one goes to visit Sawney Bean's cave anymore, neither do parents recite the chilling tales of his chomping on local residents. She had the village *sign* changed from: Ballantrae—*Home of the Feuding Kennedys* to Ballantrae—*Village-by-the-Sea...Haste Ye Back*. As librarian, Nessie reviewed the school curriculum to remove glorifications of past atrocities, and finally, last spring, she had me send Tom Hutcheson the advert for Head Gardener at Glenapp Castle under the new owners, Andrew and Eva Campbell. I got my old job back first, then wrote Tom at Findhorn Gardens. I would say her plan has worked well. The walled garden is the most beautiful damn thing I've ever seen. Everywhere you walk, the sweetness of pink honeysuckle and Star of India clematis follows you about with promises of better times ahead. Then, Nessie tells me she's certain we should celebrate Lucy's sixteenth birthday in Tom's garden at the same time she clears Glenapp's ghosts. Within days, everyone in the village agreed it was a grand idea.

What can I say? You have to understand how things are around here. When Andrew Campbell first came to Nessie's library several months back, the whole village knew every detail within hours. Once Nessie received his second call confirming he wanted to rid Glenapp of its ghosts, the news simmered to full steam at The King's Arm by noon, then steeped in the Thistle Tea Room until it reached the church pews and Reverend McCrindle himself. He cancelled this morning's Sunday service so everyone is free to gather on Ballantrae's beach where they can see Glenapp Castle on the hill and Ailsa Craig at the same time. Three hundred men, women, and children, all hoping to see the ghosts, all praying for a miracle.

My cousin Nessie is a unique woman, and I couldn't have survived this ordeal without her. You can't imagine what it's like having a child lying immobilized in a vegetative state, day after day, with no idea what she thinks, feels, sees or hears. Doctors tell me that every patient is different and all we can do is wait and hope. Wait and hope that a sight or a sound will trigger an awakening to time and place. Sometimes when I'm low, I wonder who the lucky one is.

I've dealt with neurologists, neurosurgeons, nutritionists, physical therapists, and pulmonary specialists to make sure Lucy doesn't contract pneumonia, cardiologists to monitor blood clots, three rotating shifts of nursing staff, and all with their own notions of how to manage Lucy's care. The first year I was so exhausted, I lost orientation to time and place myself.

Then Nessie stepped in. She informed me that the newly renovated Glenapp Castle Hotel was looking for gardeners and that I should return to cultivating the earth. Before I knew it she had a massage therapist working Lucy's separate muscle groups twice a week. A cranial sacral expert comes regularly now to release tissue memory while stimulating the fluids in Lucy's spinal cord. One day I walked in and Lucy had acupuncture needles in her left ear, on the crown of her head, and in what Nessie calls her *third eye*, right in the middle of her forehead. When I asked Nessie what the hell was going on, she replied, "We're stimulating the energy points in her body to maximize her ability to heal. This child is going to wake up, Cousin. You just wait."

I watched her shenanigans with amusement. If Nessie thought all this would help Lucy wake up I saw no objection. What happened next, however, made me worry Nessie had lost her marbles.

Yesterday, I walked into Lucy's room to find Nessie's hands resting on Lucy's heart. Both had their eyes closed. Not wanting to interrupt, I listened while Nessie carried on a conversation with my comatose daughter.

"Lucy," Nessie began, "your spirit guides tell me that I have done all I can. You, however, have two jobs to do before you can wake up. The first is to let go of the guilt you carry that your mother died giving you life. The second is the guilt you feel for your dad having to deal with your accident. Neither were your fault, and if you don't let go, guilt is going to eat you alive."

Nessie just stood there with her eyes squeezed shut as if she were listening to Lucy's response.

Then this… "I know you don't want to come back in this body, but you need to move through this lifetime with courage, not hide in a coma. Your dad needs you. We all need you. You're the last miracle we're all counting on. I'm doing everything I can think of to help you along, but the wake up call has to come from you. Let go of all the baggage from your previous lifetimes and come live in the present. Tomorrow is your sixteenth birthday. I'm going to ask your dad to bring you to Tom Hutcheson's walled garden. I have two requests. First, I need you to help me send Sir John McPhee to the spirit world, and second, I want you to wake up. It's your time."

I didn't know *what* to think. Nessie was implying the decision to come out of her coma was up to Lucy herself, an idea entirely new to my way of thinking. Above all, the fact that Nessie was actually communicating with my daughter left me feeling both jealous and inadequate. When I cleared my throat to announce my presence, Nessie beckoned me over and placed my hand over Lucy's heart.

"It's the heart that retains memory," Nessie told me, "not the brain. If you want to communicate with Lucy just place your hand over her heart and listen."

"What did she just say to you?" I asked, skeptically.

"She said she'd love to spend her sixteenth birthday in Tom's garden. And if you could have her there at the same time I'm clearing out the ghosts," Nessie added, "that would benefit us all."

"It's already arranged," I said, thinking, *what a pile of foolishness!* Why was Nessie getting everyone all riled up? Ghost clearings, beach gatherings, and expecting Lucy to wake up? How is everyone going to feel when nothing happens? Does Nessie really expect she can change the world with hopeful thinking? I had a bad foreboding about the whole nonsense.

I don't feel any better this morning when I drive past the church on my way to Girvan to pick up Lucy and there isn't a soul in sight. It's not natural. When I pass through the center of town, I can't believe my own eyes. Family after family is heading to the beach laden with blankets, chairs and picnic baskets at a time when they should be in church. Well, I think to myself, God's given them the day off and it's a beautiful one at that. What a shame you can't see Ailsa Craig through the mist.

The staff has Lucy in her wheelchair all ready to go, but I'll tell you the truth, my throat closes up when I see the yellow ribbons tied at the end of her braids. By God, if Nessie orchestrated this, she's gone too far.

Lucy had yellow ribbons in her hair the day of her accident. That morning she'd persuaded me to braid her hair and tie yellow ribbons on the ends before she went off to school. When I was done fumbling, she threw her arms around my neck and kissed me square on the lips. "Thanks, Daddy," she said. "They're yellow, see? They match my sandals. What time are you getting home?"

"I'm off to visit your uncle and do some errands in Maybole," I told her. "I'll be home by dinner time, I promise. Now you be good. When you get home from school, go straight to the Dunbars. Mrs. Hutcheson, Tom, Sophie...they'll all be around, too."

"I love you, Daddy," Lucy said.

Those were the last words she said to me as she skipped to the school bus, her yellow hair ribbons bouncing across her back like Mexican jumping beans. The next time I saw her she lay almost dead in a coma. When they shaved Lucy's head in preparation for surgery to relieve the pressure on her brain, the nurses cut off her long brown braids, caked with blood, and handed them to me, stained ribbons and all.

After I'm done stewing, I decide I might as well play Nessie's game, so I tell Lucy on the ride to Glenapp all that's going on—the ghost clearings, the whole village thinking that the beach was the best place to see them go to the spirit world as if they were supposed to witness some dark cloud lift through the roof, and that, above all, Nessie thinks today is her day to wake up.

"It's as good a day as any," I conjecture, well used to talking to myself. Lucy just sits there next to me, propped up in the passenger seat, motionless, staring sightlessly out the window for the entire thirty-mile ride.

When we reach the end of town, I swing by the Shore Road. You'd think it is Carnival Day—kids running barefoot up and down the sandy beach, kites swooshing and dipping through the air, half-crazed dogs advancing and retreating with the tug and tumble of the waves. Never in all my days have I seen such a sight. Not in Ballantrae, anyway.

The church bells chime half past twelve and as I don't want to keep Tom waiting in the garden, I head up the hill towards Glenapp.

To my surprise, as Tom helps me lift Lucy out of the car, Issie comes running up followed by Eva Campbell. I won't say that I mind, just that I was expecting this to be a private birthday party for Lucy.

"I hope we're not interfering, William," Eva says, kindly. "We'll only be here for a bit." She throws her head in the direction of the castle implying that she knows that I know what's going on up there, but neither of us wants Issie or Tom to know. It's complicated.

"Lucy always loves the company," I say, truthfully. "It's her sixteenth birthday today."

"I know," squeals Issie. "Kevin and I made a banoffee pie with toffee and bananas and double cream and lemon and lots of sugar. Can we take Lucy down to the garden now? Tom says I could pick a bouquet of all the flowers I know. Just one of each, right?" she confirms, looking at Tom.

"Just one of each," Tom smiles.

Issie is wearing Lucy's old clothes as she always does when Lucy comes for a visit. Today she has on the purple, sleeveless dress Lucy saved for special occasions. It shouldn't bother me; I passed on the clothes to Issie but it's a painful reminder, nonetheless.

"Tom Hutcheson," Eva delights in saying. "You've created a slice of heaven here at Glenapp. How *ever* did you do it in such a short period of time?"

Tom just laughs. "I've had a lot of help," he testifies, looking my way. "Without William and Henry, and Issie reminding me of the names of all the flowers," he winks, "I never could have done it. And remember, you were the one who hired me."

"I do," Eva recalls. "It's the smartest thing I've ever done."

"I'm grateful," Tom admits, shyly.

"So are we."

"Tom, how come you're a gardener?" Issie asks.

"Well…" Tom clears his throat, "when I was a little boy, I lived here at Glenapp. In fact, my great great-grandfather was Glenapp Castle's first Head Gardener back in 1882, so my family has lived on the property for generations. I used to beg my Dad to tell me stories about my ancestors and the walled garden, so…I suppose I've dreamed of being a gardener all my life."

"William?" Issie asks. "Did Lucy play in the garden when she was my age?"

"Nooooo," I chuckle. "Colin Dunbar wasn't one for letting children romp through his garden, was he Tom?"

"Certainly not," Tom confirms. "He was a very serious chap with a mean temper to boot. Besides, we had the glen to play in."

"Tom lets us in, don't you, Tom?" Issie says, affectionately.

"Well…" Tom ruminates, "I think of flowers as the jewel in the crown and they should be shared with everyone."

"What's the jewel in the crown?" asks Issie. "And tell Lucy, too. She can hear you."

Collecting his thoughts, Tom says, "Well, young ladies, I mean that if the earth is the crown, flowers are its jewels, the loveliest gems the planet has to offer. Can you think of anything on earth more beautiful?"

Issie ponders this for several moments, then says, "No, I can't. Can you, Lucy?"

No response from Lucy, so Issie answers for them both. "No, we can't think of anything more beautiful than a flower."

"I would agree," Tom says. "I think God created flowers to awaken our spirits, to remind us that true spiritual awareness is realized through the beauty of nature."

Issie leans over to ask Lucy, "What do you think, Lucy? Does being in the garden wake up your spirit?" Issie's effort to mimic the use of such grown-up language always amuses me. Despite my daughter's lack of response, Issie insists, "Lucy says that it does. She says there's nowhere she'd rather spend her birthday."

We stroll along a little further. Issie, apparently, isn't satisfied with Tom's answer. "But how did you *know* you wanted to be a gardener in the first place?"

"I'd like to know, too," echoes Eva.

"Well, to tell you the truth," Tom admits, "I think it evolved over time. My dad was a fisherman. He died when I was ten, but he loved the outdoors and read a lot about nature. I loved him more than life itself, so when he invited me to go out in his fishing boat, I'd jump at the chance. It was on the ocean that he taught me that certain patterns and shapes are inherent in nature, and that if I observed closely, I would discover the same shapes repeated again and again."

"Like what?" Issie wants to know.

"Well, like waves. The wave pattern creates a rhythm of movement and circulation, churning up food for the fish, for example. One sees the pattern in dunes, mountain ridges, heartbeats, light and sound vibrations. The spiral shape is another one. For snails, the pattern of their spiral shell helps them distribute and collect energy efficiently. Other spiral shapes in nature are less friendly."

"Like tornadoes," Eva contributes.

"Aye, you can think of endless examples," Tom says. "The fact is I got so seasick on Dad's salmon boat he gave up on me and sent me to the walled garden to continue my search for shapes on land."

"Oh, goodie. Like what?" Issie persists.

"Look around you," Tom challenges her.

Issie squeezes Lucy's limp hand and says, "Come on, Lucy, help me find some." In just a second or two, she picks up a fallen, rotten apple. "Circles," she says. "Circles are everywhere."

"Right again. Spheres provide the least amount of surface area for the most volume, minimizing heat loss. We see spheres everywhere: drops of water, seeds, the planets."

"Grapes, cherries, dog food," Issie adds.

"Aye, especially dog food," Tom laughs heartily, thoroughly enjoying himself now. "I didn't learn the actual purpose for all these patterns and shapes until I studied at Findhorn," Tom admits, "but as a child, I thought it was the coolest game in the world.

"Then the clincher—I noticed one afternoon in the glen that the wings of certain species like bees, grasshoppers, and butterflies looked just like the winged seed of a maple tree. The very same week our school took us to the Glasgow Zoo, and I was certain the plumage of the peacock had the same pattern as the center of a daisy. From that day on I begged my dad to ask Colin Dunbar if I could have free reign of the walled garden. Finally, when Dad died, Mr. Dunbar hired me as his apprentice. I suppose the truth is I got along with plants better than I did people. Still do."

I have never heard Tom expound on such things. I find him quite remarkable, really. Suddenly I am filled with pride that I had something to do with bringing him back to Glenapp.

I point out that there is a banoffee pie that will certainly melt in the sun if we don't eat it soon. Issie gallops off like a wild pony to pick her bouquet and in all of two minutes hands it to Lucy, who, of course, is unable to raise her hand to receive it. But Issie is not deterred—she helps Lucy wrap her fingers, one at a time, around the stems.

Just as we are headed to the table for tea and pie, we all hear an uproarious cheering from the direction of the beach below.

"Whatever is that?" Tom wants to know. "It sounds like a soccer match down there. I should think the village would be tiring of Reverend McCrindle's sermon about now. What time is it?"

"It's one o'clock," Eva informs us, looking at me with furrowed brows, for like Tom, she is unaware that the whole of Ballantrae is gathered on the shore.

I say nothing. *Whatever* are they cheering about? Perhaps they *are* playing soccer. That's when Issie starts giggling.

"Look everyone," she announces. "There's a butterfly sitting on Lucy's nose. Lucy…quick, open your eyes. There's a butterfly on your nose."

CHAPTER TWENTY-TWO

TOM

THEY SAY THAT WHEN you die a grand display of your life flashes through your mind. If I could highlight and freeze certain frames, just for the thrill of reliving them again and again, making love to Sophie would be the first, winning my high school curling championship would be the second, but the third and most remarkable is this moment, for Lucy Hobbes has just woken up.

These things never happen as one might imagine. The fact is, all the adults on hand were thinking of other things. I, for one, was pondering the influx of red admiral butterflies in the garden. They usually live in marshes and wood, preferring the sap of fermenting fruit trees. It's not common for them to congregate in gardens with a lush forest habitat so nearby. William and Eva were cutting pie when Issie starts giggling.

"Look everyone," she chimes, jumping up and down with boundless delight. "There's a butterfly sitting on Lucy's nose. Lucy... quick, *open* your eyes."

When we first hear them converse, subliminally we assume Issie is just dubbing in Lucy's voice as children do with their imaginary friends.

"Lucy, look! It's a red admiral," Issie repeats, joyfully. "Now it's on your shoulder, now your knee. Oops, there it goes."

"Who are you?" Lucy whispers, her voice sounding as if she has laryngitis. "Am I in heaven?"

"No, you're in the walled garden. I'm Issie. Lucy, YOU'RE AWAKE!" Issie whoops in unmitigated amazement.

William, Eva, and I are now captive to Issie's unfortunate game of pretending Lucy has suddenly woken up. Then, Lucy whispers, "That's my dress."

"You're right," Issie declares. "I wear it when you come from the Home for People Who Aren't Awake so you will remember and wake up, and it worked!"

When Lucy asks, "Where's my dad?" Eva, Issie, and I watch William Hobbes run to his daughter's side, then collapse to his knees. With his uncapped head in her lap, his arms around her waist, he weeps like a baby. Before long there isn't a dry eye among us.

Life *is* a marvel. It truly is. A brain, dormant for ten years, a body blind and deaf to the world, has mysteriously awakened by the touch of a butterfly. Maybe it isn't just a coincidence—a fluke born of nature. Isn't the butterfly's wing similar to those ethereal creatures we call angels or those elusive garden fairies I have yet to see? As I watch Lucy slowly emerge from her cocoon of lost time, I wonder if perhaps we *are* in heaven, after all. But no, my afterlife would include my mother and father. I am not yet to be so blessed.

My conclusion is reinforced by the sight of Nessie Brown, of all people. What on earth is she doing here?

"She's awake," William cries out. "Nessie, Lucy's awake."

"I knew it!" Nessie hollers, throwing her hands to the skies as she passes through the garden gate. "I knew it! We've just cleared the ghosts and, by God, Ailsa Craig is so clear you can see the gulls flying about. Thank God Almighty, we're free."

When Nessie reaches us she proceeds to hug Lucy, hug William. Soon, everyone's hugging, letting the emotion of the moment swallow us whole. Did she say something about *ghosts*? Andrew Campbell has just arrived looking as if he's just seen one. Whatever is going on?

"Lucy, say something. Tell me it's true, sweetheart," Nessie implores.

We are interrupted by the clatter of teacups. Nessie and Andrew left the garden gate open; Grimshaw and Rosie are helping themselves to banoffee pie in dinosaur-sized gulps.

"Grimshaw!" Eva scolds, but it is too late, not a morsel remains.

"I'm so sorry, William," she apologizes. "What naughty dogs they are! I'm afraid they've ruined Lucy's birthday pie."

"Not at all," he says. "Nothing could ruin this day, could it, Lucy?"

Lucy shakes her head and smiles, but clearly her metamorphosis has tired her.

"We'd best get Lucy home so she can start her new life," Nessie advises. "My goodness, miracles *do* happen. Did you hear everyone on the beach? I wonder what made them cheer. I've heard of dark energy visibly manifesting itself as it leaves the earth plane. Sir John that would be, certainly not Judith Hutcheson." At the mention of my mother's name, Nessie's hand flies to her mouth.

Except for the flutter of butterfly wings, not a sound can be heard in the garden. Even the birds seem to be holding their breath. "Does someone want to tell me what's going on?"

Andrew steps over and says, "May I speak with you in private, Tom?"

"We'll just be off, then," Nessie fusses and fidgets. "Thank you, Tom. Your garden was a big part of my plan and it worked."

"I've no idea what you're talking about," I reply, stupefied.

"Perhaps Andrew can explain."

"Thank you, Tom." William grasps my hand, shaking it with such effusive gratitude I almost feel ashamed. Then he breaks down and hugs me.

"I don't understand what's going on here," I repeat, irritably. "I didn't have anything to do with Lucy waking up. If anyone should be thanked, it's Issie."

"We all had a part in the events that took place here, and in the village, and on Ailsa Craig," Nessie proclaims. "We just want you to know that the beautiful work you've done here in Glenapp's walled garden has helped us all, and Lucy is the ultimate beneficiary."

"Whatever are you talking about?"

All heads turn to Andrew. "Can we chat?" he asks me again.

Nessie and William escort Lucy out of the garden in her wheelchair. Eva and Issie follow, taking Grimshaw with them. Andrew guides me towards the gardener's cottage with a kind but firm clamp on my elbow, stealing me away from a scene I have yet to comprehend.

"What's this all about?" I demand to know.

"Let's go to your cottage?" he suggests.

Noticing the garden is empty now and feeling a wee put out, I reply, "I'd rather discuss it right here, if you don't mind."

"I don't know about you, but I need to sit down."

"You look dreadful," I say, reaching for sympathy in my voice.

"I feel worse," he confesses.

I wait. Whatever he has to tell me isn't going to be easy on either of us; that is evident. Perhaps he's going to let me go. Andrew removes his jacket and wipes his brow with a wrinkled kerchief already damp with perspiration.

"I thought I had a reasonable grasp on reality before today," he commences. "But I didn't. What I am about to tell you makes no sense to me at all. None whatsoever. I will spend the rest of my life sorting this out. I expect you will do the same.

"First, I owe you an apology," my boss laments. "I've kept something from you for selfish reasons, and…because I didn't really believe it was possible."

"What was possible?"

"That there were such things as ghosts and that one of them was your mother."

"My mother! You *must* be joking? How could that be? *One* of them! Who was the other?"

"Sir John McPhee."

"Dear God!"

"They're gone now."

"Gone? Where?"

"Nessie Brown would say to the spirit world. I have no idea. But I will tell you one thing; I saw him. Was Sir McPhee bearded and wearing a kilt when he died?"

"Yes," I answer.

"I didn't see your mother," he murmurs. "The rest is a confession, Tom. Your mother wrote you a poem before she left, but when I went to retrieve it in Eva's desk drawer it was gone. I've lost it."

"What do you mean a poem? How possibly?"

Andrew faces me squarely and taking a deep breath, exhales a sigh of utter exasperation. "I'm sorry. I'm not being direct.

"I believe your mother's ghost has been trapped inside the castle since the fire. But you didn't reside in the castle, you see, so she busied herself, neatening up and such as she must have done when she was alive. Once Sir John made himself known I became frightened he might disturb the hotel guests, so I asked Nessie to help me expel them. I should have told you but I couldn't justify it, somehow. I thought it best to spare you, not understanding that it was *you* she was trying to communicate with. At any rate, she's been returned to the spirit world; I suppose for that we can all be grateful. The bad news is...I've lost your poem."

"I can grasp the idea of ghosts," I concede. "Ghosts are nothing new in Scottish castles, after all. My mother and Sir John did die a horrible death, but how does a ghost compose a poem? It seems a bit fantastical."

"Nessie went into some kind of trance as the medium, then her hand just started writing. I know it sounds absurd, Tom, but I saw it myself."

I suddenly have an irresistible urge to be alone and stand to leave.

"I cannot say how sorry I am," Andrew apologizes.

"I'm no worse off than before," I state the truth.

"Bless you," he says. Yet as I turn, once again I feel the halting pressure of his fingers on my elbow. "It's Glenapp, isn't it? It's the north turret wing that's built on the fairy path that's causing all the trouble here. And that means Sir John was the one who's responsible...Eva's been trying to tell me, but she knew I wouldn't listen. You're a sane man, Tom—you don't believe in this fairy poppycock, do you?"

"If Sir John McPhee is gone as you say, we'll see, won't we?"

*　　*　　*

Why I expect the interior of my cottage to be altered just because Lucy Hobbes woke up and my mother supposedly wrote me a poem is a mystery to me. All the faded, tattered furniture the Dunbars left behind is precisely where it was this morning. My stained tea cup remains unwashed in the sink, Rosie's muddied paw prints are dried now but they are there—a small comfort, each and every one. My hourglass empty, I lay down. Dad's book of poems lies on my bedside table and when I reach over, I notice a sheet of *Glenapp Castle* stationery resting on top. I assume it's a letter of termination—perhaps Andrew and Eva can't bear to have me around any longer. When I see it is a poem, a poem written in my mother's hand, the old scar on my right palm burns as I read—

Look not for me in hallowed ground
It is not there that I'll be found
Search in your heart for love, not fear
And wait for nature's whisper dear
I am the sparkling river's flow
I am the fairies' celestial glow
I am the spotted wings of flight
That light the garden's sky at night
But open up your heart you must
Else love's sweet nectar turn to dust
Love's tender kiss lay just beneath
The mask of pain, the veil of grief
I did not die; we did not part
My love for you lies in your heart
Remember, Son, that All is One
Life's web is thus supremely spun.

With everlasting love, Mother

I have no choice in the matter—muscle memory propels me towards the glen, along the soft forest floor, over the kissing bridge, and down the steep path towards the great towering redwood. The thunderous waterfall fills me with a longing so unbearable I strip off my clothes and let the freezing water cascade over my body. Breathe, I tell myself. One thought at a time. It is a beautiful day, and I am alive. I am more fortunate than most. My mother's ghost has left me a message. More bizarre things have happened in the history of the world, surely. Breathe.

Her missive is clear enough, but what did she mean, *Open up your heart you must, else love's sweet nectar turn to dust?* Have I closed my heart to love? Well, on consideration, of course I have! Sophie sealed my destiny when she married Hal Munro. I am thus fated to be alone—acceptance of this fact came long ago. To open my heart to someone else would forever tarnish what I hold most dear, a love transcending time. Despite Sophie's choice to the contrary, I will remain faithful to the ideal that having truly loved once is enough.

The rushing water feels wonderful. I am alive. Lucy has awakened. My garden, somehow mysteriously a part of it all, is thriving, and I have become surprisingly fond of the Campbells. My mother has, in her own befitting way, communicated her love for me. What if I am to remain a single man? It is not the worst of fates. I will, for her sake, open my heart when I can, but I will not barter my soul for mere companionship. I've done that before. If I have to wait another lifetime to be with Sophie, so be it. I will wait.

I duck out from beneath the waterfall, blinking to clear my eyes. Thoughts of Sophie are often followed by apparitions of her—soft edged, ethereal-like imaginings conjured up, no doubt, by my tireless, subliminal wanting of her, so when I see her floating down the path, a sunlit halo crowning her mane of strawberry-blond hair, I close my eyes again, imprinting her image in my memory for safekeeping. It's been a long time since I've had a glimpse of my Sophie. I am always thankful when it happens, and holding her vision close, I return to the waterfall to brand it in my memory forever. Perhaps it will be my last; I am never sure.

When I open my eyes, the apparition is sitting against the redwood tree smiling mischievously. She's confiscated my clothes.

"I was beginning to wonder if you were ever coming out," she says.

I stumble like a drunk on the rocky bottom. "Are you real?"

"Aye," Sophie replies. "I'm real. And *you're* naked."

"Would you like to join me?" I play along, willing the dream to never end.

"No, thank you," she replies, trying unsuccessfully to focus above my waist. "I'll just sit here and watch you thrash about." Then, blushing, Sophie averts her eyes, smiling in spite of herself. "You've grown into a very handsome man, Tom Hutcheson. It's a wonder some young lassie hasn't caught your fancy."

"How do you know one hasn't?" I challenge, climbing out of the water.

Sophie hands me my trousers. "Nessie Brown," she discloses. "Mum and I arrived two days ago, just enough time for Nessie to tell us every detail of what's gone on in Ballantrae for the last ten years. There isn't anything I don't know."

"Is that right?" I wipe myself dry with my shirt, feasting on her, suspended somewhere between disbelief and sheer amazement. She is wearing a pale yellow, sleeveless dress, exposing her beautifully sculpted arms and legs. She is taller, leaner, more womanly—more desirable than ever.

"You're staring," she teases.

"Why are you here, Soph?"

"That's a nice thing to ask a lady!" she declares.

"Well?"

As if not a day has passed, Sophie and I lean against the trunk of the redwood and watch the waterfall spill into the three sparkling pools. This is the woman who betrayed you, I tell myself—be watchful.

"Mum's dad died."

"I don't remember your mum having a dad," I remark.

"No, you wouldn't have. They never got along. He lived in Glasgow with his third wife who died just before he did. He left a wee bit of money and Mum is the only kin."

"That's nice for you both." As soon as I say it, I remember Hal Munro. "For the three of you."

"I'm here alone, Tom. Without Hal."

Without Hal. "What happened?"

"Hal is a good man. He was kind and he loved me. In my confusion, I took that to mean I would be happy with him."

"I loved you, too," I rebuke.

"I know, Tom, but you weren't there when Dad killed himself. You can't imagine how horrid it was. Mum and I were away in Toronto for a curling match—he'd been hanging by the attic rafters for three days. Mum mentally and physically collapsed and had to be put in the hospital, and Hal, in our despair, took over, managing Mum, managing me, *and* my curling career. I mistook his attentions for love and I married him. I shouldn't have; I know that now. He knew within months that I didn't love him. When Mum's dad died, I told him I wasn't coming back."

"Will you divorce him, then?"

"Aye."

There are unresolved matters to settle, still. "Do you know how I found out you were marrying Hal? From a curling magazine. It seems to me…"

"Before you go on and on," she interrupts, "you should know that I wrote you a ten page letter begging you to come to Halifax, that if you loved me, you'd forget about seeing the plant fairies and fly to Nova Scotia to prevent me from marrying Hal. When you never responded, I took that to be your answer. Only later did I discover that it weighed so much I hadn't put enough postage on the envelope. Hal found the returned letter on the hall table, and seeing how thick it was, and to whom it was addressed, hid it from me. It was horrible and deceitful of him, but he knew that if you loved me as much as he did, you would come. In the end, when I told him I was leaving him, he returned it to me, unopened."

Sophie reaches into her dress pocket and produces the thickest letter I've ever seen. *Insufficient Postage* and *Return to Sender* are stamped in red and black ink across the front. The seal has not been broken.

"How much was it short?" I ask.

"Was what short?"

"How much did you owe on the letter," I beg to know.

"Two cents Canadian," she answers. "What difference does it make?"

"Two more cents and we could have been together years ago. I would have swum across the Atlantic if you'd asked me to, Sophie. You should have known that. Why didn't you come see me two days ago?" I am inconsolable.

"Nessie wouldn't let me."

"Nessie? Good heavens! What's she to do with all this?" The woman is ubiquitous.

"You've forgotten she's Mum's best friend."

"But not yours!" I challenge.

"No, but she was afraid if I came sooner you might not be at the walled garden to celebrate Lucy's sixteenth birthday today, and she needed you there."

"She's right, I would have whisked you away forever," I say, tracing her thigh with my finger.

Sophie smiles. "Nessie made me promise, Tom. I waited on the beach with everyone else until I couldn't stand it any longer. I knew I'd find you here eventually."

"What was everyone doing on the beach, anyway? Especially during church?"

Sophie just shakes her head. "The whole village was gathered to see Sir John's ghost, or aura, as Nessie calls it, expelled from the castle. You'll think me daft, but I swear we could see a dark essence ascend from the northern turret wing of the castle. It was spooky. Then, when the haze lifted over Alias Craig everyone went crazy."

"Just about the time Lucy woke up, I'll wager."

"You were there. Was it amazing?" Sophie asks.

"Beyond amazing. Miraculous!" I exclaim.

I suddenly remember Iain Henry at Findhorn talking about leylines—those broad bands of energy that crisscross the earth's surface. What had he said? That when places lie at the junction of intersecting leylines, the positive and negative impact is magnified?

I understand now. Our thoughts, words, and actions affect not only ourselves, but everything around us. Nothing we do, or say, or think goes unnoticed in the universe, least of all our intentions toward others. Nessie Brown comprehends this best of all. With Sir John banished forever, she knew Lucy's best chance of revival was in Glenapp's walled garden where love and beauty coalesce in a sweeping medley of sights, sounds, and smells so seductive, even space and time lose their stronghold over the unfolding of events. My God, how have I not recognized it before? Everything in the cosmos is connected to the heart rhythm of now, to this very moment—infinitesimal yet interrelated to all things past and present, real and imaginary. *Remember, son, that all is one. Life's web is thus supremely spun.*

"Are you all right?" Sophie asks, tracing the scar tissue across my palm. To this day, I have no feeling there.

"I'd stopped believing in a supreme force when I heard you'd married Hal Munro," I tell her. "After this extraordinary day, I'm tempted to reconsider."

Sophie gathers me in her arms. "Nessie told me about your mum's poem and how it was lost."

"Not lost," I whisper, holding her so tight I can hardly breathe.

"You found it?" she asks, pulling away just slightly.

I sigh. "More precisely, it found me."

"What did she say?"

"She said that I should open my heart to love again or you'd never come back to me."

"Oh, Tom…can you ever forgive me?"

"It's not a matter of forgiveness, Soph," I say, kissing her forehead. "But if you come back to me it needs to be for good. I couldn't survive losing you twice—I truly couldn't."

"The greatest regret of my life is not being loyal to you."

It is said.

"But I want children," she declares.

"As do I. Lots of them. Being an only child was miserable."

"I agree. At least two."

"I like the idea of three. Three's a good number."

"Aye, like Orion's belt. Three it is, then."

CHAPTER TWENTY-THREE

EVA

K EVIN IS LIVID. "DO you realize I am the *only* one who wasn't on the beach? You might have told me, Eva."

"I didn't know the entire village was watching from the beach," I repeat for the third time.

"And where was I?" He is whipping the eggs to a foam. "In Wigtown with an old aunt who doesn't even know she's breathing! An honest-to-goodness ghost clearing! And what does Andrew know of such things?"

"A great deal more than he'd like," I retort, having had about enough.

"And Lucy! I missed the miracle of the century. That's what happens when you're sent away," he sulks.

"No one sent you away. Don't be ludicrous, Kevin. Really, you *are* too much!"

"Well, at least everyone enjoyed my banoffee pie."

"It was delicious," I say.

"Ah-ha! You see?" he exclaims, flinging his whisk, splattering raw egg across the wall. "You will even lie to me. Issie said you never ate it. Tell me the truth, Eva."

There is no end to the holes I dig for myself. "The truth is, Grimshaw got to it first and Rosie finished it off," I confess.

"*Grimshaw*! You fed my beautiful pie to a *hound*? Eva, how could you?"

"I didn't *feed* it to him, and it wasn't just Grimshaw; Rosie was there, too. You see, we were just about to slice it when Lucy woke up, and…"

"An event I was not there to see," Kevin interrupts.

"And…" I continue, "Nessie and Andrew apparently forgot to latch the gate behind them when they entered the garden. Grimshaw must have snuck in; you know how fond he is of Rosie. There was nothing any of us could do. I'm sorry to have lied to you, Kevin, but you're so hysterical over these things, I was trying not to hurt your feelings."

"You were trying to prevent another scene," he mopes, wiping the wall of egg.

"Why don't you fix a banoffee pie for Issie's birthday next month? It's on the tenth of September. Please, she would love it."

"I'll think about it."

"You do that."

"I will."

"Kevin, we have other things to discuss," I say, exasperated.

"Do we? I can't think what."

I have him now. "I thought you'd like to know that Glenapp Castle Hotel is the newest member of the Relais & Chateaux group, one of the most coveted honors in the hotel business worldwide. And, we've just been awarded Five Stars by the Scottish Tourist Bureau."

Kevin pretends to be unimpressed. "Humph! What's that to do with me?"

"The exceptional cuisine was the decisive factor," I say, offhandedly.

"Number one!" he whoops with open delight. "What was number two?"

"The grounds, the walled garden in particular."

"Well deserved," Kevin concedes.

"As was the first prize. Congratulations, my friend. You've made us proud."

＊   ＊   ＊

Indeed, things are going well for us. Andrew's mother has settled in, making friends with Nessie Brown and subsequently half the village, her fame sealed, as is Andrew's, as the heroes who helped Nessie clear the castle of its evil spirit. Tom found his mother's poem, much to Andrew's relief, and Issie will start Primary Two next week. For me, the most welcome news of all—Issie seems to have forgiven me for the disappearance of Maria and Vicente Flor. In fact, I hadn't thought about them for quite some time until the post arrived this morning. There were actually two letters of interest: Vicente's and another from Judge Sinclair. I left them both sitting on my desk. When I return to the office, Andrew is seated in the swivel chair, both opened letters in hand.

"Which one should I read first?" I ask, trying to lighten his surly mood.

"Vicente's," he murmurs, not looking up.

"What is it? Is something wrong?" Andrew nods, urging me to read for myself.

Vicente's letter is short and written in his own hand.

> *My Dear Friends,*
> *I've lost her. Maria died of heart failure last Friday. I am broken-hearted and plan to return to Ecuador as soon as arrangements are made to bring her home. I will never forget your friendship. Please give my devoted love to Isobel.*
>
> *Pray for me,*
> *Vicente*

"I can't believe it!" I exclaim. "I never really expected…"

"Read the judge's letter."

"Andrew, aren't you shocked?" I ask, reeling from the news.

Standing up to give me his chair, he repeats, "Just read, love. Then we'll talk."

"Does it have to do with Issie?"

"No, not that," he attests.

Dear Mr. and Mrs. Campbell,

It is under quite extraordinary circumstances that I write to you both. After serious consideration, I have concluded there are times in one's career when breaking with protocol is appropriate. This is one of those times.

You shared with me that Vicente Flor revealed himself as Issie's biological father. Though, as I said, I have never met the gentleman, I recently received information related to his late wife, Maria Flor. No doubt you will find it of interest.

My old friend from Oxford, Mr. Bradford Morgan-Jones, is a cardiovascular surgeon in London and the one, ironically, who performed Maria Flor's heart transplant last spring. Whose heart she received, of course, would normally be held strictly confidential. However, upon her death, and because Morgan-Jones and I were both close friends of the Campbell family, he shared with me that Maria's donor was Kitty Campbell.

In all my professional life, I cannot recall such a coincidence.

I hope this missive finds you well. I should think Issie would be starting school soon. Please convey to her, and to Grimshaw, my very best wishes.

Sincerely,
Judge Sinclair

"Andrew, how is that possible?"

"Maria must have been a waiting and ready recipient when Kitty was killed," Andrew surmises.

"It's unbelievable! Did Vicente know, do you think?" I wonder.

"I doubt it, but it explains a great deal," Andrew reflects. "Remember Vicente telling us of the nightmare Maria kept having of being in a foreign land with wild ponies along the side of the road and seeing the whites of the drunk driver's eyes before he rammed his lorry into her car? She was reliving Kitty's accident in her dream. It was the New Forest ponies she saw. They wander freely all through that area, and Kitty was killed by a drunken lorry driver."

"You're suggesting that Kitty's heart retained the memory of the accident even after it was transplanted into Maria?"

"I'm suggesting that the memory of Kitty's heart would have lived on in whomever received her heart. Remember all the observations Vicente made concerning Maria's new behaviors—the change in food preferences and suddenly not wanting to eat meat? Kitty was a vegetarian. Maria's sudden love for children, her changed tastes in music, her altered personality from someone who was quiet and private to someone who loved crowds, and her unprecedented yearning for her own child—I remember thinking that Maria had two personalities: happy one minute, sad the next."

"And it would explain Grimshaw's behavior," I add. "When he first saw Maria he jumped and twisted like a crazed monkey, acting as if he'd found a long lost friend. I couldn't get over it."

"In a manner of speaking, she *was* his previous owner. Amazing that he felt it, don't you think? Remember, Vicente bought Grimshaw for Kitty as a going away present," Andrew reminds me. "And Eva, think about it. This explains why Issie and Maria became so easily attached. The hearts of a mother and child recognized one another. They were literally genetically connected."

"You're saying that Issie thought Maria was her mother?"

"I think Issie was irresistibly drawn to Maria's heart, not Maria. It makes sense that, of all the organs, the heart would retain memory from one human to another. It's fantastic, really. I actually read in a medical journal once that a young girl received the heart from a donor who was murdered. Night after night she'd have recurring dreams of her death. Her parents finally reported it to the police and the child identified the murderer. It was a true story."

Could it be that our personality is imprinted in our hearts, and not our brains, after all? Have I been raving mad with jealousy over a network of cells that I thought comprised Maria, when it was really Kitty? But why didn't I recognize Maria's heart as Kitty's? No, Kitty and I weren't close, nor were we biologically related. Issie knew. She couldn't explain it, bless her little heart, but she knew intuitively that Maria's heart loved her.

"One can easily understand why Vicente was confused," Andrew muses. "His two lovers shared the same heart. Poor fellow, he's lost the same heart twice."

"We'll have to tell Issie eventually, don't you suppose?"

"I'll wager she already knows," Andrew sighs. "She brought in the mail this morning."

*   *   *

I find her sitting on the stone wall of the terraced garden, her gaze cast to the Irish Sea. On such a clear morning, one can see thousands of white gannets flying about Ailsa Craig like an astral shower of shooting stars, but she does not seem to notice. Grimshaw's head is nestled on her lap. Soft, empathetic whimpers emerge from his throat and I know for certain that Andrew is right.

"May I join you?" I ask, scooting close.

"Maria's dead, isn't she?"

"Yes," I say, tenderly wiping away her tears.

"I loved her soooo much," Issie effuses.

"She loved you more than you'll ever know," I say. "But you must remember, Issie, that love is eternal. Just because someone dies doesn't mean they stop loving you, ever."

She considers this for several moments. "You're my real mum now, aren't you?"

It is her turn to wipe away my tears. "Yes," I answer. "I'm your real mum now."

"Then I have three mums who love me."

"Indeed you do, and two dads, too."

CHAPTER TWENTY-FOUR

GRIMSHAW

LUCKILY FOR ME, BANOFFEE pie has become the standard party fare here at Glenapp. The last time Kevin made one was the day Lucy Hobbes woke up. Rosie and I had a wonderful time. Today is also an important day—it's Issie's sixth birthday. Kevin made these pies just for Rosie and me this time, I'm sure of it. In the tea room, just inside the greenhouse, he even put blue and yellow balloons on the table to attract our attention. The problem is—how to get into the walled garden before the guests arrive and mistakenly think the pies are for them. Through the iron gate, Rosie and I are discussing the matter.

"We got into a heap of trouble last time, Grimmey," she reminds me.

"It was worth it, don't you think? And besides, I think Kevin feels guilty and made these for us this time. Certainly, he didn't make *two* pies just for Issie's birthday party."

Rosie considers my point. Her sleek, majestic white nose sniffs the air as the irresistible aroma of banana drifts our way.

"Well," my beauty replies, "quite a few are coming to the birthday party. There is Issie, of course, and Eva and Andrew, Tom and Sophie. William's bringing Lucy and his cousin Nessie. Kevin will have worked his way in, I'm sure. Oh, and there's Mary, Andrew's mum, and I overheard Eva telling Issie she could invite several new school friends. And …" she flutters her long eyelashes.

I am thinking about those pies Kevin made for us. All this talk of company was entertaining enough, but what about my grumbling stomach?

"Rosie, don't you think," I propose through the gate, "that you could slip the latch and let me in? The party's going to start soon and Kevin will be furious if someone else eats our banoffee pies, don't you agree?"

"Shouldn't we share?" Rosie asks, ever the thoughtful one.

"Absolutely not! Clearly, Kevin would have made four pies if he intended anyone else to have any."

Rosie attempts to lift the latch with her paw. "Try your nose," I coach, hoping for a lick.

"I know what you're doing, Grimmey. You're trying to kiss me," she reads my mind.

Steadily, Rosie nudges the latch, and the gate swings open. No human in sight. "Let's go!" I bark, waddling my way along the garden paths.

"What about that kiss?"

I can hear voices coming down the path from the castle. "Rosie, can it wait? Aren't you hungry?"

"Somehow, I've lost my appetite," she sulks.

"I'm warning you. If you don't want yours, I'm going to eat them both," I threaten, incredulous she would forego such an opportunity.

I ingest both delectable pies in a record ten seconds flat. Already my stomach is turning somersaults, a dress rehearsal for the volcano of nausea yet to erupt, when Kevin enters through the gate.

"No! No! It cannot be! Tell me this isn't possible," rails the chef. "Where is Grimshaw? I know it's him! Rosie?" he glares at her with fire in his eyes. "Tell me the truth. Did you do this?"

Rosie quickly sits on her haunches, regally shaking her muzzle to the contrary.

Kevin grabs my collar. "There you are! If you didn't have such long ears, I'd think you were a pig. Look what you've done! Can you deny it?"

Deny it? Certainly I can. What proof does he have?

Breaking loose, I stride away defiantly, assured Rosie will defend my honor, when she says to me, "You have pie across your forehead, on both ears, and on the left side of your muzzle, Mister Piggy. You're cooked."

"Come back here, you beast," Kevin scowls, taking hold of my collar again. "How dare you eat Issie's pies! Have you no couth? You're doomed, Grimshaw. Out!" And he drags me through the garden gate weaving exaggerated serpentines through the incoming guests.

"Kevin, what did Grimmey do?" Issie begs to know, concerned I am being unfairly punished, which I *am*.

"He ate your birthday pies!" Kevin testifies, all in a dither. "It's too much. Lucky for him I made two extras for the staff. What will I give them now? This dog has no manners, Issie. You must learn to discipline him. I cannot have Grimshaw filching my delicacies every time I turn around."

"I'll come get you later, Grimmey," Issie promises me. "For now, you can watch us through the gate." She leans down and after giving me a hug, licks the pie off my forehead.

But she doesn't come get me later. In the excitement of the festivities, she forgets. Eva forgets, too. Even Andrew forgets. Not only did they forget to feed me dinner (not that I could have eaten it), but they left me out all doggone night long.

Believe me, this isn't the first time I've been cast to the wolves. Nearly ten years ago now, a young man with dark hair and skin saw me in the pet shop window, shivering from the cold draft. He looked nice enough; maybe he could get me out of there. I barked to get his attention. Before I knew it, he'd picked me up and, of all things, started examining my privates.

"You're a little boy," the man said in a funny accent. "What's your name?"

"Grimshaw," I barked, not that I expected him to understand dogspeak.

"Does he have a name?" he asked the young sales clerk.

"Grimshaw," she said. "Isn't he cute?"

"Well, *buenos dias*, Grimshaw. *Me llamo Vicente*. What breed is he?"

"He's a purebred basset hound," she bragged on my behalf. "We have his papers."

"How old is he?"

"Let's see, what's today—29 March. That makes him almost nine months old. If you can put up with their inherent stubbornness, they make wonderful family pets. Is he for you?"

"No, for a lady friend about to move to London. Will he be all right living in a flat, do you think?" the man inquired, rubbing my back with long, slow rhythmic strokes from the top of my head all the way to the tip of my darling tail. I was asleep in seconds and woke up to find myself curled in his lap with my back braced against a steering wheel. Not having had time to do my business before leaving the pet shop, I looked around for some newspaper. No luck. I licked my new owner's face, then my hindquarters so he'd get the point. No luck there, either.

"Hello, Grimshaw. Have a nice siesta? I was hoping to drive straight to Glasgow with you, but I have, most unfortunately, an errand to complete, then we'll be on our way. You're going to love your new *mamá. Se llama* Kitty, and she's the sweetest, loveliest *señorita* in the world."

We drove in silence for a few minutes when he started up again. "She's taught me a great deal about being a good boyfriend, Grimshaw. Listening is the thing! *Señoritas* love to talk. They don't want you to give advice or solve their problems, just to listen. It's easy enough. And you can't force the sex thing. If they don't want it, don't press the point; it's bad form. They desire intimacy and candlelight, to be wooed, wined, and dined. If they don't *feel* that you love them, it's all over. It's a delicate matter—*muy delicada*. Perhaps it's different for dogs," Vicente said, giving me a hearty pat on the hindquarters. "I envy you, boy."

My new human seemed to be enjoying himself. "The thing about Kitty is she's had terrible trouble getting out from under the likes of Sir John McPhee. But she's clear of him now, and we're going to move you both to London tomorrow before I return to Ecuador. I've wanted to buy her a going away present and you're *just* the thing! She'll love you.

"But first I have to go to Glenapp Castle to say adios to Sir John myself. He's not a good man," Vicente warned me. "In fact, he's the dregs of the earth. You wouldn't believe a person could be so horrible and deceitful, so cruel and conniving. Do you know what he does? He pretends to be saving the souls of impoverished children from the streets of Guayaquil, but he is importing them to London to be sold on the child pornography market. All the while he hides in his *castillo grande*, king of the hill, and pretends he's a decent human being. He makes me ill. And he's running drugs. He had *me* running drugs. He *sido un tonto*— a real idiot I've been! I don't think people like Sir John McPhee should be allowed to populate the planet, do you?" he asked me. "I'll tell you one thing: if he so much as touches my Kitty again, I'll kill him. I'd be doing the world a favor."

It seemed to me the driveway to the castle went on forever. There was a beautiful wood with peeing trees everywhere for me to mark my territory. Why didn't he just let me out to do my business and play around for a bit? Nothing doing; this was a man on a mission. When we finally arrived at the castle, there were a lot of people hustling and bustling about. I thought to myself, there must be some sort of celebration going on—maybe a puppy show.

Vicente parked right by what I now know to be the croquet lawn. William, the gardener, was there, placing two cans of some sort by the turret stairs. Vicente got out of the car, leaving me all alone. Abandonment numero uno.

"You'd better not leave me here," I barked.

"No, Grimshaw. You cannot come. This will be quick, and then we'll go for a walk, I promise." I showed him; I peed on the rubber floor mat.

I quickly realized if I stood on my hind feet, I could just see out the driver's side window. An old man with a white beard was closing the curtains on the second floor, then he walked to the rooms next door and did the same. Boy, he must like it dark. Glad I wasn't trapped in *there*. Suddenly, William shoved Vicente against the castle wall, and they just stood there as if they were listening to something. Before I knew it, Vicente was back in the car, shaking like a wet Chihuahua.

"*¡Dios mio!*" he cried out, slamming his fist against the dashboard. "The bastard's made a porno tape of Kitty! Let's get out of here, Grimshaw." Then we drove out into the countryside past fields of black-faced sheep and cows of all colors for what seemed like hours and hours, all the while Vicente talking and talking and talking. Boy, was he mad!

"*Necesito*—I have to go back, Grimshaw. I have to. I need to know if it was consensual. I pray it's not the case, but if it is, *no la varé jamás*—I will never see Kitty again."

Never see her again? What's to happen to me, then? Doesn't he know there are laws against inhumane cruelty to animals, especially to hounds? Wait until PETA hears about this!

"But, if Sir John forced himself on her, I swear I'll strangle him. What sort of a person would do such a thing? She's always claimed she's rebuffed his advances. Maybe I've been duped." He turned the car around and headed back to Glenapp Castle.

"Ruff, ruff," I doggedly objected. "I'm starving to death."

My human seemed oblivious. "The gardener with the green woolen said they were all going to the curling championships around seven. I'm going to sneak back in. I may get caught, but what choice do I have? If he's taped Kitty, whom else has he filmed? Innocent children? Other helpless women? Is there no end to the evil this man can conjure up?"

I must have fallen asleep because the next thing I remember was the crunching sound of plastic as Vicente repetitively stomped on a black box of some sort. We were on a beach. I howled to be let out. Really, I'd had enough for one day.

Finally, by the light of that big, white ball in the sky, we walked along the sandy shore—my virgin stroll along Ballantrae's beach. "Oh, Grimshaw," he wailed, falling to his knees. "Such terrible things he did to my girl." I licked away his tears, but they were falling so fast I couldn't keep up. On and on he moaned and wept, moaned and wept. The human was clearly in crisis!

"What am I to do? Call the police? And tell them what…that I broke into Sir John's private quarters and watched a videotape of my girlfriend, raped and drugged by narcotics I likely procured myself? And I found a list of his victims, their names all crossed out but one—someone named Judith. *Santa Madre de Dios*, what am I to do? Whoever she is, she's his next victim."

For a very long time, as I romped about and licked salt from my paws, Vicente just stood, still as a dead tree, staring at the black, rippling water.

Then without warning, like a bitch in heat, his mood suddenly shifted. "It would be easy, Grimshaw," he mumbled as if he were really only talking to himself. "There are two diesel cans sitting right there. All I have to do is pour the petrol up and down the turret stairs, light a match and drive away. No one will ever know."

He picked up the video tape, hoisted it with great determination into the sea, and we got back in the car. Vicente started the engine and didn't say another word until I heard him ask for a box of matches at Marsden Frew's petrol station. This time we parked behind a tree next to a graveyard, and then I saw it—the same gate we'd passed through twice already that day. But we didn't move. One by one we watched the steady stream of car lights sweep across the windshield. When the last car had passed, Vicente said, "*Que raro*…it seems early for everyone to be leaving the party; it's only just after ten. Well, never mind, Grimshaw, here we go. Stay calm, amigo. We're doing the right thing. Now listen, you mustn't tell Kitty about this. She must never know what we've done."

We? How did I get involved in this?

For the third time that day, Vicente and I wove up the driveway to Glenapp Castle, but this time he turned off the car lights as we approached. Sure enough, there was the old man drawing the curtains in his chamber, just like before.

"*Sí, este es el momento.* Now's the time, Grimshaw, before his next victim arrives," Vicente announced with steely resolve. But as he started to climb out of the car, already clouds of black smoke were pouring out of the north turret stairwells.

"*Dios mio*, the gardener beat me to it!" he stammered. But I knew better. In the dim stormy light, only a hound's eye would sight the gleam of the long silver braid as it faded like a ghost into the night.

*　　　*　　　*

At present, however, I'm feeling despondent and woefully underfed. I wander aimlessly through the chilling, predawn air, missing my Rosie, missing Issie, even missing Vicente! Dare I say, even chef?

Dog tired, I keep to the gravel path, as on this night there is no moonlight to guide my way. Only the hoot of an owl and my long nails scraping the pebbles do I hear as I pass the lily pond, pass the boathouse, all the while reminiscing how Rosie and I sometimes lean into each other, pressing our coats together through the garden gate.

But what's this? The big sea mountain is lit up. I turn towards the walled garden, naturally wanting to share my vision with Rosie, when I notice the garden is all lit up, too! I howl. Rosie barks back. My heart thrills at her voice. Running towards her call, I discover the gate is open.

"Look," she smothers my muzzle with licks. "It's the plant fairies. They've come back."

Never in my lifetime have I seen such a beautiful sight. Hundreds upon hundreds of fairies, all with wings the color and shape of red admiral butterflies, illuminate the garden as Tom and Sophie laugh and dance along the garden paths. Round and round they waltz, until Tom, exultant and out of breath, hands Sophie a trowel, and says…

"Come, my love. We have work to do."

CHAPTER TWENTY-FIVE

TOM

I
T TOOK ONLY EIGHT months for Sophie's divorce to go through, expedited by the fact she left everything to Hal and required no financial support. Judge Sinclair, a lawyer friend of the Campbells, took care of the details on her behalf. Things were going exceptionally well until Victoria, Sophie's mum, insisted we marry before living together. A bit outdated, I should think—we are, after all, nearly thirty years old. It's not a problem, really. We just moved up our date several months, and on 27 August we are to be married in the walled garden with Reverend McCrindle presiding.

This morning William informed us that my uncle Roddie is in the hospital with an inflamed liver. Not surprisingly, the cumulative effect of losing my mum, of remaining a prime suspect in the murder of Sir John McPhee, and for him, worst of all, being robbed of the chance to compete in the Curling Nationals, was too much to bear. But it is guilt and remorse that finally broke his spirit, for during the criminal investigation, Officer Gavin Gillespie discovered that those trips my mother embarked on twice a year "doing good works" for Sir John McPhee, were in fact aiding and abetting the illegal importation of innocent children from Ecuador to the red light district in London. She would greet them on arrival, settle them into a local parish for the night, and believing they were headed to Catholic foster homes the following day, she would return to her duties at Glenapp Castle, none the wiser. Roddie sensed something was awry, yet he did nothing—a decision he will regret for the rest of his life. And alas, when Roddie publicly celebrated Colin Dunbar's suicide, he lost the sympathy and respect of most everyone. Eventually his drunken bouts cost him his captain's license.

Sophie and I drive to Girvan straight away. Our entrance is acknowledged with a disdainful groan.

"Hello, Roddie," I attempt a cheery voice. "How are you feeling?" He looks at me with an expression of utter hopelessness. Dark rings circle his eyes giving him the expression of a trapped raccoon. His sallow cheeks are concave hollows; his lips are cracked and bleeding. Even Sophie is stunned into silence.

"You kids married yet?" he mouths, a mere poof of air forging his words.

"Not yet," I say. "In three months time. We're planning on you being there, Roddie."

An unlikely prospect.

"Tommy," he says with enormous effort, "I want you to contact a lawyer. Not that I have anything much to leave you, but I want to die properly, with things in order. I've my house and the ferry. It was your dad's, and I want you to have it."

I think of *Red Runner* and the times Roddie and I floated aimlessly after the last run to Ailsa Craig, sorting out the past and conjuring up dreams for a brighter future. I have realized mine; Roddie hasn't been as fortunate.

Suddenly he turns to Sophie. "Your mum's been in to see me," he surprises us both. "She's a nice woman, Victoria," he muses. "She brings me a comfort I don't deserve. I don't know how she can even look me in the face, especially this face." Roddie attempts a smile, then reaches for the suave to moisten the deeply cut fissures in his lips. His hands shaking, he manages to raise himself up on one elbow to sip some water while avoiding the saline drip tubing in his arm.

"Don't blame yourself, Roddie," Sophie protests. "Dad did it to himself. She knew that from the start."

"I don't. I just don't know why she's being so nice."

"What? You mean she's been a regular visitor?" I tease.

"Aye. She brings me baked sweets and home-brewed tea as if I was somebody special. Tells me it's premature for me to be dying, that I should get off my arse and live a little."

"Sounds like Mum," Sophie laughs.

"Maybe she's right."

"Right about what?" Roddie growls.

"Right that you might still make something of yourself. It's never too late, but you'll have to give up the whisky."

"Victoria said she'll help me," he says.

"How many times has she been to see you, Roddie?" I ask, nonchalantly.

"Don't meddle," he shoots back.

"You brought it up," I remind him. "You've only been in here two days. Sounds like you two have been talking before this."

"I don't deserve her."

"That's nonsense," Sophie shushes us both. "She's lonely, Roddie. She hasn't had a loving relationship since long before Dad took his own life. If you are fond of her, tell her so. And she's right, there's no reason to wallow away your life. It would be a hard journey to sober up, but what's to lose? It beats the alternative."

"What if it's too late?" he replies, sullenly.

"Well," Sophie continues, "you'll never know if you don't give it a go, now will you? That would be the greatest tragedy of all time, Roddie—if you have a chance for love in this life, and you didn't even try."

"Who said anything about love?" he retorts.

"Saints like Mum don't come along every day," Sophie comments.

"She is a saint," Roddie agrees. "It's me I don't trust."

"Maybe you ought to consider living at Glenapp again. I'm sure the Campbells would find something for you to do. Maybe even in the garden…" I suggest.

"No," he grumbles, "I want my Captain's license back." He glances wistfully out the window at Ailsa Craig. Rumor has it that Roddie was found time and time again circling the sea mountain at night, hoping for a glimpse of the fairies.

"Anything's possible," I say.

"I can't stop shaking," he stutters. "How the hell am I ever going to manage?"

"You're just detoxing."

"God awful!"

"Aye, but it too shall pass."

"The doctors say if I don't quit I'll die," he states, matter-of-factly. To that...there is nothing to say.

Then, he adds, "I'm not much interested in that."

Overcome with exhaustion, the curtain closes and he drifts off to sleep.

*   *   *

It's unusual that when Sophie and I return to the walled garden Rosie isn't there to greet us. She often naps in the shade of the conifers, but always, always hops up, contorting her long frame in a full-body jig to welcome us home. Even Sophie notices.

"Maybe she's in the cottage."

"I left her out, but I'll look. Could you check to be sure the gates are all shut? If she's gotten out, she could be halfway to the Highlands by now," I worry.

Sophie and I head in opposite directions. As my imagination scans the possibilities, Sophie cries, "Oh God, Tom. She's here, just outside the gate. She's all right, but...Oh God!"

Rosie has dug a hole three feet under the stone garden wall to get to Grimshaw who lies still as a summer's night on the walkway. When she sees us, she whines woefully, beseeching us to raise him from the dead.

I cannot express how I feel at this moment. Relief that Rosie is alive, yet devastated for the loss she will feel with Grimshaw, her closest canine companion, gone forever. Needless to say, the one who will be most crushed is Issie.

"Can you help me lift him up? Let's get him inside the garden, then I'll find Andrew or Eva and ask them what they want us to do." But as I try to ease Rosie away, for the first time in our lives together she snarls at me, bearing her teeth as if to strike.

"Rosie, girl, we're only going to carry him into the garden so you can watch over him."

Then the most extraordinary thing happens. Raising her regal nose to the sky, Rosie howls her heart out, expelling her grief for all to hear. On and on she cries, until finally exhausted, she lays down with her muzzle resting on Grimshaw's, and after one last trailing whimper, she quiets.

It is too much for Sophie; it is too much for me. If ever I thought animals incapable of expressing emotion, I now know their hearts grieve in equal measure. And why not?

Soph and I hold one another for as long as we can before obligation kicks us into action. "You stay here. I'll find the Campbells. Thank God Issie's in school for another few hours," I say.

Andrew and Eva are in the office, the former answering the endless e-mails that come from guests all over the world each day. It is several seconds before they notice me standing in the doorway.

"Hello, Tom," Eva says, always enthusiastic in her greeting. When she sees my expression, however, she senses the ill-fated nature of my visit. "What is it? What's the matter?"

Andrew, hearing the concern in her voice, turns to face me. "You look awful, Tom. Whatever is it?"

"I'm afraid I've sad news," I manage to choke out. "It's Grimshaw. He's died, just outside the garden wall."

"Oh, dear," Eva exclaims, bringing her hands to her mouth in shock.

"Oh my!" Andrew echoes.

Words defy us. We stand idle and disoriented, each letting it sink in, thinking of Issie, pondering what we should do next. Andrew glances at his watch.

"It's a quarter past one—two hours until Issie's home from school."

"She has to say good-bye to him," Eva insists. "We can't just bury him; it wouldn't be fair."

"I heard someone howl like a coyote a minute ago," Andrew comments.

"It was Rosie. They were close."

For several minutes I listen as they discuss the best way to manage. Finally I say, "I would be happy to dig a grave inside the garden wall so Issie can visit him there."

"I think Issie would love that," Eva says.

"All right," Andrew agrees. "Tom, maybe you could dig a grave now and lay Grimshaw there until Issie comes home, then she can say good-bye, and we'll all bury him together." He shakes his head and sighs, "I'm not looking forward to this."

Right alongside me, Rosie digs her grieving heart out, spraying dirt all over the place. When Sophie and I gently lower Grimshaw into his resting place, Rosie watches, then carefully, one limb at a time, lies down next to him. An hour later, walking down the path and through the garden gate are not just Eva and Andrew, each holding one of Issie's hands, but Mary, William, Kevin, and the rest of the castle staff in one long procession. I am doing fine until Issie breaks away and runs into my arms.

"Oh, Tom, I'm going to miss Grimmey soooooo much," she cries. "I didn't think he'd die so soon." The poor child weeps and weeps, her shoulders heaving against my chest. Finally, she gathers the courage to look at her lost pet and bends down to stroke his side.

"Bye, Grimmey. You were the best dog anyone could ever have. I will never forget you. Never."

I can hear muffled cries, the most pronounced being Kevin's, a close second being my own.

Issie draws my Rosie close to her side. "You're going to miss him as much as I am, won't you, girl?" Her bravery spent, she stands up and buries her face in Eva's skirt. Gently, Eva urges her to take a handful of dirt and toss it over Grimshaw's prostrated body. One by one we all follow suit, then William and I fill the grave while Issie watches her first pet disappear into the earth forever.

*　　　*　　　*

Sophie and I have decided to forego bridesmaids and ushers, and asked only two favors of the Campbells: to be married in the walled garden and for Issie to be our flower girl.

You would have thought she was the one getting married. Once invited to be in the ceremony, she talked of nothing else. The biggest decisions we left to her—what she would wear and what flowers she would choose for her bouquet. Each day she gathers a fresh arrangement from the perennial cutting bed then sets it on display on my kitchen table for inspection. When Sophie informs her that she is also the keeper of the rings, and as her dress is apparently without pockets, she returns to the garden in search of a sturdy, non-wilting flower so she can run the weddings bands up the stem for safekeeping. After much deliberation, and to our delight, she settles on sunflowers.

*   *   *

Many claim their wedding day to be a murky blur, but I have vowed to remember every last detail. Because of the Gulf Stream's moist air, Glenapp's garden is at its peak of color. By this, the second summer, there are foxglove and phlox of every variation, Pink Lady zinnias alongside Crystal Orange daisies, and Blue Billow hydrangeas so large they require a bed of their own. From the fruit orchard, the heady, succulent aroma of peaches and pears drifts by so fleetingly, the casual passerby might miss it altogether. To me it smells like love.

In formal Scot's attire, I await my bride beneath the canopy draped with morning glory and black-eyed Susan, Rosie at my side. With a moment to observe our guests, I notice each dons a sprig of white heather, worn as a traditional token of good luck—Eva's contribution, no doubt. And there Mary Campbell sits with Nessie Brown and her family. William is nestled close to Lucy's wheelchair. Lucy, who has gained partial use of one arm, excitedly points out that Rosie is licking the palm of my right hand. I see no harm in it; the tingling sensation feels wonderful, and I let her lick to her heart's content. If nothing else, it will keep her occupied. And wouldn't you know, just in front of Chef Kevin and the staff sits my Uncle Roddie, grinning like a circus clown. Beside him, Victoria's empty seat awaits her return after she gives Sophie away. Andrew and Eva are, I know, with Issie as she readies to lead the processional. There are forty-seven guests in all—Sophie and I know each and every one.

"Nervous? It would be only natural," Reverend McCrindle comments.

"Not in the least; I've waited for this all my life," I reply, wiping my saliva covered palm along the pleats of my kilt. Several times I repeat the motion as I can still feel the sticky residue through the thickened, sinuous layers of scar tissue. I nudge Rosie's muzzle with my open palm, certain I am mistaken, urging her to lather my burned hand once again, and with each passage of her tongue, the tingling turns to prickling, and the prickling starts to tickle, and the tickling surrenders to the fantastic realization that I am feeling every luscious stroke of her adoration as if never had I grabbed the scalding door to Sir John McPhee's bedroom suite.

"Well…" the Reverend smiles, relieved. "I believe it's time to begin. At least Miss Campbell appears to think so."

"Aye," I agree. "It's time." I lean down to kiss Rosie's nose. "Thank you, girl," I whisper. "You've performed a miracle. You and the fairies, I'd wager. Am I right?"

The bagpiper, jolted by Issie's premature appearance, quickly begins his processional. Only a few of us recognize the purple, sleeveless dress that Issie wore the day Lucy Hobbes woke up. Her black hair is fastened in a bun, secured with baby's breath and a White Rose of Scotland. My eyes well up when I think of how much I've come to love this little girl. Our gold rings with the inscription *Mo ghaol ort,* Gaelic for *I love you,* hang by a stem, and I pray Issie won't drop them on her way to the altar. She must have read my mind because, ever so proud of herself, she carefully removes them from their hiding place and holds them up for me, and everyone else, to see.

Not far behind, Victoria and Sophie, arm in arm, float down the garden path as if on a flying carpet of summer air. Closer and closer they come until my bride's hand is placed in mine. I have imagined this moment since I was a boy of thirteen. Sophie must have been thinking the same thing because Issie begins to giggle as the Reverend clears his throat several times to get our attention.

Of the actual ceremony, I will admit some distraction. I think about my parents and how proud they would have been to have Sophie as their daughter-in-law. My gratitude for Sophie's return, for the generosity of the Campbells, and for the opportunity to cultivate Glenapp's garden is overwhelming, really. But above all, I lose myself in the beautiful woman standing by my side.

When the time comes, Issie carefully slips the rings down the sunflower stem, then hands me Sophie's first.

"With this ring," I begin, but just then, a brawny zephyr thrashes through the garden, dislodging several of the ladies' hats. Reverend McCrindle dutifully slaps his hand on his Book of Order as the pages blow helter-skelter. Issie, smiling broadly, stands on her tip toes and intones, "It's your mum."

"His mum?" Sophie echoes a wee bit loudly.

Mum. Aye…it makes sense that she wouldn't miss this day.

"With this ring …" I continue, happier than I've ever been in my life.

*   *   *

I've only one more short story to tell. Issie's seventh birthday was on 10 September, just two weeks after Sophie and I were married. Kevin prepared his traditional banoffee pies for the small gathering planned in the garden conservatory. Issie, I will say, is still saddened both by the losses of Grimshaw, and her mum, and Maria Flor and, I believe, by what she fears will be different now that Sophie and I are living together. These changes are subtle and difficult for young ones to navigate sometimes. As a result, Issie didn't want a lot of people at her birthday party this year—no school pals, no frills. She hadn't even dressed up in one of her usual flamboyant outfits for the occasion.

We were all standing around waiting for Eva who was, for some reason, delayed. Issie was wandering about the garden naming flowers when Eva finally snuck in, cradling a wee basset hound puppy. Ever so carefully she placed the cute thing on the ground, and it plodded down the path towards Issie as if it knew exactly who would love her the most.

"Happy birthday, sweetheart," Eva said. "It's a little girl."

"She's soooo wee," Issie exclaimed. "Is she really mine?"

"She's really yours."

"This is the best present in the world. Thank you so much."

Issie paraded her new puppy over for all to see. Then, with Rosie at her side, she ran over to Grimshaw's grave to introduce her new friend.

*   *   *

I am not a philosopher, and unlike some people I know, I cannot predict the future or communicate with spirits. What I can tell you is this: life is an organic, ever-changing proposition. Sometimes it hardly seems worth the effort. Yet, Mum was right. Just beneath the veneer of everything, love awaits our notice. And I was right, too. Time doesn't heal—the remedy for a broken heart is to love and to be loved. Only then can the grandeur of life's odyssey unfold like the White Rose of Scotland.

I believe this.

Related Readings

Allen, James, *As you Think*, edited by Marc Allen, The Classic Wisdom Collection, reprinted 1991.

Andrew, Ken, and John Strawhorn, *Discovering Ayrshire*, John Donald Publishers, limited, 1988.

Browne, Sylvia, *Visits From the Afterlife, The Truth About Hauntings, Spirits, and Reunions with Lost Loved Ones*, Penguin Group, 2003.

Cheape, Hugh, *The Book of the Bagpipe*, The Appletree Press, Limited, 1999.

Coventry, Martin, *A Wee Guide to the Haunted Castles of Scotland*, Gobinhead, 1996.

Crockett, S.R., *The Grey Man*, Alloway Publishing, reprinted 1990.

Doczi, Gyorgy, *The Power of Limits, Proportional Harmonies in Nature, Art, and Architecture*, Shambhala, 1994.

Foreman, J.B., M.A, General Editor, *The Poems of Robert Burns and Selected Stories, The Alloway Bicentenary Edition*, Collins, 1959.

Hansen, Warren, *Curling: the History, The Players, The Game*, Key Porter Books, 1999.

Heinrich, Bernard, *Mind of the Raven,* HarperCollins Publishers, 1999.

Herman, Arthur, *How The Scots Invented The Modern World*, Three Rivers Press, 2001.

Lancaster, Roy, *What Plant Where*, Dorling Kindersley, 1995.

MacLean, Fitzroy, *Scotland, A Concise History*, Thames and Hudson, 2002.

Maine, G.F., *A Book of Scotland*, Collins, 1962.

Pearsall, Paul, Ph.D., *The Heart's Code: Tapping the Wisdom and Power of our Heart Energy*, Broadway Books, 1998.

Rickard, Bob, and John Michell, *Unexplained Phenomena, Mysteries and Curiosities of Science, Folklore, and Superstition*, Rough Guides, Ltd., London, 2002.

Stevenson, Robert Louis, *The Master of Ballantrae*, Dover Publishers, Incorporated, 1889, 2003 reprint.

Wright, Michelle Small, *Behaving As If God In All Life Mattered*, Perelandra, 1997.

For more information on Glenapp Castle Hotel, please visit:

info@glenappcastle.com